Aleutian Grave

Aleutian Grave

by

William Doonan

2014

BookYear Mysteries, First Edition 2014
www.bookyearmysteries.com

ALEUTIAN GRAVE
Copyright © 2014 by William Doonan
www.williamdoonan.com

Other Titles by William Doonan:
GRAVE PASSAGE
MEDITERRANEAN GRAVE
GRAVE INDULGENCE
AMERICAN CALIPHATE
THE MUMMIES OF BLOGSPACE9

This novel is a work of fiction. The characters and events depicted herein are derived from the author's imagination.

ISBN Number: **978-1499186154**

Printed in the USA.

for Carmen

ACKNOWLEDGMENTS

I am indebted to a number of people who worked to help bring this project to life. Bob Bernstein consulted on several drafts and provided countless edits. Dan Stuelpnagel ripped the first draft to shreds, saving my readers from an unpleasant reading experience. And my family gave me the support and encouragement to keep both myself and Henry afloat.

CHAPTER ONE
DAY 1 - ANCHORED OFF GURBKA ISLAND - 5:30AM

I met Brice Laird twenty years ago, shortly after he killed his first wife, not after he killed his second wife as he remembers it. So when I heard about the murdered girl on the cruise ship, and I saw Brice's name on the passenger list, I put two and two together and figured I had already solved the case. As it turned out, I was wrong.

A twenty-four year-old cabaret dancer by the name of Rose DeSilva had been stabbed to death onboard the arctic adventure ship *Nikolai Gorodish*. Two hundred and ninety-two passengers midway through their Bering Sea voyage had all been notified. Security was tightened, counseling provided, free liquor poured, and one top-notch investigator called in – me.

The ship was anchored off the island of Gurbka, a fishing outpost in the Russian part of the Bering Sea. Captain Boris Tolstoy had crossed the international dateline on the night of the murder, so it was unclear if Rose DeSilva had been killed in US or Russian waters. Crimes at sea are tricky when it comes to jurisdiction.

"Not much down there," the helicopter pilot told me as we approached the island. "Gurbka doesn't have a lot to offer tourists. Most folks only go so far as Dutch Harbor or maybe Attu, but this, this is out there. This is the last of the Aleutian islands. Next stop; mainland Russia."

"Is that right?"

"Want to hear something strange? Couple of guys I been flying out to a campsite on Nunivak – they got a claim up there and they been coming for years – two dentists from New York. I think they got one of those special relationships, but that ain't my business. In any case, I flew them up early last month, then I come back two weeks later like we planned, and guess what I find?"

"I don't know. Two dentists?"

He stared at me. "Well, yeah, but they was dead. Both of them covered in blood, knives still in their hands. They killed each other. With knives. They had, I don't know, six or seven grand worth of hunting guns with them, and they kill each other with knives."

He stared at me as if to make a point. I tried to think it through, but I just kept willing him to turn his head forward and concentrate on flying the helicopter.

"State trooper flew in the next day. Damnedest thing. They had been friends for years, and like I said, I think they might have been, you know . . ."

"So you've said." I didn't know why two friends might kill each other after so many years, and it wasn't my concern. I stared down at the little ramshackle town of Gurbka. It wasn't much more than two muddy streets lined by rusted pre-fab buildings. "So what's down there?"

"In Gurbka?" The pilot shook his head. "Not much. Just a bunch of Aleuts, some Russians, but there's not shit to do other than fish or drink, unless you like rabbits."

"Can't get enough of them," I said. "I like fishing and drinking. Actually, not so much fishing. But rabbits, send them my way." It was raining but we were close enough to see the ship anchored in the harbor. "They're delicious."

"No, no. You can't eat them. Not this summer. Some local tradition – you're not supposed to eat them some summers, this being one of them."

"Why is that?"

"Don't know, some mythology, but up here in these parts, people take that kind of thing seriously."

"Even you?"

"Even me, you can bet on it. Last thing I need is to be flying my ass through a white-out with some arctic demon coming for me. No to that." He pointed toward the ocean. "That's your cruise ship down there."

There she was, anchored just outside of Gurbka's tiny dilapidated harbor.

"Hey, I got a joke for you." He brought the helicopter in toward the town.

"I can't wait."

"OK, so this tourist visits Gurbka and has a look around at all the beat-down pre-fab buildings, and all the rusting-to-shit fishing boats, and the down-on their-luck sad-sacks going about their business or what-not. So he goes up to a local guy and says, 'Hey, is it always so miserable here in Gurbka?' And guess what the guy tells him?"

"I have no idea." I had no idea.

"The guy says, 'I don't know, I'm only forty-eight years old.' You get it, right? Like Gurbka has been miserable for at least forty-eight years!"

"Yeah. Listen, I'm not seeing a helipad on that ship. That's the ship, right?"

"Yeah, that's the *Gorodish*. There's only the one cruise outfit up here doing this run. She starts out in Anchorage, sails the Aleutians, does two nights in Russia, then back to Anchorage. Same route, all summer long."

"Still no helipad."

"Yeah, there's no helipad. She's too small. So I'm going to put you down just by the sea wall."

And he did just that. "Watch yourself," he warned as I stepped out of the helicopter. "Everyone is on edge this summer."

I assured him I would.

They ran me out to the ship on a Zodiac that looked to have been patched together from lesser Zodiacs long past their prime. By the time I climbed on board the *Nikolai Gorodish*, I was exhausted, starving, and thankful that the heat was on. I could already tell that the extended daylight hours were going to take some getting used to. I hoped my cabin had some heavy drapes.

"First time in the Bering Sea?"

"What, now?" I looked around the reception lobby, but I didn't see anyone. The desk was unmanned. Either that or whoever was back there was so short they couldn't see over the top, but that rarely happens. I didn't know what to make of my situation – no security, no welcome.

"I am watching you on the monitor," came the voice again, female, heavily-accented. "Please take the elevator to the Puffin Deck and I will meet you in the lobby."

"Which one is the Muffin Deck?" I called out. "I'm asking because I haven't had anything to eat in quite some time."

I got no answer. "It has been really a long time," I called out. "I'm really hungry and a muffin sounds nice."

"Puffin," came the voice over the loudspeaker.

"Yeah, no. I would prefer a muffin. I can't do poultry in the morning; it gives me gas." Before heading for the elevator, I had a walk around. Nice carpets, they looked brand new, but they were grey, and that's a bad color for a cruise ship. Grey is a sad color, somber. And nobody comes on a cruise to get somber. I passed a number of prosperous looking passengers wandering around. None were somber.

"Good morning," I called out. I got some replies, and I got some Russian in there and some German. I said good morning to a chambermaid as she popped out of a stateroom. I think I scared her a little because she nearly jumped.

"Sorry," I told her. I leaned in to read her name tag. "Petula. Sorry about that, Petula. I didn't mean to sneak up on you like that."

"No, no," she said as she smoothed her uniform. "Is my fault. I was just cleaning the stateroom, that is all."

"Is that right? You get started early around here. I like that. Hey, don't forget your cart. Where is your cart? I think you left it in the room."

"What? Oh, oh yes. I will go back and get it just now."

"Petula, if I didn't know any better," I began, "I'd think you had something to hide."

She blushed.

"But I don't care. I hope you enjoyed yourself. I'm just trying to finish my thought and find the Puffin Deck."

She pointed me to the elevator and I kept walking.

Twos and fours, that's how passengers moved. No threes, never threes. Cruising is for couples. Seventy percent of cruise ship passengers are couples, and another twenty percent are families. Ten percent are lone wolves such as myself, looking for love or riches on the high seas. But no groups of threes. It just doesn't come together.

Somehow I walked right past the elevator, but it worked out just fine. There was food to be had. The cozy piano bar was closed, as one might expect at 5:30 in the morning. The lights were off in the Explorer lounge, the gift shop too, but the dining room was open for business.

"Not yet open for business," said a young waiter who was folding napkins at the maître d' station.

"I was led to believe there would be muffins."

"Muffins, yes. And eggs and sausage. A large assortment of food delights will be provided, but not until 6:30."

I leaned in to read his name tag. "I have to tell you, Vadeem from Yakutsk, I was kind of hoping for an early-risers breakfast. Do you think you could scare me up a muffin or a blintz or two? I have the diabetes and I would hate to drop dead on your watch. I'll work on the napkins while you're gone."

He looked up at me, the distress evident on his face, but Vadeem understood as well as I did that cruise ships are in the business of pleasing passengers, and passengers do not enjoy being displeased. "And if you can scare up a Bloody Mary," I called out as he wandered off to the kitchen, "I'll put in a good word with the captain."

I took out my briefing packet, figuring I would do a little light reading while I waited. Rose DeSilva's photo had been taped to the cover. She was a beautiful girl.

Hailing from Montreal, Rose had been onboard only three months, but she had worked four other cruise ship contracts, receiving satisfactory ratings each time. Still, things couldn't have been going that well. You don't move from Crystal Cruises to Carnival to Contessa and then to this little polar ship voluntarily. No, more than likely Rose had some issues.

Maybe she drank. Maybe she flirted too much with the passengers. Maybe not enough. But she didn't deserve what happened to her. I shook my head looking at the crime scene photos. So much blood.

"Excuse me, sir."

I looked up to find a woman coming down the hall. She wore a crew uniform, and wore it well. Nice black hair all up in a bun. She was cute and I told her so. "I'm good," I told her. "Vadeem is hunting me up a muffin."

"Mr. Grave, sir? Were we not going to meet up on the Puffin Deck?"

"What, now?"

She held out a hand. "Irina Bok. I'm head of onboard security."

"Is that a hint of a smile, I see, Irina? Am I not what you were expecting?"

She blushed. "It is only that . . ."

"It is only that I'm an old man, Irina, that's it. You

weren't expecting someone old. I'm eighty-five years old, but I have the stamina of a fifty-eight year old."

"Yes, OK. That is . . ."

"And to be honest, I wasn't expecting someone so young and so female."

"My father wasn't expecting me to be female either," she said. "He cried for weeks when I was born. Most mornings, he still weeps. But here we are."

I've always loved the sound of Russian women speaking English; it's melodic and a little angry. "Yes. Hey, this is new to me. I've never been on a Russian cruise ship before. I'm looking forward to trying out some Russian food, like kebabs and those little pancake things. Listen, what say you and I go take a look at the crime scene as soon as I get my muffins?"

She shook her head. "No, we cannot do that. I'm sorry to have to tell you. I can only let you see the photographs."

Vadeem returned with my breakfast, and my beverage. I thanked him and turned back to my new friend Irina Bok. "I want to see the crime scene. I don't care about the photographs."

"The crime scene has been sealed by the authorities."

"Here's how this works," I told her. "I am the authorities."

"You're not," she said. "I will take you to your stateroom. Then the captain will meet with you shortly afterward. If you will come this way."

"Then I'll make my request to the captain," I told her. "It's his call."

"No," she said. "It is my call."

We were getting off to a rocky start. I drank my Bloody Mary and I stuffed a couple of muffins in my pocket before setting off after her. "I like to get a lay of the land when I'm at sea," I told her. "This is a small ship and I intend to walk it, every corridor, every hall, every . . ."

"Corridors and halls are the same thing," she said.

"Unless my English is less perfect than I had hoped."

"Fine. Corridors, decks, and public venues. As I was saying, this is a small ship. Six passenger decks and one crew deck. Am I right?"

"You're not. Six passenger decks, staterooms on four of them, 146 staterooms in total including suites. And two crew decks including the Engine deck. Any more questions?"

She kept walking and I followed. "How many public venues?"

"That depends on what you consider a public venue. We have one dining room, one cafe, one theater lounge, and four bars including the one by the pool."

"How many people on board, total?" I asked. "Staff, crew, officers, passengers, the whole lot?"

"Including you - 382."

"In my notes, I had 383."

"There was a murder, you might have heard."

"Right. Right. Hey, there's a passenger I want to talk to. His name is Brice Laird. He has a history of violence against women."

She stopped and turned. "A history of violence against women, that is interesting."

"Isn't it? So unless you have a suspect in custody already, I'd like to start with him."

"I have met Mr. Laird. He is quite popular with the female passengers."

"Don't get too friendly with him."

"Oh, I won't, but you have been misinformed. He is not a guest; he is an ambassador host, one of the gentlemen who the company hires to dance with the ladies."

"Brice? You're kidding me. Can he dance?"

"I would imagine."

"Has he killed any passengers yet?"

"Not to my knowledge." She led me down a stairway through a narrow corridor where she swiped a door lock.

"Your stateroom."

I stepped inside. It was grim. I turned around slowly, taking in the bed, the little desk, the little TV, the little chair. Everything looked new and perfectly functional, but it was drab. Grey walls, grey bedspreads, and a framed photograph of a greyish owl; my spirits were not lifted.

"Hey, what's with all the grey. Did this used to be a warship or something, like a destroyer?"

"Are you dissatisfied with your stateroom?"

"No, it's very nice. Is there a minibar?"

"Minibar is under the television. Satellite television is currently down but you can watch movies on channel seven or shipping news on channel eight."

It was time for my litmus test. I gingerly pried open the minibar door only to find two splits of wine, two liters of vodka, two bottles of Tinkoff beer, and a candy bar. I was impressed. "What's Tinkoff? I've never had that before. Is it nice? Is it one of those beers that's made from wheat? Because I don't like that. Is it nutty?"

Irina Bok stared at me. "I don't drink beer."

"You've never had a Tinkoff? Never? Not even in college?"

"No. I am going to leave you to freshen up. I will be back in half hour to take you to the captain. And you will be interested to know that we do have a suspect in custody."

"Is that right? Who?"

"I won't tell you."

CHAPTER TWO
DAY 1 - ANCHORED OFF GURBKA ISLAND - 6:30AM

In my line of work, you have to be ready to pick up and go at a moment's notice. And I can do that. I like to see new places, and I like to meet new people. I'm a social man by temperament. I make friends easily. And because I've been in this business for many long years, I know a lot of people who work crew on these luxury ships that ply our seven seas.

Cruising gets in your blood. I read the statistics recently, I think it was in the newspaper, or on the radio station that plays classical music if you turn it on at the wrong time, that 80% of passengers on their first cruise plan to take another. And I can see why. The food is first rate, the scenery second to none, the service beyond compare, the dinner theater unmatched, and the flow of premium liquor ample.

What those other 20% of passengers are thinking, I can't be certain. Maybe they're among the few who actually get seasick, which is nearly impossible given the size and complexity of the stabilizers below. Or more likely, they're among those younger folk who have not yet learned one of life's most astonishing secrets - that you don't have to move so quickly to get places, you can catch mice just as nicely by waiting until the mice come to you. Relaxation is not a character flaw.

Here's my advice to young people today, though I doubt they stay still long enough to listen to an old man - sit still now and again. Have a nice beverage and some pistachio nuts, and just sit. It won't kill you.

That's all really. I don't have too much else in the way of advice, except don't kill someone on a cruise ship, because if you do, I'm going to come for you. And you don't want that.

A more thorough inspection turned up some crackers in the minibar, and a couple of packets of cheese, so I made myself a snack as I read through the crew and passenger manifests. I almost always see someone I know, and that's a comfort because otherwise I'm kind of on my own. But this time, only Brice Laird stood out, and I doubt he'd be much help. I tried to send him to prison once, so he might still be mad.

I started reading about our cruise ship, which was built in Finland. That's as far as I got. I think I dozed off because when I woke up, all the ice in my Bloody Mary had melted. I heard a knock, and I opened the door to find Irina Bok standing there.

"How many times do I have to knock?"

"Ten times," I suggested. "After that, just feel free to use your key. Hey, is it time for breakfast yet?"

She checked her watch. "It is, but the captain is waiting for you. Then, if your stomach can still handle it, I will take you to breakfast."

"Believe me," I told her, "my stomach can handle it."

I met Captain Boris Tolstoy in the lounge – the Beluga Bar it was called, no doubt because of the framed Beluga whale photographs that lined the walls, and the grey upholstery on the couches, the bar stools, the benches. Why pick a grey animal for your theme when this could just as easily have been the Parrot Bar, the Tiger Bar, or the Butterfly Bar? "I'm just asking," I said, but Captain Tolstoy didn't have any answers.

He was one of those super-fit guys who looked like he ate vegetables all day long. Late fifties, good-looking, clean-shaven, he belonged on TV.

"You asked to see the crime scene," he said, in lieu of introducing himself. He opened a door and pointed into the storeroom behind the bar. "Over there," he continued, but he didn't need to. Crusted blood covered the bar surface, the counter behind it, and much of the floor. It was everywhere.

"One of our bartenders found her early yesterday morning, at about this time." He pointed behind the bar. "That's where she was found. There was blood on the bar itself, so the doctor thinks she was killed on the bar, and then at some point, she might have . . . slipped off."

I took a look around. "The bar is closed, right? It would have been closed yesterday morning as well. Bars aren't open in the morning. So why was there a bartender here?"

"That same concern occurred to us." Tolstoy exchanged a glance with Irina Bok. "We spoke with the bartender about this. He explained that he was looking for cocktail onions for a passenger who demanded cocktail onions for his morning cocktail."

"It's a crying shame." I sipped my Bloody Mary. "Where is the body?"

"In the walk-in beverage refrigerator. We wanted to move her to our morgue, but we were instructed by our managers in Moscow not to disturb the crime scene."

"In the walk-in beverage refrigerator," I repeated. "What can you tell me about Rose DeSilva? What kind of person was she?"

"She was nice." Tolstoy appeared to be measuring his words.

"Nice?"

"Nice, yes. She was a dancer. She was friendly, she laughed easily. She was a nice girl."

"Did you know her well?"

He took a deep breath and shared another glance with Irina. "It is against company policy to engage in a romantic relationship with anyone in one's supervisory capacity," he said. "So for me, as captain, that would include everyone on board."

"Yet sometimes things happen," I suggested, "like two ships passing in the arctic night."

"Something like that," he said softly. "We were together only a short time; it was over. It was over a week ago."

"Who made it over?" I moved over to the beverage refrigerator and peeked through the window.

"She did," he said. "Rose. She broke it off."

"Makes you a suspect," I told him. "Maybe you killed her. Is that her in there? Under that tarp?"

"Yes, she is there."

"Why did she break it off?"

He took his time answering. "There was someone else she was interested in. I don't know who."

"You were upset. You liked her, didn't you?"

He nodded. "I was upset. I liked her very much. And yes, I understand it makes me a suspect."

"And?" I rubbed some of the frost off the window to get a better look.

"And I didn't kill her. And no, I don't have an alibi. I spent the night alone in my cabin. I did some drinking, which is unusual for me."

I reached for the refrigerator door and noticed the padlock. "I want to see her."

"No." Irina shook her head.

Tolstoy stared down at the grey carpet. "Due to my potential conflict of interest, I have ceded all authority in this investigation to Ms. Bok."

"Yeah, that's grand," I said, "but here's how this works; when I come onboard, I go wherever I want to go. I think you'll find that this point was made explicit in your security certification papers."

"No," Irina Bok said.

"Stop with the 'no.' Look, if you prevent me from doing my job, my organization will pull your security clearances. You won't be able to enter any US port. Kind of puts a kink in the arctic cruising business, but I'm sure you can have your way with North Korea. I hear they're starting up an acorn jelly festival."

Tolstoy shook his head. "You don't understand. A Russian naval frigate has been dispatched. It will arrive later this morning. Onboard is a maritime investigator who will assume control of this process."

"The Association of Cruising Vessel Operators has jurisdiction," I told him. "They sent me."

"Technically, no," he said firmly. "This ship is sixty percent owned by the Russian state, which gives the military paramount jurisdiction. This means you will have a partner. You will be working hand in hand with our investigator."

I didn't like this at all. I put down my drink. "I don't like this at all," I said. "Is it too much to ask if I can see the body, really?"

Irina Bok shook her head. She might have some authority in this situation, but I could see her looking for cues from the captain. He was, after all, her boss.

"Due to the nature of the attack," he began, "the ship's doctor has requested that the body not be touched."

"Of course. I just want to look."

"Due to the nature of the attack," he said again, "the details of the assault have not been made public."

"Is that right? She was stabbed, right?"

He nodded. "Yes. Initially."

"What do you mean initially?"

He produced a key and opened the padlock. "I was a naval officer," he said. "I have seen people under my command killed before. But I have never had anyone eaten."

"Excuse me?"

He pulled open the door and motioned for me to enter

the refrigerator. "If you don't want to look, I'll understand. For your part, I hope you can understand that I don't wish to look again at the cannibalized body of my former lover."

At first I didn't believe what I was hearing, but the looks on their faces were enough to give me pause. I've seen a lot of things in my eighty-five years on this planet. But I've never seen the work of a cannibal before.

I lifted the tarp to reveal the face. Rose DeSilva had been a beautiful girl. Frost clung to her eyelashes, but her eyes were open wide. She was staring, as if unable to comprehend what was happening. I pulled the tarp further down. She had been stabbed repeatedly. But even warned, I was unprepared for what I saw when I uncovered her stomach. A pack of wild dogs could do no worse.

"I'm so sorry, Rose," I whispered to her. "I'm going to find who did this to you." I covered her up. "And I'm going to kill him."

I stepped back outside but the captain had already left. I turned to Irina. "I assume you made sure there wasn't a pack of wolves on board."

"Wolves?" She shook her head. "No, it was a human who did this. The doctor confirmed a knife was used."

"I've never seen anything like this."

"Nobody has," she said, but I was pretty sure that wasn't true. Somebody knew something about this. Even a lunatic driven mad by some chemically-induced frenzy follows some suite of norms."

"You said you had a suspect."

"I did say that."

"Can you not play games with me? The clock is ticking. If you wanted someone else investigating, then he should be here already."

She stared at me. "You are quite right about that. Inspector Belov should have been on a plane, but the genius at shore command decided to ferry him here by ship. It was a terrible decision, I agree. But we have rules to follow. And for a Russian, rules are more important than results. I'm sorry to say that. Many would disagree."

"So what? So you're going to prevent me from doing my job?"

"Of course not. But I cannot actively assist you."

"Then you can inactively assist me. I need to talk with your suspect. Hey, I'm going to have a stroll on down to the brig just for the hell of it. Want to come with? We could chat along the way."

She seemed to be giving it some thought, so I took that opportunity to refresh my beverage from the ample liquor supply.

"You didn't like her, did you?"

"Excuse me?" She looked up as if I had slapped her.

I gestured to the body. "Rose. You didn't like her."

"No," she began, but then she paused again. "No, I didn't not like her."

"That's not a ringing endorsement. How well did you know her?"

"She had not been on board long, but we are a small group, a small community."

"That means you knew her."

"I knew her."

"Why did she end things with the captain?"

She looked around. It might have been a subconscious gesture, but she made certain we were alone before she continued. "I don't know. We were not close. You could speak with her roommate Michelle. They were inseparable."

"Any boyfriends after the captain? New loves or new lovers?"

"Very likely."

"I see. Now let's leave poor Rose for now and go find her killer. You can start by telling me who you have sitting in the brig."

CHAPTER THREE
DAY 1 - ANCHORED OFF GURBKA ISLAND - 7:30AM

The *Nikolai Gorodish* was a midsize cruise ship, small by today's standards but spacious enough to accommodate 292 passengers. Ninety staff and crew worked on board tending to everything from propellers to paper umbrellas. Technically, eighty-nine worked on board now. Eighty-eight if you consider the fact that James Ember, the ship's award-winning executive chef, wasn't doing a lot of cooking in the brig.

On most cruise ships, the brig is down below, deep in the bowels of a ship, far removed from pleasure and room service. But not here. Here, the brig was just off the bridge, across the hall from the captain's office. "Easier to keep an eye on a prisoner," Irina told me. "On the bridge, there is always someone."

I couldn't argue with that. I went in alone and pulled up a chair so I could line up on the prisoner.

He was eating. He looked up at me and chuckled. "What are you, like a hundred years old?"

"Two hundred." I opened my briefing packet and started reading. "James Ember of Manchester, England, age fifty. Numerous awards, yes. But not any I've heard of. Cooking school, that sounds like fun."

"Who the hell are you?"

I introduced myself. "So what did you do to get yourself into this mess?"

"Nothing," he said, munching away. "It's absolute bullshit. I would never hurt that girl."

"You slapped her," I said, reading Irina Bok's report. "The night she died you two had an altercation."

"I didn't slap her. I kind of pulled her hair. I was talking to her and she kept trying to leave, and I don't know. I was trying to keep her from leaving."

"What were you talking about?"

He set down his silverware. "If you must know, I kind of dug her. I'm sure you've seen her picture by now, so you know what she looked like. She was a knockout."

"Go on."

"OK, so we had been partying, and she had something of a reputation."

"Go on."

"I don't know. I suggested maybe we could get together, you know, maybe head back to my cabin, which I know is nicer than hers because she has a roommate and I don't. So I was telling her about this nice bottle of Pinot I had been sitting on, and how I might be willing to share it with her, and she laughed at me."

"That's not nice."

He nibbled at a potato. "Exactly. It wasn't nice. That was a ninety dollar bottle of Pinot, and I was willing to open it for her, for us. But no, she has to make fun of me. She told me I was too fat. I'm not fat."

"You're a little fat."

"I'm big-boned. I'm robust. But I'm not fat."

"You could lose some tonnage around the middle, and you're kind of getting a wattle. But to focus, you slapped her because she called you fat?"

"I didn't slap her." He shook his head. "Look, you didn't know her. She could be mean. She humiliated me in front of the other girls. I've been onboard for a year and a half, then this little saucy girl comes on three months ago, and it's like she's the new queen bee. And then she goes and starts talking trash about me."

"Still not OK to slap a woman."

"Enough." He smacked his hand against the bars. "I didn't slap her. I pulled her hair, and she got all bent out of shape. That's when I left."

"And shortly after that, she was killed."

"I know. That's what I'm hearing, but I didn't kill her. I wandered around, went back to the kitchen, and then went back to my cabin."

"Alone?"

"Yeah, alone."

"Sucks for you."

"Tell me about it. And I made quick work out of that bottle of Pinot."

"How was it?"

"Tight, nice dried-cherry notes, light tannins, but I couldn't get into it. I was grumpy."

"Because of the girl or the tannins?"

"The girl."

"Are you going to eat those crackers?" I could just see them peeking out over the edge of the tray on the little table.

"What?" He looked back at the remains of his lunch. "Goddamn Pang, he has been wanting my job for a long time, and now that he is in charge he serves me up a garbage game hen, old potatoes, look at these. These are not roasters, and soup from a can with a little wrapper of crackers. It's inhumane."

"Can you send them this way?" I asked. "Are they Saltines?"

He nodded and handed them over.

"Any thoughts on who the killer might be?"

He stood and moved over to the bunk. "I don't know. Maybe the captain; he had her to himself for a month or so before she got tired of him. Or Sasha at the piano bar. I'm pretty sure he's gay, but Rose wasn't the kind of girl who would let that stand in the way. Or you might have a look at Lonagan, the naturalist. Rose had a huge, major, giant crush on him. And I don't know why; the guy is a prick. I cooked a nice swordfish last week, really nice, ginger marinade with a little white wine, and he sent it back, told me he wouldn't eat it."

"It sounds delicious." I shook my head.

"It was. What are you shaking your head for?"

"These are not Saltines."

"They look like it to me."

I held up the packet. "Sunshine Krispys," I read. "They're almost like Saltines but not as good. Some might argue. Back home at Rolling Pines I've become involved in some roiling debates, but I stand by my guns."

He stared at me.

"OK, tell me about this Pasha."

"Sasha."

"That's what I said. Did Rose have a thing with him?"

"Look, Rose had a thing with everybody. Also, I'd look into goddamn Pang if I were you, because getting me locked up was the best thing that ever happened to his sorry Malaysian ass. Other than that, I have no clue. I don't know anyone who might want to kill her."

But I did. I left James Ember in the brig and took the elevator up to the Caribou Deck. I had some serious doubts about James Ember's guilt, but not enough to suggest he be let back loose in the kitchen. After consulting my passenger list, I gave a knock at cabin 534. "Housekeeping," I called out. But I got no answer. Evidently, Brice Laird had already headed out for breakfast, and it was high time I did the same.

Vadeem from Yakutsk met me at the entrance to the dining room. "A table by yourself, Mr. Grave, or would you prefer company?"

"Company," I told him. "And a Bloody Mary when you get a minute, easy on the tomato juice."

A few passengers were still mingling at the entrance, but most of the breakfast herd had already been seated. I heard conversation and chewing, and it made me happy. I love the idea of breakfast and that fact that at breakfast time, a great many people are eating breakfast. It's magical. Vadeem led me to a table by the window where an Oriental couple, about my age, had already started in on their feast.

"They have noodles?" I frowned. "Noodles. Soup too, is that soup? I'm not a huge breakfast soup fan."

"Our menu is very comprehensive," Vadeem assured me as a waiter named Jimmy handed me a menu.

"Give me time, Jimmy," I told him, but he didn't move. I don't like to rush food-related things. Breakfast is one of the most important meals of the morning, I reminded Jimmy, and I like to get it right, nail it the first time, so that I don't have to revisit things until at least brunch.

"May I recommend the Denver omelet?" he asked with a thick Russian accent.

"Really? A Denver omelet on a Russian ship? That sounds dicey. What say you bring me three eggs over hard, bacon, sausage, some hash browns. Hey do you have those pigs in a blanket?"

Jimmy looked momentarily lost as he scanned the menu.

"Never mind. What say we just round things out with a side of waffles and half a melon."

"Very good, sir. Can I bring you some coffee?"

"That would be swell. Make it an Irish coffee, and if you could find an extra tot of whiskey to bring it to life, I would be forever in your debt."

He was still writing when he left, which was fine. I didn't want him to forget anything. I turned to my breakfast companions. "Nice morning we're having." I introduced myself.

"Connie Watanabe." The woman shook my hand. "It's very nice to meet you. Yoji is shy. Fifty years he's been living in Bakersfield, and he's still nervous about his English."

I gave Yoji a wave. "So where are you folks from?"

"Down in California," she said. "We raise alpacas. Used to have some llamas too but they got too mean."

"Is that right? Can you eat something like that or do you just use the wool."

Yoji cleared his throat. "The meat is very lean," he said. His accent was Japanese, unlike his wife's. "To be honest, I don't enjoy it as a steak, but when seasoned for stir fry, it is quite delicious."

"Is that right?"

We chatted.

Jimmy returned with my beverage, which, once sampled, turned out to be right on the nose. Nothing ruins an Irish coffee like too much coffee, and Jimmy seemed to understand that.

"So what brings you up to the north pole?" I turned back to my table mates as I grabbed some toast from the basket.

"Oh, I don't think we're going that far north," Connie said. "And at this rate, we're not going anywhere at all." She gestured out the window with her thumb at the little island town, little Gurbka from which an oil-streaked fishing boat had just departed for parts unknown.

"Have you gone ashore?"

She stared at me. "No, I don't think there's anything there to see."

"Is that right?"

She frowned. "Why? Have you gone ashore?"

"No, no."

"I didn't know we were allowed to go ashore. I thought we were just here waiting for some detective."

"That's what I'm hearing." I folded my grey napkin on

my lap. "Actually it looks kind of drab."

"Yeah, drab," she said. She went on for awhile, talking about drabness. I kind of lost track but I tuned back in when my breakfast arrived, some of it. I had to remind Jimmy about the hash browns.

"Apparently it's just a little fishing town," Connie said. "Russians and Aleuts. And they're not really set up for tourists."

"Russians, really? Over here?"

"Over here? Over what here? We're in Russia, right? This is a Russian island."

I nodded as I chewed. "Very true. I guess I just wasn't thinking about it like that."

We watched as a helicopter circled the town, then set down behind a long building with a rusted tin roof.

"So what brings you to the Russian fishing islands?" I asked. "Anniversary? Birthday? How about it Yoji? The big eight-five?"

"I am eighty-seven." He shook his head "I expected we would come to this."

"I expected as well."

Connie paused, her fork halfway to her mouth. "Expected what?"

There's a special kind of relationship that men my age participate in. It is one based entirely on respect, even when it comes to interacting with men who are German, Austrian, or Japanese. We are gentle with each other, but we shared something, and it cannot not be spoken of.

"I was a soldier in the Imperial Navy," Yoji began. "I was part of the Japanese expeditionary force sent to Alaska. We came ashore in Dutch Harbor."

"Dutch Harbor, I remember it fondly," I told him. "I was just there this morning. I was in a little plane from Anchorage, and they left me off at Dutch Harbor. Nice little town, though not Dutch. Then I was on a helicopter to Gurbka."

Connie frowned. "This morning? We were at Dutch Harbor three days ago. What helicopter? What are you talking about?"

"What, now?" Nuts. I was blowing my own cover. "That's what I meant, three days ago - delightful town, Dutch Harbor. So picturesque."

She frowned. "Picturesque? Are you serious? It's nothing but canneries and shipping containers."

I dug into my potatoes. "I have a weakness for shipping containers. Also canneries."

She turned back to her meal. "Honestly, I think this whole part of the world is pretty bleak. We did a Greek cruise last summer. Those are nice islands. But this . . . so far, what, we've been to Kodiak, Dutch Harbor, and Attu, and each one has been bleaker than the last."

"I thought Attu was kind of pretty," I said. "Cute little downtown."

She stared at me. "It's uninhabited."

Nuts.

She squinted. "How come I haven't seen you onboard?"

"I eat mostly in my room," I told her. "So I don't do mealtimes. Plus I sleep a lot. To be honest, I mostly came onboard for the minibar."

I ate to pass the time, and also to obtain calories. "So Dutch Harbor," I said to Yoji. "That must have been something. I got sent to Belgium, but I got captured right away. Some good I was!"

He nodded sagely as he ate his soup.

"So wait, you were posted up here during the war and you wanted to come back? Brave man."

He looked over at his wife. "I made some friendships, you see. Several dozen of the local inhabitants, the Aleuts, returned to Japan with us. Some stayed for years. They were prisoners, you understand, but after a time it became something else."

I knew what he meant. "I was in a prison camp for five months. There was this one guard. We weren't friends or anything, but we were two guys, you know, in the middle of something."

"That's right."

"We became friends afterwards. I even went to visit him once in Berlin, years later. He took me to a dance club filled with Polish girls. They were pretty." My hash browns came, and I ordered another beverage. "So this trip is like a reunion?"

Connie laughed. "It was meant to be. Yoji had a friend from the war who died some years back, only now Yoji figures he needs to be friends with the man's loser grandsons as well."

"They are not losers. They maintain a traditional lifestyle. They still speak the Aleutian language. They tell the old stories."

She shook her head. "Those two scamps, Benny and Short Lewis. We came up here to visit them. We planned this trip for months, and we showed up at Dutch Harbor and they weren't there. They were out on some seal hunting boat."

"A fishing boat," Yoji corrected her. "They are deckhands. They cannot predict when the ship will return to port. They cannot give orders to their captain."

"Fishing boat, whatever. My point is, we came here to see them. They could at least show us some courtesy. It's not like they're not down in Bakersfield for a month every winter drinking our beer."

"They are trying to earn money," Yoji said, standing up for his friends.

"Yeah, you know how much money you can make watching HBO and burning that damn incense?" Connie pushed rice around her plate with a set of chopsticks. "Fishing, you say. We'll maybe they can finally make some money instead of coming up with yet another stupid scheme. They had this brilliant idea of importing alpaca clothing up north."

"I can see that," I suggested. "It gets cold up here."

"It does, but nobody here has any money."

Yoji reached over and put his hand on hers. "We'll . . ."

"He thinks he owes them something." Connie pulled her hand away.

"I do owe them something," he said, and I got the impression it was a fight they'd been having for decades.

She wouldn't look him in the eye. "Twenty years, we have been flying them down for the winter. Short Lewis last year finally ups and marries Margarita Bustamante from Turlock with whom he now has three children, and what does he contribute by way of support?"

Yoji closed his eyes. I think he was finding his quiet place.

"Let me ask you something." I was ready to change the subject. "Are you all a little nervous knowing that a girl was killed onboard?"

Yoji's eyes crept open now that the tension had been dialed down a notch.

Connie took a deep breath. "Not really. Listening to the gossip, one gets the sense that this was a personal thing. Like a lovers' quarrel."

"Did you meet her?"

She shook her head. "No, I don't think so. I'm not sure which one of the dancers she was. We went to the shows because Yoji likes the slinky costumes."

Yoji looked out the window as a helicopter rose from behind the fishing docks.

"I'm off then," Connie told us. She had a cigarette in her hand before she pushed her chair in. "I have dominoes."

Yoji waited until she left the dining room, at which point Jimmy brought him a gin & tonic. I got the impression it was a standing order kind of thing. "That is the second helicopter I have seen today," he said.

"Any idea who might be on it?"

"We have been told an investigator was to come aboard. I should expect this is his helicopter. Now, perhaps, we can continue to the mainland."

"An investigator," I repeated. "Do you think he'll figure out who killed the girl by the time the cruise is over?"

"Oh, yes." Yoji took a healthy swig of his beverage. "Oh, yes. Yes, he probably will, but unfortunately not before another person is killed."

I stopped chewing. "Why would you say that? I thought this was a crime of passion."

He shook his head. "In fact, it is something else. They are not telling us much, but word travels. Something got to her, and it wasn't human."

I stared at him. "You think an animal did this?"

"I do not. I saw something once, the last time I was up in this part of the world, on Attu island back in 1943. A thing like this happened. It is a thing that happens from time to time in the far north. And I saw it."

"What are you talking about?"

"A demon." He finished his drink and stood. "I wish it were not the case, but it is. Please forgive me. I have Bingo to play."

"At this hour of the morning?" I waited for him to leave before I finished his toast. A surprising amount of rice had been left on his plate but I didn't touch it. I'm not a fan of wasting food, but rice in the morning isn't really my thing.

I've tracked down numerous killers over the years, some more evil than others. But I've never come up against a demon. I was certain that whoever killed Rose DeSilva was a garden-variety human. I was certain too that I was going to find him.

CHAPTER FOUR
DAY 1 - ANCHORED OFF GURBKA ISLAND - 9:30AM

After stopping by the cabin to don my outdoor wear, I took the forward elevator up to the Lynx Deck, to the top of the ship, and stepped out into the arctic morning. And I nearly froze to death. I saw half a dozen passengers gathered by the railing staring at sea gulls, which upon close inspection appeared to be eagles. A pair of heavily-garbed joggers came around the bend and then quickly disappeared behind me. There wasn't much of a jogging track onboard, but people make do.

Consulting my handy deck plan, I learned that there wasn't much up on the Lynx Deck except high-end passenger cabins and a fitness studio. The fitness studio was closed, so I took the stairs down to the Puffin Deck. An older gent, maybe my age, was plastered up against a Plexiglas dome staring down at an empty swimming pool.

I moved in next to him. "What are we looking at?"

He grinned. "Maud Munvez. She does her late morning laps at this time every day."

I fished out my glasses and took a look.

"There's nobody there."

"Settle down."

Sure enough, a moment later I spotted a woman enter the pool. She took her time doing so, stepping gingerly down the steps as she stretched. I smiled as she tossed her towel aside. "She's a looker."

"You can say that again. I've had my eye on Maud since the day we boarded. She's from Coral Gables, retired librarian, a widow to boot."

"She could probably use a little comforting."

"That's what I'm thinking. Fifty-five years old, which in my book is the perfect age for a woman."

"I won't argue with you there. A woman that age; she knows what she wants and she knows how to get it."

"And she knows how to please a gent."

"There is that," I agreed. We watched as Maud gracefully swam back and forth, back and forth, then started climbing up the ladder. "What? Only two laps?"

"Yeah, she only does just the two." He held out his hand. "I'm Murray Abramowitz. I don't think I've seen you around."

I introduced myself just as Maud Munvez settled into a lounge chair. "Is she really going to do the tanning oil? She is. Look at that. That's right, don't forget the legs."

"And don't forget, I saw her first. I'm working up the nerve to ask her out. I'm a little shy."

"What's there to be shy about?" I frowned. "You're a good-looking man, Murray. Virile, powerful, you're in the prime of your life. How old a man are you?"

"Ninety," he said.

I shook my head. "Ninety is the new eighty. I say you walk right up to her, tell her she's the most beautiful woman in the whole Bering Sea. Tell her that if you were an Eskimo out hunting a whale and you saw her . . . No, don't say anything about whales. I don't know, maybe just ask her to dance."

"I might do just that. Yeah, you're right. I'm going to do just that. After I have my nap, I'm going to do it."

"Tell her you'll keep her safe," I suggested. "There's a killer afoot. A young lady could do worse than have a man at her side all night long, just to be on the safe side."

"You're right about that. I've been pumping a little iron in the fitness club. Just let that bastard try to get to my Maud,

I'll show him a thing or two."

"What makes you think it's a he?"

He turned away from Maud. "Come again?"

"She's turning over," I whispered as a couple strolled past us. I pointed down to the pool.

"Holy, mother." Murray shook his head.

"What makes you think it's a he?"

"The killer? Oh, I don't know. A beautiful girl gets her head chopped off, that's not something a girl does. It's a romantic thing."

"I didn't hear anything about her head getting chopped off," I said. "Where did you hear that?"

"Did that not happen? I can't remember, but I do remember thinking that this was a romantic thing. Someone cheated on someone, and someone got mad, something like that. Did you ever have an affair, Henry?"

"Nope."

"You were a married man, I'll wager. You're here by yourself ogling a strange woman. You're wearing gloves so I can't see your ring finger but I'm going to bet you're not wearing a ring. So maybe you got divorced, which would be a statistical anomaly for a man your age- you're in your eighties if you're a day. No, you're a widower, Henry. Ever cheat on your wife?"

I turned. "What the hell?"

"Sorry." He shrugged. "I'm a retired statistician. I like working the odds. So how about it, ever cheat on your wife?"

I took a deep breath. "I got married in 1943. Six months later I shipped out to Belgium just in time for the Battle of the Bulge. I got captured several weeks later and waited out the war in a rancid stalag. Opportunities to cheat were few and far between. My wife died before I got back home."

"I'm sorry to hear that," he said. "Didn't mean to bring up sad memories."

I turned back to Maud but I was still thinking about

Emily, about how little time we had together. Sixty-something years later, and I think about her smile every day.

"It could have been a rival?" I suggested. "Another girl. She was mad because Rose stole her man."

"Possible. And you're saying that whole head-cutting off thing didn't happen, right?"

I nodded.

"Then yeah, maybe. But girls killing girls, statistically, it wouldn't be a stabbing. That's an anger thing, a man's thing. The fairer sex, they're more likely to sneak something up on you, poison your martini. No, it was a man who did this, and I'll be damned if I let him get anywhere near Maud."

So we watched in silence, just two men enjoying the air, taking in the view, for about forty-five minutes. Then I headed in.

I stopped back at the cabin to drop off my coat and found a message waiting for me. Irina Bok requested that I meet her in the captain's office. Something had come up. The message was about an hour old, so I got myself together, ate some nuts from the minibar, and headed out.

I must have gotten turned around in the hallway, because instead of the elevators, I found myself in front of the Arctic Spa. Soothing seashore noises and the smell of jasmine hit me as I pushed open the door.

"I was afraid you wouldn't show up," a young lady said by way of greeting.

"What, now?" I found my glasses and had a closer look. "Hey, you're quite pretty." I leaned in to read her name tag. Priscilla was from Gdansk. I introduced myself.

"You're just in time for Core Surfing," she told me. "Most of the group is already here, so go ahead and get changed. I'll be back in five."

I walked through the double doors into the fitness center where a row of surfboards lined the starboard wall.

"Well I'll be goddamned."

"There's an open one right here," a young woman at the end called out, so I walked past a group of limber folks wearing tracksuits to have a look. Upon closer inspection, it wasn't really a surfboard. It was kind of a surfboard machine. I pushed it with my foot and it wiggled.

"First time?"

"No, that was many years ago," I told her. "But I still get shy taking off my clothes."

She stared at me. "No, I mean is this your first time on a Core Surfboard?"

"Oh, god no. Back in Gdansk, Priscilla and me would go at it for hours."

She wrinkled her nose. "I think you just made that up. I'm Dot. Don't be afraid. I can help you through your first lesson. You'll love it. You'll come out feeling the elongation in your spine."

"But my spine is already long enough."

She shook her head as I sat on my surfboard. The rest of the group had already climbed up onto theirs, and were gently rocking back and forth when Priscilla returned. She had changed into a flattering leotard. I couldn't leave.

"We're going to start out with some basics to help energize your core. Sir, Henry was it? Climb on up." She turned on some old surfing music from the fifties as I tried to stand up.

"Everybody, let's start gently rocking our boards from side to side. What we're doing Henry, since this is your first time, is simulating the athleticism of surfing without having to worry about finding the right wave."

I've never been surfing, but I have to say, once I got myself up there on the board, I found it extremely uncomfortable. I almost fell twice, and I was still holding on to the railing.

Dot reached over from the surfboard next to mine and grabbed my hand, "to help you balance," she said, but I was pretty sure she was hitting on me.

"Now engage your core," Priscilla commanded me when I finally got myself up straight. "You should feel the elongation in your spine."

I think I felt it at about the same time I saw Irina Bok step into the room. She hooked her finger at me.

I let go of Dot's hand. "I'll never surf without you," I promised as I climbed down from my mount. I hugged Priscilla on my way out and joined Irina in the hall.

"Can I ask what you were doing in there?"

"Elongating my spine," I told her.

"Did you not get my message?"

"I did. I did. I was on my way; I just got caught up."

"Yes, I saw. Belov has arrived ahead of schedule. I thought you would want to know."

"Belov? Isn't that one of those arctic weather systems, like all the warm air gets sucked up and then it makes all those weird lights in the sky? Because I've heard about that. I thought you could only see it at night. Is it scary?"

She stared at me. "Victor Belov is a Russian maritime investigator. His ship ran into some mechanical difficulties, so they helicoptered him to Gurbka."

"Is that right?"

"Inspector Belov is anxious to begin his investigation. He is quite a professional, as I'm sure you will see. He is here to do a job, and he does not lose sight of that. He does not waste time. He does not frolic in the spa."

"What are you trying to say?"

She kept quiet as we moved through a throng of passengers. They were wearing towels and beach gear, very likely on their way to the pool for a morning of napping and mystery novel reading.

"Let me ask you a question," I said. "What were the passengers told about the murder?"

Irina led me to the elevator lobby. "Only that a member

of our staff had been found dead, possibly the victim of a homicide."

"That's all? No details?"

She shook her head as the elevator arrived. "We revealed her name, but no details of the assault."

"And nothing about the fact that she was eat . . ."

"Of course not." She held open the door for me. "But it seems that some gossip had already spread before we put a stop to it. The bartender who found her, who found Rose, he told his friends, who then told others."

"I'd like to talk with this bartender."

"Of course." She inserted her keycard into the elevator panel. "His name is Georgie Orbelani. I will take you to him. Inspector Belov is questioning him as we speak."

CHAPTER FIVE
DAY 1 - ANCHORED OFF GURBKA ISLAND - 11:00AM

The elevator took us down, and the door opened onto an entirely different world. Gone were the shimmering carpets, the textured wallpaper, and the soft lights. This was a world of linoleum, of glossy grey paint slathered onto the walls like butter, only lumpier. Fluorescent lights lit our way, nine times as bright as they needed to be. I followed Irina Bok down an immaculate hallway half as wide as the hallways upstairs. This had to one of the cleanest crew decks I had ever seen. "No scuff marks, no trash, not litter," I noted.

"Many of our crew are ex-navy," Irina said. "They become accustomed to rules and procedures."

"What's in here?" I opened an unmarked door on the port side before she could respond. Inside, a bald woman in a kimono was applying mascara to a woman sitting in a barber's chair. Both frowned when I stepped inside, so I stepped out.

"Informal economy," Irina said. "Sultana does makeup for many of the girls."

"Did she do Rose's makeup?"

"I would have no idea."

Just past the forward elevator lobby was the ship's hospital, the only place on this deck that a passenger would have any reason to visit.

"You don't have a morgue onboard?" I asked. "Most ships have morgues, just in case."

"We do, two beds. It is behind the hospital."

"Then why is poor Rose still upstairs in the fridge with the club soda?"

"I told you. We were instructed by our managers in Moscow not to disturb the crime scene until Mr. Belov had a chance to examine it. She will be moved down here this afternoon."

"I'm going to need to speak with her roommate," I told Irina. "Can you set that up?"

She led me down the hall. "Her roommate is a bartender, Michelle Parker. I don't know if I can make her talk with you. She is . . . she is difficult."

"I can do difficult."

I tried to keep up with Irina Bok but we were by this point encountering crewmembers walking past us, and because the hall was barely wide enough for two people, I had to frequently pause. "Something smells good." I looked ahead, and sure enough, there was the crew mess. "Hey, let's go see what they have?"

Irina stopped and then started up again without turning around. "Have you not already eaten?"

"I just thought, you know, maybe a nosh." I grabbed the next fellow who tried to pass. He was wearing the standard engine-room garb, the overalls still vaguely blue after years of bleaching to remove the grime. "What did you have for breakfast?" I demanded of him.

He frowned, then said something in Russian to the man in front of him who began laughing. "Breakfast," I repeated. "What did you have? What's good here? Can you get fries any time of day? I like to be able to get fries any time of day. I don't eat them a lot. I just like knowing."

He said something again in Russian, then stood up a little straighter when Irina approached him and started talking to him.

"He says he had cereal." She turned to me, and if I didn't know any better, I'd think she was angry. "He likes cereal. As well, he enjoyed a pastry. Did you have any more questions about his meal, or can he return to his duties?"

"No, that's fine. Honestly I would be interested in learning more about the pastry, but no. Tell him thanks."

She sent him on his way, and led me further down the hall. Instead of heading into the crew mess, which I now saw was filled nearly to the breaking point with late breakfasters coming off the morning shift, we turned into the crew bar.

"Tempo." I read the neon sign over the entrance, and I followed Irina into the darkest smokiest crew bar I had ever seen. It featured a dozen tiki-style tables complete with palm frond umbrellas, and one ping pong table pressed up against a wall in a way that would effectively prohibit play.

The walls were decorated with old Jamaica travel posters, and at the far end was the bar itself, its mirrored surface doing nothing to brighten the mood.

"This makes me very sad," I told the man standing behind it. "Given such a promising name, I'm finding this Tempo bar grim, very grim."

"I am sad all day long," he said. "I pray for an early death."

Across the room, an older bald gent sat at one of the tiki tables talking with a younger man. And across from them, two attractive peroxide blondes bounced ping pong balls toward the open mouth of a snoring man who had passed out on the ping pong table. The blondes were gaining in skill and precision. It would not be long. "So where is everybody?" I asked the bartender.

"More will come later when the need is felt, when the thirst becomes unbearable, and when the next shift ends. Then I become a well-loved man."

Irina took a seat at a tiki table table next to the older bald man, and she beckoned me to do the same. "Mr. Grave," she said, "I would like you to meet Inspector Belov."

Far be it for me to judge a man on the basis of his age, but I have to confess, I did just that. I was expecting a much younger man, and he was at least my age if he was a day. "Call me Henry."

"Victor." He grinned as he shook my hand. He spoke with a thick Russian accent. "I suspect we are sharing a thought."

"This is Mr. Orbelani." Irina Bok indicated the younger man. "He is a trusted member of our staff, a bartender. It was he who discovered the body."

"Call me Georgie," he said, looking around nervously. "I'm not sure what else I can tell you. I was shocked, as you can imagine. I knew her. Rose, she was one of the family, you know. We all hung out together, nothing more."

"Georgie Orbelani of Tblisi," I read his name tag out loud. "We're a long way from Ukraine, Georgie."

He looked up at me as if he was confused. "Georgia, not Ukraine."

"I'm just saying."

Belov cleared his throat. "And you insist that you were not romantically involved with this woman, Rose," he said, continuing his interview.

"No, never," Georgie insisted. "No, I'm a married man. Second marriage, coming up on our anniversary, I'm not going to do anything to screw that up, no way. With Rose, it was like we were good friends, nothing more. Besides, she was all hung up on Oscar Lonagan. You might want to talk to him."

Belov motioned to the bartender and held up four fingers. "This may come as something of a culture shock to you," he told me. "But I am a Russian man, and we celebrate new friendships. It is perhaps too early in the morning for you, I suspect?"

Irina shut her eyes.

"I can make an exception," I told him. "What did you

have in mind?"

"Tuzemsky," he said when the bartender delivered a clear bottle and four tumblers. "To my own surprise, it is all they serve here."

"We are passionate about our liquor here at Tempo," the bartender told us. "This bottle of Tuz will delight. A finer beet liquor cannot be found anywhere in the Bering Sea."

"Beets?" I frowned. "Beet liquor; that's a new one for me."

"It takes some getting used to," Georgie told me as Belov poured. Irina shook her head but he filled her glass anyway.

"To a speedy resolution of this case." Belov raised his glass. And we drank. Even Irina.

"You lied," I told Georgie after draining my glass.

Belov slammed his empty glass down onto the table. "Yes, he lied. That is very astute of you. How did you know?"

"What, now?"

Georgie looked up, clearly alarmed. "I didn't lie about anything."

Belov refilled our glasses. "Mr. Grave is clearly a professional at this line of work." He stared the man in the eye. "But I myself could tell that you are lying. It is in your eyes, Georgie."

"No."

"Yes. You killed her, didn't you? It is time for you to be admitting that you did this thing."

Nothing else could be heard in the room, except the bouncing of a lone ping pong ball as it headed out into the hall.

Georgie's mouth hung open. "No," he said finally. "No, I didn't do anything. Nothing."

Belov stared at him hard. "When I asked you about the victim, you indicated that you were simply acquaintances, that you hung out together, good friends, nothing more."

"That's right," he said defensively. "Come on, there's a party every night down here, in one cabin or another. Usually six or seven at a time, it's how we blow off steam."

"Na zdrovje," I said, and I tossed back my drink.

Belov drank his slowly. "Nobody really says 'na zdrovje.'" He took his mobile phone from his pocket. "When first I heard about this murder, I sent a message to Captain Tolstoy requesting the entire previous month's surveillance files. Nineteen hours of footage, I was sent, including this."

I leaned over to get a look at the tiny screen. The image wasn't very high-quality, but it didn't need to be. Two naked people were going at it on top of the bar in the Beluga Bar, right where Rose DeSilva had been killed.

Irina's eyes opened wide.

"Of course it does not have audio," Belov noted. "We might have heard some interesting things, but I'm certain we can all agree that this is you, Georgie, upon whom that young lady is mounted. That is the late Miss DeSilva, is it not? And on top of the bar, no less, which is unsanitary. I find myself becoming quite disappointed in you."

Irina frowned. "I don't remember seeing this on the file footage. We scoured every scene for entire week leading up to the murder."

"Which is why I asked for the entire month," Belov told her coolly. "This encounter is taking place three weeks ago. It was not the night of the crime, for certain, but doesn't it seem a little strange that he was with her in the same place where she died? Did he grow angry when she rebuffed him?"

"What? No." Georgie shuffled in his chair. "Look. Look, you know, it was just one of those moments. You saw what she looked like; she was gorgeous. You know, we had both had a little too much to drink. It was weeks ago, like you said. It was just a hookup, nothing more."

"Things aren't looking so good," I told him, "at least as far as that second marriage is concerned."

Georgie shook his head. "Come on, I've been two tours without a break. That's six months. That's a long time to go without . . . you know. And so what, so we hooked up? Doesn't mean I killed her."

"It doesn't mean you didn't." Belov stood. "I am only just arriving. You are now my number one suspect." He turned to Irina. "Arrest him. Put him in the brig."

"Hey, no. Wait a minute," Georgie begged. "No, look. I don't know what happened to her, really." He gestured to Belov's phone. "After that night, we barely spoke. She was dating the captain, so she was being careful. It was a little awkward, I'll admit. I wanted to see more of her, OK?"

"But you did see more of her," Belov told him. "You're the one who found her body."

Georgie nodded. "I did, but I had nothing to do with it. I swear."

Our conversation was interrupted by a series of cheers. Over at the ping pong table, a drunk man sat up. He was choking, but once he coughed up a ping pong ball, we could all see why.

"Put him in the brig." Belov checked his watch. "I have appointment with the chief engineer. Perhaps, Mr. Grave, we will share our dinner together tonight."

That sounded good to me. "My treat," I told him.

CHAPTER SIX
DAY 1 - ANCHORED OFF GURBKA ISLAND - NOON

I didn't know what to think about Georgie Orbelani, but I was definitely developing a mental picture of Rose DeSilva. She was a saucy thing.

Let Belov have his own suspects, I certainly had mine. I took the elevator to the Caribou Deck and delivered a healthy knock to door number 534. "Housekeeping," I shouted.

I heard movement from within, but nobody said anything. I knocked again, and somebody told me to go away. I wasn't going to go away.

Part of the deal that a cruise ship operator makes, when I am called in to investigate a crime, is that I am allowed extraordinary access to information, to files, and to physical space. You'll remember that I work in international waters, where national jurisdictions do not apply.

Think you have rights at sea? Think again. Do I need to read you some kind of warning before I question you? I do not. Do I need a warrant to read your personnel file, access your e-mail, or enter your cabin? Guess again. I am a one-man law-enforcement bureau, and I always get my man.

I used my master keycard to unlock the door, and I stepped inside.

Brice Laird popped up in the bed. The puzzled look on his face betrayed a troubled mind churning through unhappy memories in search of recognition.

"Hey there, Leslie." I moved into the room. "Remember

me?" Some thoughts occurred to me at this moment. I have never felt any attraction for men, but I think if I was going to, it would be for a man like Brice Laird. He was the picture of manly gorgeousness. Seventy years old, and he looked fifty. Fit as a masculine fiddle. If I had a look like Brice's, I would have moved through the female fauna of this world at some greater pace. Not that I've done half bad.

"Good God," Brice said as I sat down next to him. He looked as if he had seen a very unpleasant but handsome ghost.

"I have this same cabin," I told him. In the bed, a lady friend sat up, gathering the sheets up to her chin. "I mean, my cabin is identical, down to the artwork. But I have to say, Leslie, I didn't get a beautiful girl in my bed. I need to talk to someone about that."

"What is this about?" The girl was not pleased. "Can you leave? Can you see that I'm not dressed?"

"Oh, I can see." I patted the edge of the bed. "So are you the new Mrs. Leslie Wayne Humholtz or just a friend?"

"What are you talking about? Brice, who is this man? And who is Leslie Wayne Humholtz?"

Brice Laird shook his head. "Darla, I'd like you to meet a very old, very sad man who has been stalking me for years.

I held out my hand but Darla didn't shake.

"We had an unfortunate incident some years ago in the South Pacific," Brice continued. "Henry made some unfounded accusations."

"Leslie killed his wife," I told the girl.

"I had nothing to do with it," Brice explained. "I loved her."

"Actually he killed both his wives. Listen, Darla is it? I'd love to catch up some time. Maybe you and I could get together later on, have a tot or two, maybe tie one on and talk sports. But for now, I have to have a chat with Leslie, and I'm pretty certain he'll want that to be private."

"Who is Leslie?" She reached over to collect her her clothes from the sofa. "I think you might have the wrong man. This is Brice Laird, the movie star."

"Movie star? Movie star is pushing it. He was in four movies, maybe. Two if you only count speaking parts."

"Seven." Brice held up seven fingers. "Seven critically-acclaimed films. I was called the next Cary Grant."

"By your mother." I turned back to Darla. "His real name is Leslie. Last I checked he was still living with his mother. How is she these days?"

"She passed away some years back. I don't remember receiving your condolence card, now that we're talking."

"Killed her too, did you?"

"Natural causes." He folded his arms. "And after all these years, I assumed that you had passed as well. I'm sorry to see that's not the case."

I turned to Darla. "Have you seen any of his films? I doubt they're still around, but at best you could call him a bit actor in low-budget Mexican horror films."

"'Pyramid of Wax' was re-released." Brice smiled at Darla. "They added a new musical score. I received a Best Actor Award from the Academy."

"He did," I agreed. "Best actor from the Mexican Academy of Motion Picture Monsters. What did they call that little trophy they gave you, a Paco?"

Brice shook his head. "It's more than you've ever won. And 'A Bride for Count Yorga' remains a cult classic. Henry, please don't let your complete lack of success make you bitter."

"Count Yorga - wasn't that the one where you played a werewolf? I had never seen a Mexican werewolf before." I turned to Darla. "He was wearing a sombrero."

"I was not. Can you leave us now, Henry?" He grabbed a bottle of tonic water from the minibar. "Darla and I had plans to enjoy our afternoon. But if you prefer, I can call security."

"Oh, you can try," I told him, "but I'm afraid I am

security. When I heard about this girl being murdered, and you being onboard, well, I put two and two together, Leslie."

"You have got to be kidding me. You're still working? If you really need the money, I'm sure you could find some job down at a local pie shop or something. But to work as an investigator at your advanced age . . . it just seems unseemly. I feel sad for you."

"You and me both. Believe me, I'm weeping on the inside. I would like nothing more than to find my own Darla and sail the seven seas. In fact, I may even try to steal her away from you. But for now, I have to focus on the case."

He sighed. Then he turned to Darla. "Sweetheart, would you mind if I dealt with this unpleasant thing now and then meet you in a little bit?"

"Fine," she said. "Turn around."

I did. When she left, I moved over to the couch and pried the lid off a tin of cookies.

Brice sat at the edge of the bed. "There was no call for you to be rude. I'm just an old man trying to make a living. Why do you need to hassle me?"

"Somehow I'm having a hard time seeing you as a dancing host. How long have you been at that?"

"Coming on two years now."

"Nice. You dance with the ladies, make sure they're having a nice time. I get it. I'm pretty sure you're not supposed to sleep with them. Hey, these cookies are first rate."

He held out his hands. "You know, what can I tell you? Darla is lovely. What could I do?"

He had a point. "You know, Leslie . . ."

"Brice. It's Brice. That's my legal name. If you want to talk to me, you'll have to use my name."

"Brice, when I heard a girl had died in your vicinity, I have to admit, my mind started putting the pieces together."

He sighed. "Yes, that poor girl. She was lovely, Henry. You should have seen her."

"I did."

"What? Oh, right. I see what you mean. But really, she was a truly charming girl, one of uncommon beauty, also very loose morals. Very loose, which I admire."

"Did you get to know her?"

"No, no, not in the way you're suggesting. But since I am technically part of the entertainment staff, I did attend events that she also attended. I can't say that I ever had a conversation with her."

"Not even when you killed her?"

He didn't even respond.

"Where were you two nights ago?"

"Right here in my cabin."

"Can Darla confirm?"

"No, but Murial Orlovsky can, though she won't be happy to do so. She gave her husband an extra dose of whatever he takes at night so she could slip out. I'm certain if you spoke to her discreetly she would confirm that she spent the night with me."

Nuts. I wrote down the name. "I'll be sure to check. So who do you think killed her?"

He finished off his tonic water. "I haven't given it much thought, but you might do well to question Oscar Lonagan, the naturalist. Rose had something of a crush on him, though he was clearly attached."

"Who is Oscar Lonagan?"

"He's our featured onboard lecturer, some kind of botanist. I haven't been to any of the talks, but he's popular. He has an assistant, if you will. Lovely girl, half his age, a student I believe."

I closed my notebook. "I'm not going to have to worry about you, am I?"

"What do you mean, Henry?"

"I mean I already have one murder to investigate. I don't want to wake up in the morning to learn Darla has been killed and you're yammering on about how she tried to stab you so you stabbed her first."

He held up his hand. "Henry, haven't you found that a man mellows with the passage of time, becomes more relaxed, less impulsive?"

"No," I told him, and I left, taking the cookies with me.

I rode the elevator down to the Polar Bear Deck and headed to Reception. There I found a placard promising that someone would return in ten minutes. I used the house phone to call Irina.

"Where can I find Oswald Lonagan?" I asked her.

"Oscar Lonagan. Hold on a moment. Let me check. Where are you?"

I told her.

"Turn around."

I did just that.

"Do you see the entrance there to the Vitus Bering Theater?"

I nodded.

"Do you?"

"Yes, yes."

"Do you really?"

"I do."

"Do you see the giant poster with the words 'Oscar Lonagan' printed on it?"

"Let me get a closer look." I took a full step away from the reception desk. I read the poster and checked my watch. "Wait, that's right now."

"Yes."

"That's quick work," I told her. "Hey, I can't spend the whole day yakking it up with you. I'm off."

"Wait," she said.

"What, now?"

"How did you know he was lying?"

"Who?"

"Our suspect; Georgie. You said he lied. You and Belov both knew. But Belov had the video. You didn't. How did you know?"

"Yeah, I tell you, Irina, if you live long enough, you develop skills, mad skills, the kind a tiger uses to hunt elands and savanna dworkins and glockenspiels. And I've spent a lifetime honing my considerable intellect so that . . ."

"Just tell me."

"You know that beet brandy we just had?"

"Tuzemsky. Yes, so what?"

"Well I've never had it before. Georgie said it would take some getting used to, but it didn't. I took to it immediately. It was delicious. It was crisp. Briny, yet there was a hint of nutmeg there. I found it very refreshing."

"So that's what you meant when you said he lied – that he was lying about the liquor."

"Pretty much," I admitted.

She hung up.

CHAPTER SEVEN
DAY 1 - SAILING FROM GURBKA ISLAND - 1:00PM

I felt a slight roll underfoot. A glimpse out the window confirmed that we were underway, leaving Gurbka in our wake. I would like to have spent more time staring out at the sea, but I had work to do.

I quietly slipped into the Vitus Bering Theater and took a seat in the back. Oscar Lonagan paced the stage. Behind him, on the screen was an image of an Alaskan woman smoking a pipe. Lonagan was a big man, maybe sixty years old, ruggedly handsome with a thick head of hair. 'Shamans, Sagos, and Sagas,' read the sign in front of the podium.

"Mrs. Kiliak is among the last of her kind," Lonagan told the assembled crowd. A giant gold watch slipped up and down his arm as he ran his fingers through his hair. "She is among the last of the Umaquiut Aleut shamans. And if you're among the six hundred inhabitants of Romanoff Island, you're going to need her sooner or later."

On his next slide, the same woman, smoking the same pipe, gave a young native boy an injection. "Lest we think that shamanism is nothing but superstition and sleight of hand," Lonagan continued, "we need remember that it is these local healers who provide a range of medical functions. They are public health professionals trained in the healing arts."

The next slide was blank and the theater was suddenly dark. "But we didn't come here to talk about that," Lonagan told his audience.

Gasps from the audience accompanied the next slide, which featured a young Aleutian whale hunter covered in blood, his lips pulled back to reveal bloody teeth, but it was the eyes that held our attention. Bulging and nearly black.

"This young man is Edward Littlemore," Lonagan said quietly. "He had a bad day. You see, this far north, normal rules of time and space hardly apply. Day can become night for a very long time. I'll tell you, I have been out there at sea in a baidarka, a native canoe, when the wind began howling in unnatural ways. The cold suddenly becomes colder, as if your heart were made of ice. Have you ever had a polar bear talk to you? Tell you to turn around? I have."

"In this next slide," he continued, "you'll note Edward Littlemore's baidarka. And this is the photograph that the police took just before they took Edward into custody. Can someone tell me what that is sitting on the seat?"

I heard grumbling and light conversation. Honestly, I couldn't see anything but blood and maybe some hair.

"Is that a head?" Someone asked.

Lonagan nodded. "That is Edward Littlemore's grandfather's head. At his trial, Edward told the jury the same thing he had been saying all along, that he had no idea what happened to his grandfather, that he had nothing to do with it. But he had. We can know this for sure."

He said nothing for a full minute. "We can learn a lot from DNA," he said finally. "But can DNA prove this man killed his grandfather? Tell me how?"

Hands went up all around the room. Lonagan was doing great. I've seen a lot of lecturers in my day. Some were good, and some were coma inducing, but I would have been willing to bet money that nobody was going to leave Oscar Lonagan's lecture before it was over.

"You could test the DNA to prove they were related," came a voice from the front.

"You could," Lonagan said. "But we already know they

are related."

"The kid had blood all over him. You could test the blood to see if it was the grandfather's DNA," offered a young woman.

Lonagan nodded. "Closer. But first, we already know it was the grandfather's blood because there would have been no other place to acquire human blood out in the middle of the Bering Sea. Second, blood doesn't have a lot of DNA in it. Red blood cells don't have any."

"Oh no," came a voice from the back. I turned to find on older woman shaking her head. "Oh no. They did find the grandfather's DNA didn't they?"

"Yes." Lonagan nodded. "In the only place that could positively prove that Edward Littlemore killed him."

Some speculation ensued.

"In Edward Littlemore's stomach," Lonagan said softly. "He killed and partially ate the old man. And afterward he had no memory of it. He died twenty-nine years ago in the psychiatric ward of the Spring Creek Correctional Facility in Seward. His body was exhumed seven years ago, as was the grandfather's head. That's how the DNA match was made. Otherwise, we might still not know for certain that it was Edward who did this."

On the next slide, the old woman with the pipe was leading a ceremony in which thirty or so people held their hands in the air. "Modern science has no explanation for Edward Littlemore's behavior," Lonagan told the audience, "but Mrs. Kiliak does. Like the shamans of the Amazon, like the healers of the South African veldt, like the medicine men of the Shoshone, Mrs. Kiliak has answers to questions we humans have been asking for millennia. And Mrs. Kiliak knows about the Pribilof Sago, which will be the topic of my next lecture. Thank you all for coming."

After a lengthy question and answer period that I somehow managed to sleep through, the theater started to empty out.

I couldn't have been down for long because I awoke to find Oscar Lonagan with his arms wrapped around a young woman. She had her back to him as she coiled a pair of electrical cables. There must have been an argument, I surmised, because she was doing her best to ignore him, even as he kissed her neck.

My stomach rumbled forth from the back, startling the semi-amorous couple. "Goodness." I pried myself out of the seat. "I didn't realize how hungry I was."

Lonagan released the girl. "My apologies. I thought we were alone."

"No, no. Hey, I enjoyed your talk. That's quite a thing, the thing that you spoke about." I turned to the girl and introduced myself. "You must be Mrs. Lonagan."

"Really?" she said. "You think I'm his wife? Well I'm not. His wife is his wife and he won't divorce her, so here we are. I'm Grace Redfield. I'm Oscar's research assistant."

"Is that right? Were you there when that boy ate his grandfather?"

"What? No, of course not," she said. "That was in 1943. I was not even conceptualized."

Lonagan closed his laptop and placed it in his case. "Grace is one of the most talented botanists I have ever known. She is vital to my work."

"And I hope she will be to mine as well," I said. Of the three of us, nobody was sure exactly what I meant by that, so we let it pass. "Let me ask you something, why do you think he did it, that kid who ate his grandfather? Did he just run amok?"

Lonagan grinned. "Interesting choice of words. Amok is a culture-bound psychosis, first identified on the Malay archipelago. A seemingly-introverted, calm, subordinated young man would suddenly be gripped by a strong urge to kill, which he very well might act on."

"Our postal workers do that all the time," I joked.

"No they don't," he said firmly. "That's a myth, and an unkind one. But like most myths, it encapsulates a grain of truth. What will the average American postal worker never achieve?"

"A smoking hot research assistant." I winked at Grace.

"No. No, think about it. What does it mean to be an American? What does an American man grow up wanting?"

"Liberty and justice for all," I ventured, "also, a recreational vehicle."

"Power." Lonagan slammed his fist on the podium. The girl jumped, startled, but you could tell she liked it.

"Power, my good man. He wants power. He wants great wealth and power over other men, which is something a postal worker will never have. And for a small percentage of such men, the absence of power can slowly become maddening, until one day it becomes too much."

"Is that why women rarely kill?" I asked, "because they don't care as much about power?"

He stared at me. "Of course. What does an American woman want more than anything in the world?"

I turned to Grace.

"Don't look at me," she said. "I'm Canadian. And I would be OK with power and great wealth."

"She wants to be thin." Lonagan answered his own question. "She wants to be interesting and creative, but more than anything else, she wants to be thin. So badly in fact, that this desire may warp her mind in much the same way as the Amok victim. She may do violence to herself. She may refuse to eat, even if it leads to her death."

"Anorexia," I said.

"Yes. Another culture-bound psychosis. We scientists still have so much to learn about the mind, about its weaknesses. What is schizophrenia really? Is it nothing more than the distance between a cultural ideal and a mind that finds itself lacking?"

Grace finished coiling her cables. "We need to move along," she said. "They need to set up the room for Casper's Follies."

"What is Casper's Follies?" I turned to find two Filipino technicians carrying a miniature piano.

"I have no idea," she said. "But we are due in the Beluga Bar, where we are contractually required to be social."

I put my hand on Lonagan's arm as he tried to follow her. "The girl who was killed on board - what's the chance that this had something to do with one of these culture psychotics?"

"Culture-bound psychoses," he corrected me. "And I have seen no evidence to suggest that one would be involved. Unless dear Rose was obese, power-crazed, or partially eaten, I suspect her killing was of a more mundane nature. If you will excuse me."

I watched him leave, following the girl. He didn't know what had happened to Rose, and I was going to have to tell him. Oscar Lonagan was going to help me find the killer.

CHAPTER EIGHT
DAY 1 - AT SEA - 4:00PM

L eaving the theater, I nearly lost my footing as a swell lifted the ship. I looked out the window and saw the waves below us. We appeared to be at full steam, and the sea was not peaceful.

I walked past the inexplicably-named Havana Bar, in which a couple of gents smoked cigars. The card room was empty, not even a tray of cookies on hand, but the gift shop was open. I went in and perused the fine assortment of bathrobes, watches, semi-fine jewelry, and paperbacks. Two Russian women were trying on dinner gowns. From the looks of them, I made two conclusions: these women were lifelong friends who had stopped liking each other decades ago; and the gowns didn't work for either of them.

"Can I help you?" The nearest woman frowned.

"No. No," I told her. "I was just looking around, trying to pick out some watches, semi-fine jewelry, and paperbacks."

"You should not stare."

Apologize or engage; I understood these to be my options. To apologize would be the honorable choice. And had I been on land, I would have chosen that option. But I was at sea. I am a pelagic man, at home on the oceans. And I am a hunter, having dedicated the latter portion of my life to catching those rare criminals who haunt my beloved cruise ships. As such, I must engage whenever possible. Apology not offered. "I couldn't help myself," I said. "You're a beautiful woman."

But I think I waited too long. She was already halfway to the dressing room by the time I got my line out. "What?" she called back.

"Nothing. Just trying to pick out a bathrobe."

I left quickly and continued my walk. I passed a woman pushing her older husband in a wheelchair, and another even older couple who half-stumbled along, enjoying the last legs of the ambulatory portion of their lives. I also saw a couple of younger couples; men and women in their twenties, maybe thirties, honeymooners perhaps, and I was glad to see that. It's important to have young people on board. Otherwise cruising becomes something that old people do, and nobody wants to do the things that only old people do. It's too depressing.

The vast dining room was soon before me, and there was no line in sight. I would be the first for lunch!

Vadeem greeted me with a frown as I threw the great doors open.

"What, do you sit here all day?" I asked him.

"No, Mr. Henry. I fold the napkins. It is work that gives me solace between meals."

"Now that you mentioned it," I said, grabbing a napkin and tucking it into my shirt, "I could use a good meal. I'm famished. What's for lunch?"

He frowned again.

"You're bringing me down, Vadeem. Hey, what say you bring me a gimlet and find me a table where I can meet girls. Just set me up."

"But it's four in the afternoon, Mr. Henry. Lunch is over."

"What, now?" I looked at my watch but it was still set to Pennsylvania time. I looked out the window. "It's the middle of the damn day."

"The arctic sun; it can trick a man. It feels like noon, but it is in fact already close to evening."

"So what happened to lunch?"

He shrugged. "It was eaten."

"All of it?"

He nodded.

I gave him back the napkin. "No gimlet?"

He shook his head. "And no girls."

"Can I get room service?"

He smiled. "You can always get room service. Just call from your stateroom. You will find a menu in your welcome packet."

"Do I have to dial 9 first?"

"Don't do such a thing. Dinner is at 8:00, Mr. Henry, so be sure to eat only a small portion. Perhaps some crackers, a little cheese."

"That's a fine idea," I told him.

Back in the cabin, I took out the passenger profile folder that Irina Bok delivered, as well as the staff profiles. Then I called room service. I didn't have to wait long. Two Bulgarian beers proved a fine accompaniment to the cheese plate. The pate required a stronger tot so I found a split of white wine in the minibar and gave that a sample. The pound cake was normal pound cake, but that was OK. What's not to like about pound cake?

I got myself settled, opened up the profiles and decided to learn a little more about our featured lecturer.

Oscar Lonagan, age 60, of North London, was a British ecologist of some minor international fame. From his bio, you would think he was next in line to be Pope.

"Often called the greatest naturalist of modern times, Dr. Lonagan has conducted ethnobotanical fieldwork on all seven continents. Although he was awarded his Ph.D. at Cambridge University, it was in the university of the Amazon jungle that he earned it, Lonagan is quick to tell his students. As an apprentice to the great Jivaro shaman Quin-'siwe, Lonagan spent more than two years at the banks of the Maranon River learning the ways of the ancients.

A pioneering researcher in the field of ethnomedicine, Lonagan is perhaps best known for his best-selling books *The New Way of the Old Shaman*, and *How I Became One with the Cactus at the Center of the World*, both of which recount his experiences with tropical hallucinogens.

Current research interests include arctic and subarctic pharmacology as well as indigenous medicine. Dr. Lonagan maintains homes in London, and in coastal Maine."

And just for fun, I had to have a look at the bio of my old nemesis.

"Original, old school, romantic, peerless; Brice Laird is all this and more. One of the most talented actors of his generation, Brice has graced screen and stage, garnering an international reputation as both a character actor and a leading man. The recipient of the Rodolfo Manuel Ignacio award for best actor in a motion picture, Brice has also garnered nods at Cannes, Aspen, and of course, Hollywood. Classically-trained, Brice still graces the stage when not traveling or filming.

Brice was born and raised in Los Angeles. As a teenager, he was an assistant to the great Bela Lugosi who became a close friend. Indeed it was Lugosi who encouraged Brice to take to the stage. And once he began, there was no stopping him. In addition to acting, Brice Laird is also an award-winning dancer, taught by none other than Ginger Rogers, his companion of many years. Brice enjoys cognac, old movies, and the company of women."

Yeah, Brice is peerless all right. Not many people can say they killed two wives and got away with it. I've paid a lot of attention to Brice over the years, so I had some sense of what was real and what wasn't. The Ginger Rogers bit was new to me, so that was likely made up. I'm pretty sure he raked leaves at Lugosi's house once or twice; that being the likely extent of the lifelong friendship. Rodolfo Manuel Ignacio was a Mexican horror film producer who prided himself on never spending more than $100,000 on a film. And almost everybody enjoys cognac, old movies, and the company of women.

All things considered, I wasn't too impressed with Brice's bio, but apparently it was fat enough to get him this gig.

I must have nodded off at some point, because I woke to find a beautiful woman standing in front of me. "Am I dreaming?" I asked her.

"Your bed, sir?"

"Yes," I said, patting the mattress at my side.

"Would you like me to turn it down before dinner?"

"What, now?"

"Or if you like, I can perhaps do it while you are at dinner if you prefer."

I was getting a little confused. The sunlight was shining right into my eyes. "What time is it?"

She pointed to the clock on my bed table. "8:15."

I felt my chest tighten. Adrenaline surged through my abdomen. I jumped out of bed and ran out into the hall. "I'll be back after dinner," I told her. But in truth, I was back a moment later to collect my pants and shoes, and the envelope that Irina Bok had slipped under my door. Then I raced back down to the dining room.

"Girls, Mr. Henry." Vadeem greeted me excitedly. He pointed to a four-seater by the window where two lovely women were enjoying their shrimp cocktail. One blonde, one redhead; they were the kind of women who watched their figures, who ate daintily, delicately, and who would always leave a little something on their plate. And that would mean more shrimp for me.

"You're my main man, Vadeem. If I ever achieve enlightenment, I'm coming back for you. I want you to know that. No Nirvana for me, not until we get you all sorted out. Then it's you and me taking on the afterlife." I clapped him on the shoulder and started on my way, eager to sample my own crustaceans. I was halfway there when Belov waved at me. I had forgotten I promised to eat with him.

"I was worried you had forgotten our dinner," he said.

"No, no," I told him, as he pointed me to a chair. "I've been looking forward to this meal."

"It looked to me as if you were about to be sitting with those women over there. Do you know them?"

"Not yet." I took my seat. "But I'm hoping to. So what's good here? Hey, I see you've already started on the juice. I was hoping we could have more of that beet bourbon. That was nice, kind of tangy. It had an interesting afterburn, kind of earthy."

Belov tucked his napkin into his collar as I did the same. "Tuz," he said. "Yes, it has some life to it. I'm surprised you enjoyed it. Most Americans find it too caustic."

"Caustic is my middle name." I smiled as a waiter placed a menu in my hand. "Hey, can you bring us more rolls? Belov ate all of ours."

Belov shook his head. "I did not."

"You lie." I pointed to the crumbs next to his chair. "You ate them all. No shame there, I'd have done the same if I got here first."

"A true detective." He clapped his hands. "Tell me, how is it you are not retired? I always thought you Americans were pensioned off at a young age. No move to Miami for you? Poolside, surrounded by blondes and breasts; it is an image I am clinging to for years."

"You and me both."

"Is it not real?"

I told him about Rolling Pines, up in Bethlehem, where I hang my hat. "Things can really heat up, especially in the summer. But you're right about the ladies. They are lovely and they are many. About a month ago, I'm sitting on my back porch. Not the front porch, because it gets the sun in the late afternoon. So I'm sitting there and this bus pulls up. 'Cortland Manor' I read. Do you know what Cortland Manner is?"

Belov shook his head. "Is it the residence of an ancestral count or a duke?"

I shook my head. "It's only the most posh ladies retirement community in eastern Pennsylvania."

Our waiter was still standing there so I had to make a quick decision. Belov beat me to the punch. "The chef's salad, please, the tomato bisque." He frowned. "I am torn between the salmon and the venison. Perhaps I might not have to choose. Perhaps I might eat both?"

I was starting to admire this man. "I'll have the same." I shut my menu. "Also shrimp cocktail."

Belov poured me a tumbler of bourbon.

"I thought you Rusian guys only went in for vodka."

He sighed. "I cannot stand it. All my life, I have been hating it. This has made me unpopular on many a social occasion, but what can I do?"

"The liver wants what the liver wants."

"It is true. Now tell me more about this Cortland Manor."

I drank some of my bourbon. "Right. I had forgotten all about this social event that was on the calendar, so I cleaned up and headed over to the clubhouse just as the ladies were getting off the bus. And they were lovely, let me tell you. These women were refined, not to mention rich."

Belov grinned. "What a life you must live."

"So I got to talking to this one sweet thing by the name of Cadence. She was from Queens originally, and she walked like one too, all regal. She'd had work done, a lot of it. Nose, cheeks, and a boob job. You would swear she was seventeen except for the goiter."

Our basket of rolls arrived, and I beat him to it. "Anyway, me and Cadence get to talking and it turns out we have a lot in common. She had an aunt up in Albany, and I did too. We both enjoyed romantic comedies, though me not so much. And we both liked wine. So we did a little drinking, did a little dancing." I took a moment to savor the memory.

"And?" Belov had an expectant look in his eyes.

"Yeah, so that was pretty much it. After the drinking and the dancing, I sat for a while, and I think I nodded off because when I woke up, they were gone, all the ladies. But she sent me a note about a week later telling me she had a nice time."

"That is all?"

"No, no. We met up again a few weeks later. We went into the city and saw a show. It ended late so I suggested we should stay overnight in the city. She didn't know it, but I had already booked a room. So we went traipsing into the Ritz Carlton and I demanded champagne for the lady. Everyone at the desk was staring, so I slipped the guy a twenty and my driver's license and asked for their finest room, whatever the price."

Belov grinned. "I am enjoying your chicanery."

"Thanks. Yeah, so the guy behind the desk, he's playing along. He apologizes and tells me they only have a junior suite left. See, I already know this because I booked the room the day before. I even used a coupon I found in the AARP magazine, so I got a really good price, but I cursed him out anyway, asking him if this is the kind of lady who looks like she belongs in a junior suite. And he didn't know what to say."

"I would not know either."

"So the upshot is that Cadence was quite impressed. We drank champagne and stared out at the lights of New York City, and I swear I felt like a spry septuagenarian that night. I made love like one too."

Belov clapped. "This is a wonderful story you are telling me."

"Thank you very much. So what about you? What's life like for a Russian fellow? Boiled turnips and beet beer, or do you live large?"

Our soups arrived. Food moves quickly in a cruise ship restaurant. It's wonderful food, but it is dished and served with assembly-line speed and precision.

"One year ago," Belov tasted his soup, "I was living in a beautiful dacha about an hour outside of St. Petersburg. A short walk down the road lived a widow of sixty-one years calling herself Sarah Ivanova. Each day I am making a point to walk by her door, at which time she would invite me in for schnapps and energetic lovemaking. Her family was from Minsk, you see, so I always spoke slowly so she could understand."

He roared with laughter. "That is old Russian joke that I enjoy very much."

I grabbed another roll from the basket. "Tell me more about Sarah."

"Yes. So one day after the schnapps and the energetic lovemaking, I was enjoying a shower in Sarah Ivanova's shower with Sarah Ivanova, and I fell down, breaking my hip."

"Ouch."

He shook his head. "It was more the embarrassment than the ouch. I have three step-bastards who conspired against me. They sold my dacha and moved me to a disturbing bleakness in central Moscow where lunatics cry out from street corners."

"An asylum?" Our salads arrived, which was a good thing. The soup wasn't going to last long.

"No, it is a residence for retired soldiers, but the neighborhood is bad. Many drunks called it home. Many of us still do." He roared with laughter again. "But also there are a great many lunatics who are walking around, for reasons I cannot know."

"You were a soldier, weren't you? You would have been there, back then, in the big war."

"I would have been," he said, "but my father pulled a fat piece of string connected to a powerful general, and I spent the war at a signals desk in the Kremlin."

"Lucky guy. Hey, so tell me more about the widow Sarah. Was that the end of the story?"

"No," he said, his mouth crammed with salad. He paused to chew. "No, she visited me once in Moscow. It was nice. We ate boiled fish and played cards. But no energetic lovemaking."

"That's a terrible thing. And now here we are, two old men trying to get a few crumbs to eat as we solve a murder."

Belov nodded. "So do you know yet who murdered poor Rose?"

"I think it was Oscar Lonagan," I lied. "I think he's a cannibal."

Belov shrugged and refilled our beverages. "I doubt this very much, though I have intentions to speak with his assistant. I will be meeting with her in the morning."

"Who do you think did it?" I asked.

He wiped his mouth with his napkin and tossed back the vodka. "The bartender Georgie, the man we have in custody. I am planning to interrogate him further."

"You don't think it was the cook, the other fellow we have in the brig?"

Belov shook his head. "I do not."

"Then maybe we could spring him," I suggested. "My salad lacks zing."

CHAPTER NINE
DAY 1 - AT SEA — 10:00PM

My dinner companion was quite a drinking man. I realized this as I hobbled out of the dining room. I've been known to imbibe a drop or two from time to time, but I was no match for Belov. I headed up to the Puffin Deck to take in the evening air, and I nearly froze to death once again.

Although the sun was still out, the air had cooled considerably, and I wasn't dressed for this. I ran back inside, thinking maybe it was time to visit the bridge.

Passing the brig, I had a peek inside and spotted the chef and Georgie Orbelani sharing a space meant for one. Neither looked happy, but I was in no mood for their gloom. I kept walking and knocked on the unmarked door.

On most cruise ships, the door to the bridge is unmarked because anyone who has business there already knows where it is, and anyone who doesn't have business there isn't welcome. But if you look closely, you can usually spot the differences in the door. It will be heavier than most, and the hinges more substantial.

Piracy is rarer than most people imagine, but it's still a threat. And if someone came on board to hijack the ship, the bridge would be the last line of defense. Inside, in a locked cabinet, waits an assortment of weapons.

That being said, a cruise ship isn't an airplane. And no captain is going to let passengers fall in harm's way. No, he'll hand over the keys to the ship to the pirates, but only after sending a series of emergency signals that will be immediately picked up by a number of military services around the globe.

You can't do much with a hijacked cruise ship except demand ransoms and eat good food. And with the chef in the brig, even that much was going to take some work.

I knocked and nobody answered. I knocked again and held my ID up to the peephole. "I can stand here all day," I called out. "But it was very cold outside. I think one of my toes fell off. Also, a testicle. Can you please open the door and invite me in?"

Nothing, until Captain Tolstoy emerged from the office behind me. He was talking in Russian on his cellphone. "Mr. Grave," he said. He slipped the phone into his pocket. "How can we help you this evening?"

"Thought I'd have a look at the bridge."

"Of course." He led me to the door and pushed a series of buttons on the keypad.

"Hey are you any relation to the other Tolstoy, the poet?"

"The novelist," he said, as he led me onto the bridge. "Leo Tolstoy was a novelist. He is a great uncle of mine."

"That's a fine thing," I told him as I wandered over to the forward window. "Hey did I ever tell you I have a famous writer in my family?"

He frowned. "We only just met this morning."

"OK, so if you've heard this before, just tell me to be quiet. My son Teddy was looking at genealogy, and he was tracing back on my father's side, and you'll never guess what he found." I took a seat in front of a large array of dials. "Hey, all the writing is in Russian. What does this one do? Is it radar?"

Counting myself and the captain, there were six of us on the bridge. The other four were apparently engaged in sailing the ship.

"It's a thermometer; eleven degrees Celsius. What is it I can help you with, Mr. Grave? It's a beautiful night, and a beautiful view. You're welcome to stay here as long as you like, but I have to complete my paperwork."

I stared out at the calm Bering Sea. "Hey, do you ever get polar bears out here?"

"Not at sea, no. Polar bears are land animals."

"Very true. Hey, I was watching a program the other night about a bear. It wasn't a polar bear, just a regular bear, black one. So there was this orphan boy named Krishna who got picked up by a traveling circus and he was helping out the tiger trainer, but the tiger trainer was a very mean man who used to beat him."

The captain took a deep breath.

"So one night, when the train was heading toward the south of India, they were on a train, you know, the whole circus. It's how they got around the country. Anyway, so one night after the boy had been badly beaten, the tiger trainer's wife put on her best sari, and came to visit the boy. She told him she was sorry, and also that she loved him. And then she taught him all the things that the tiger trainer wanted her to do to him but she never would do. And let me tell you, Captain, these were nice things."

"And this was on the TV? This is the sort of program they have on the TV in the US?"

"Yeah, well, it's cable. Spicy Bombay; you have to pay extra, but it's worth it."

"What did the story have to do with a bear?"

I thought about that for a moment. "Not sure. I remember the bear but I don't think he was worked into the narrative very well. Not that I was complaining."

He took a deep breath. "Is there something I can do for you, Mr. Grave?"

"Yes, yes. That's what I came up to talk to you about. I want Chef Ember released from the brig. He doesn't have anything to do with anything."

"It was Ms. Bok's decision to take him into custody. You will have to take it up with her. And Mr. Belov has ultimate authority in this matter."

I shook my head. "I'm not convinced that's the case."

"And the other man in the brig, the bartender? What about him? You think he should be released as well?"

"Not so sure yet. Let's keep him on ice."

Tolstoy leaned in. "A piece of advice; you had best be careful with that one. He has some powerful relatives. And if you think that doesn't count for much in this part of the world, you should think again."

"I'll keep that in mind." I pointed out at the sea in front of us. "So what's out there?"

"Mother Russia." He nodded. "We were hoping to arrive in Petropavlovsk by morning, but there's a storm system in front of us. So we'll be holding up for a few hours to see if it passes."

"I want to catch this killer before we get there."

He shook his head. "You won't make it. We are two hundred and twenty miles away. You have only just fourteen hours left. Do you even have any leads?"

"No, no, not yet. But I still have the evening. I'm kind of a night owl. I hunt by night. But not too late; I get tired."

He stared at me.

"Also, Captain, I want all public areas locked down at night. Beluga Bar, the lounges, the cigar bar. They shouldn't be open this late. You have to close them down earlier, get the passengers back in their cabins after dinner. Nobody should be moving around at night. I want to degrade the surface area of the killing field, if I can put it bluntly."

He shook his head. "This was a crime of passion. I think we have established this much. I have no reason to believe our passengers or crew are in danger."

"I'm not convinced. Crimes of passion normally don't

involve any post-coital, post-mortem nibbling. So we leave open the possibility that we are dealing with something else entirely."

"What? A lunatic? A monster of some sort?"

"That's right."

He looked off over the bow and shook his head. "So what would you have me do?"

"I just told you. First, get the chef out of the brig. Second . . ."

"No, not on your orders. No."

At this point in my life, I do not enjoy people getting in my way. "You know what, Captain, I have bosses too, just as you do, and they sent me here to do a job. If you get in my way, I'm going to do whatever I can to have you removed from your command. You think I can't do that? You might be right. But I damn sure can try. I'm persuasive."

He didn't say anything.

"Now get the chef out of the brig, and shut down all public areas at night."

He shook his head, more to himself than to me.

"And one more thing, one of your dancing hosts is a man named Brice Laird. He's sleeping with passengers. I'm pretty certain he's not supposed to do that."

Tolstoy turned to me. "Do you suspect this man? Because if you don't, I have more important things to do than worry about sleeping arrangements."

"No, I don't suspect him. Not exactly. But he's done a lot of bad things. He is a monster in his own right. He might be able to spot a kindred spirit."

"What do you want me to do about this?"

I had a plan. "I would like you to downgrade his living arrangements, starting tonight. Transfer him to Georgie Orbelani's cabin. It's currently not in use. He can have a look around. If Georgie is a killer, Brice can help me prove it."

An officer approached with an open notebook, and the

captain spoke with him in Russian. "I am scheduled to take a call from the Petropavlovsk harbor pilot," he said. "I have to leave you now. I will consider your requests."

"That's a fine thing," I told him. "Hey, so I never did finish telling you my story. OK, so Teddy traced our family tree back to England in the 1850s, and he came across this fellow named Isadore Grave, the illegitimate son of a penniless tenant farmer named Presscott Grave. He drank himself to an early death, the poor fool. But that Isadore, why I'll be damned if he didn't grow up to be the assistant editor of the East Winkfield Observer."

Tolstoy stared at me.

"Only the second largest bi-weekly in the entire Winkfield area." I clapped him on the shoulder. "See, we both have writers in the family."

CHAPTER TEN
DAY 1 - AT SEA — MIDNIGHT

L eaving the bridge, I took the stairs down to the Beluga Deck, where several parties were taking place at once. A quiz game was being played at the pool bar. It was highly disorganized. One of the hostesses stood on a table shouting out questions to a gaggle of seniors reclined in deck chairs.

"So far the Golden Girls are winning," she called out. "Maritime Mavens are in second place, yet the Lords of the High Seas are holding a distant third place."

A group of men cheered at that announcement, holding their beverages high.

"OK, the first question in round three," she began. "This Dominican diplomat was already the world's most famous playboy before he started dating Zsa Zsa Gabor."

Five hands popped into the air simultaneously. I knew the answer. Every man my age did. I didn't have time to stick around.

Although the overhead plexiglass dome kept the cold out, nobody was swimming at this time of night. But I noticed some teenage couples dangling their feet into the water. Nobody paid any attention to them, which is exactly what teenage couples want.

Moving inside, I walked past the library. On most cruise ships the library has set hours of operation, but here it was more casual. A self-service scanner was available to check out a book, but several comfortable chairs were occupied by several comfortable passengers as they made late-night progress into their mystery novels.

I kept walking. The Beluga Bar had been taken over by ballroom dancers, lots of them. A quartet of Filipino musicians was doing a pitch-perfect Duke Ellington big-band thing, and it was going over well. Over at the bar, the liquor was flowing.

I spotted Brice Laird out on the dance floor. I knew he'd be there somewhere; a host's contract requires attendance at all dancing events. He wore a tuxedo and he looked good as he gently led an elderly woman. I would get back to him later. I had some thinking to do.

I turned around and headed back the way I came, passing the library, passing the pool. I stepped around the shuffleboard courts where courting young adults drank liquor furtively and toyed with the paddles. Anyone of them could have been a cannibal, but I wasn't seeing it. Making my way toward the stern, I came to the Lido Café. This late in the evening, there wasn't much in the way of food, but a bar at the back beckoned. A lone hostess watched my approach. She didn't wave.

"So where is everyone?" I asked. "Looks like it's going to be just you and me."

She leaned forward. "They've got free wine and champagne up at the Beluga Bar, so why would anyone come here?"

"Ambiance," I suggested. "I enjoy food-themed bars. Just looking around, I can tell there's usually food served here, and that makes me happy. Hey, do you have anything to nosh on?"

Without looking, she produced a bowl of nuts from under the bar. "I have popcorn too if you want."

"Please. And can I get some of that beet booze? I can't remember what it's called. Over ice, and maybe you could toss in some lemon, and a splash of gin."

She frowned.

"Don't frown," I told her as I read her name tag. "You're adorable, Michelle, but when you frown you look kind of angry."

"I'm not sure what you're asking for," she said.

"Hey, you know what I'm noticing here? Your English is good. Not much of an accent."

"Thank you very much. I'm American."

"You're welcome. And no you're not. You have an accent, a little bit. I think you're a Russian girl. I spent a lot of time with Russians when I was in the service. I can always spot a Russian accent. Say this for me; say, 'what's that up in the road ahead.'"

She said it. And she said it perfectly, no accent at all. But she took a moment to plan it out before she said it, so I knew.

"Nope," I told her. "You sound Russian. Ahead is pronounced 'a-head.' And you said it like this; 'a-heeyad.'"

"I did not."

"Did too. In any case, I want to have some of that beet vodka I had down at the crew bar with the half-assed Hawaiian theme. It was good, very tasty."

She frowned. "Are you talking about Tuz, that diesel swill they serve the cretins who work in the boiler room?"

"Maybe. I like to try new things. So what do you say?"

"We don't serve garbage up here," she said. "This is passenger bar."

"This is *a* passenger bar. You have to slow down and use articles. An English speaker would never say 'this is passenger bar.'"

If I was bothering her, she didn't let on.

"We only serve real liquor here," she said. "Tuz is nasty Anatolian moonshine, distilled by goat herders in distended goat bladders. Most of it is poured down the throats of convicts who've done terrible things. The rest is used to fuel the power tools of the desperate poor and the nearly dead. And if any is left over, it's smuggled over porous mountain borders in filthy porous gourds to be served to seamen."

"I'm impressed," I told her. "You know a lot about your liquor. You kind of like this Tuz don't you."

She shrugged. "It grows on you. It's like Sterno but with more of a pop. It's nice if you get a cold or TB."

I leaned in to read the fine print on her name tag, but I didn't have my glasses on so I had to lean way in over the bar to get close. She pulled away, but not quickly enough. "New York?"

She nodded. "Big apple."

"Well I'll be goddamned. Hey, if you're going to pretend you're an American, that's as good a place as any to pretend to be from. So what are you doing up here at the top of the world? It's dangerous. We could sail over the edge of the earth at any moment."

"I'll take my chances. I wanted to see the world."

"OK, OK. Let me think. First, bring me a gimlet, and maybe some more food. Little sandwiches if you have them, or those little cocktail franks. I like those. Then we need to talk. You just became my new best friend."

"I'm delighted to hear that."

"No, seriously, you will be. I'm charming."

I read through my notes as she prepared my drink and delivered it with a basket of popcorn. "I'm going to need to ask you some questions." I handed her my ID. My beverage was first rate.

"*Cat Fancy*," she read.

"What, now?"

"You're an investigative journalist for *Cat Fancy*?"

I frowned, but that's exactly what the card said. "Sorry." I grabbed it back and handed over my investigator's license. "Sometimes I get them mixed up."

She shook her head. "I want to talk about the other one.

It's fake, right?"

"Sadly, no," I told her.

"What could a journalist possibly investigate about cats?"

I ate a few mouthfuls of popcorn, cleverly giving myself a moment to think. "You would be surprised. Cats are having a tough time of it; there's a lot of homelessness. I spent most of last month living with a pack of ferals outside of Philly. It wasn't easy, but as the weeks passed, they began to see me as one of their own."

"I'm sure." She picked up my investigator's license. "So you're here about Rose. Ha, now the tables are turned. You're supposed to be Russian. We were told the investigator would be Russian. So, it would seem that of the two of us, you're the one who is Russian."

"Da. I'm a huge Bolshevik. Did you kill Rose?"

She looked up. "Me? No."

"Who did?"

"Don't know." She walked to the edge of the bar as a young couple approached. Upon learning that the drinks here weren't free, they elected to return to the Beluga Bar.

"Did you know her?" I asked.

"Of course. There's only like ninety people working here, and thirty of them are oily little Filipino guys who oil machinery and don't speak English. So yeah, I knew her."

"She was your roommate."

"How did you know that?"

"I'm a little bit psychic. I also know that your last name is Parker. How about that?" I showed her the page that Irina Bok had slipped under my door. "So what was Rose like?"

"Is this like an official interview? Am I a suspect?"

"Hardly. Hey, why are you even working? Shouldn't you get some time off to grieve? Geez, your roommate! You didn't get shaken up?"

She nodded. "I am a little shaken up. But like I said,

there's only like ninety people working here."

"Still, they could give you some days off."

"They offered, but I don't want to be sitting around the cabin. And the food downstairs is disgusting. I would rather be up here."

"Were you and Rose close?"

"You're interrogating me? So I am suspect after all?"

"No, no, you're not a suspect. The only thing I suspect you of is being too good-looking to hide away in an empty bar. But I still need to ask you questions. Were you and Rose close?"

"Yeah, a little. She was new but she was cool."

"What was she like?"

"I don't know. She was fine. Pretty, she was a party girl. You know; bubbly, whorish, laughed a lot. She was fun."

"Did you know she was dating the captain?"

She shook her finger at me. "Aren't you a gossip?"

"So did you know?"

"Everyone knew. She dumped him, and then everybody started joking about how the captain was going to ram an iceberg out of despair, or like spend the rest of his life chasing a whale."

"He was upset."

"You know, anyone will get upset when they get dumped, but he was really pretty upset."

"What about you? Do you get dates on board?"

"For sure." She pushed back from the bar and twirled around. "Do you have any idea how good-looking I am?"

I nodded. "I've already commented. How well do you know Brice Laird?"

"OK, now that one is bad news. Has to be seventy years old and he thinks he can ask me out? That's disgusting."

I frowned. "Seventy isn't really all that old, and what are you, about thirty-five, thirty-six? It's not so much of a ..."

"I'm twenty-four."

"Is that right? All I'm saying is that sometimes a mature man . . ." She was shaking her head, so I stopped.

"You have to have suspicions. Who do you think might have done it?"

"Don't know," she said.

"You're not scared to be here all alone, a murderer on the loose?"

"I'm not alone. I have a big powerful man to watch over me."

I had to give her that one. "I am powerful, big too, but not too big. But you're not afraid?"

"No." She pointed to a figure sitting at the back of the room. "I was referring to him."

As if on cue, the man flipped open a lighter and lit a cigarette. I couldn't see much in the dim light.

"Who is he?" I asked.

"That's Rurik. He's one of the ship's security guys. He doesn't say much but he's cool. He has steel teeth. I've been throwing corn nuts at him all night but he doesn't respond."

"Tell me about the corn nuts?" I waved to Rurik as she went into the back for a box, but he didn't wave back.

"Ms. Bok, our head of security made a rule that nobody can be on duty alone."

"That's a good rule. I like that. And you feel safe with Rurik around?"

"I do."

"So if you had to guess, who killed Rose?"

She took a handful of corn nuts and twisted around on one foot as she ate. "I would say Georgie, maybe. He comes off as all chill, but he's got an attitude. He fell pretty hard for her, not that he isn't married, right?"

I took out my notebook. "Georgie," I repeated. "I'm going to have to look into him. Do you have his last name?"

She shook her head. "I don't remember. But he's the only Georgie onboard."

"No, there's a Georgie in the brig right now."

"Yeah, that's him."

"It's all coming together." I crossed Georgie off my list of one name. "Who else might have done it?"

"Don't know. Could have been you. Or maybe that big outdoorsy chick that came with the botany lecturer. Rose had a crush on the lecturer and his chick wasn't happy about it."

"I met her," I said. "She isn't big, and she didn't seem outdoorsy to me."

"Are you serious? She's got a face like a horse. If you look closely you can see her little beard."

I finished my beverage and held it out for a refill. "You're a little mean, you know?"

"You think? Why do you think I'm in here by myself and not over at the Beluga Bar, where the tips are? By the way," she reached behind for an empty jar and placed it in front of me, "tips are appreciated."

I fished through my wallet for a ten-dollar bill as she mixed me another drink. I was getting nowhere when the bar phone rang and she took the call. "It's for you."

It was Irina Bok. "Can you meet me in sick bay? In the hospital?"

"Who?"

"Belov."

CHAPTER ELEVEN
DAY 2 - AT SEA - 1:00AM

The ship's doctor was a former Russian naval officer named Karmov or something approaching that. I never actually met him, though we would cross paths several times. When I arrived in the ship's hospital, he was shining a penlight in Belov's eye.

"Enough," Belov howled as he sat up. He had two black eyes, and he was wearing only a T-shirt and thong underwear. It wasn't a good look. "Where are my clothes?"

"What happened to you?" I asked. "And what made you go with the thong? A sensible man wears boxers. They give you some breathing room."

"I am being beaten up is what happens to me," he howled. "A coward who hits a man from behind should be shot. Where is my gun?"

The doctor gestured to a shelf where the clothes and the gun could be found.

"You said it was dark." Irina Bok questioned him as he dressed.

"I did say that, yes, because it was dark."

"Why was it dark in the hallway?" I asked, but nobody paid me any mind.

"And yet you were in a public corridor," Irina continued. "You said you were on your way to your stateroom."

"I was on my way out of stateroom," Belov spat, angrily buttoning his shirt. "I have told this to you already." Then he switched to Russian and I learned nothing from the rest of the conversation.

The doctor asked him to stay in the sick bay for another hour but Belov refused.

"And you walked only a few steps until you were attacked from behind," Irina continued in English, which I assumed was for my benefit.

"As I am arriving in front of the elevator, a man is coming from around the corner. I am thinking nothing of it, but as I am turning, he hits me. After that, I know nothing until I am woken up by a grouping of old ladies."

The doctor tried to detain him, but Belov was having none of it. "I will be in my room planning vengeance," he said. "I wish that nobody will be bothering me."

I followed him to his cabin, passing a couple of technicians who were busy replacing the lights in the elevator lobby. I gave Belov thirty seconds before I knocked.

When he opened the door I found myself looking down the barrel of his gun.

"Forty-five caliber." I opened my jacket to show him my holstered gun. "That's a Smith & Wesson. I have the same one."

"It is a dependable weapon." He walked back to his desk and I followed him inside. "Back home, they are issuing me a Makarov, a Russian automatic pistol, but I became convinced that my directorate saved much money by instead buying the inferior Bulgarian models. When I would shoot, it would never not jam."

"That's disappointing."

"Sit." He handed me a glass of bourbon and I sat on the edge of the bed. "I am feeling this feeling . . . what is the word for when you are feeling ashamed but yet you know there is no shame to be felt?"

I stared into the liquor for a moment. I knew what he was talking about. It's an old man thing, and we were two old men. "Anybody can get attacked from behind."

He sat heavily on the bed, his shoulders slumped. "A younger man would have fought back."

I thought back to that night nearly seven decades ago when that German scout took me prisoner, then walked me through half of Belgium's forests. All night, and I didn't do a thing. I didn't start fighting until I got older. And at this point, I was very good at it.

"We may not pack a punch, my Russian friend." I was trying to cheer him up, "But we get the job done. If you were a younger man, you might have fought back but you might have been killed. At least you're alive. And that's worth another tot."

That got me a grin at least, as well as a refill on the beverage. "What did he hit you with?"

"What? Nothing. The elevator he hit me with. I am smashed head first into the elevator. This is what knocks me out. It was like a wild animal crashing into me."

I thought about that for a moment. "Could it have been unintentional?"

"What is unintentional? Most people do not crash others into elevators and then leave. No, he was growling."

"Growling?"

"Yes, growling. I can see a little bit his reflection in the polish on the elevator door, a man who is wild. And he was growling."

"Growling," I repeated. Belov's phone rang but he didn't answer it. In fact, I think he nodded off a little, still holding the cup in his hand. I drank quietly, giving him some space. After a time, I stood up, thinking I might leave, but just as I stood up, the ship lurched and I nearly fell over. I took Belov's drink from his hand, got him under the bedspread, and I left quietly.

I took the stairs up a flight and found some commotion. Apparently a lady or two had fallen, and a number of other ladies had not enjoyed the sudden change in course. And I can understand that. We seniors pay a lot of attention to balance and traction. When we fall, it isn't pretty.

I know more about cruise ships than your average passenger. I know that cruise ships rarely make sudden moves. In fact, you probably won't sense much in the way of motion at all. Sure, on a rough day, you might feel a gentle rocking, but that's about it. The stabilizers take care of that. There are rumblings when the engines first awaken, and some vibrations perhaps when the anchors are deployed. But that's about it. No lurches, not ever.

There's nothing to lurch at. All manner of radar and depth finders and satellite positioning systems allow a comprehensive understanding of the position of the ship and anything that might be nearby. So why the lurch?

My knees were aching from all the climbing, so I took the elevator, and when I arrived at the bridge, they let me right in.

Captain Tolstoy was wearing a robe, and he didn't look happy. He scanned the horizon with a huge pair of binoculars. "Nothing," he said. "There's nothing there."

"It was there a moment ago, Captain," the bridge officer insisted. "Pavel saw it too."

At the helm, another man nodded. "I saw him, Captain. He was right in front of us."

"Show me on the radar," the captain said, handing me the binoculars. "Give me a history of the last ten minutes."

"That's the thing, Captain," the first officer continued. "We didn't see anything on the radar. Look, right there, there is a small event, perhaps a pod of whales, we thought."

"And you insist you saw a boat?" The captain lit a cigarette and stared into the monitor.

The man nodded. "A baidarka, sir."

"A baidarka?"

"Yes, sir, an Aleutian canoe; sealskin over driftwood. They are relatively uncommon in these . . ."

"I know what a baidarka is," the captain said quietly.

"But I don't see one. And why would a baidarka be out here? There's nothing here, no islands, no nothing."

"And traveling at ten knots," the helmsman added. "He was moving at least that fast."

"Impossible," the captain insisted.

"With my own eyes, Captain," the first officer insisted. "Pavel watched him as well. He crossed our bow, a single figure in the canoe, moving at least ten knots. We had to heave to the starboard to keep from hitting him."

The captain shook his head. "Nobody can row a boat at ten knots."

"He wasn't rowing."

The captain puffed on his cigarette. "He wasn't rowing? Was this a motorized baidarka?"

"See that's the crazy thing," the first officer continued. "He was just sitting there. He wasn't rowing. There was no motor. But yet he was moving very fast."

The captain shook his head.

I hefted those giant binoculars and scanned the Bering Sea. The weather was definitely deteriorating. Storm clouds menaced, and there was enough sunlight left to see the rain in the distance.

The captain peered at the instrument panel. "That storm system is impressive," he said. "I thought we could get around it by now, but it has grown somewhat. Mr. Yevgen, is there any communication from Moscow?"

"No, sir. But there is a weather advisory. Shipping is advised to hold fast east of the storm system, or to move north if necessary. The storm system is slowly moving south."

The captain plugged a tablet computer into the instrument panel and uploaded some data. "Then we will resume our course heading. Continue north, making our speed five knots. We'll wait this thing out. We'll be a day late making port. I don't like this. I don't like sitting still."

"I don't like it either," I noted. "I get antsy."

"And if you see anything on the radar," the captain told the bridge officers, "anything, even a pod of sardines, you come and find me. If your mystery baidarka sailor returns, we'll take him onboard. If he exists at all."

He left. I stayed.

"Tell me," I said, standing next to the helmsman. "You're certain? It's not those arctic lights playing tricks on you, like that aurora thing?"

He shook his head.

"You're Pavel, right?"

"I am Pavel, yes. And no it was no trick. There was a man. I saw him through the binoculars, as did the first officer. There was a man. He had a beard. He was sitting in his boat, moving very quickly and we nearly rammed him. We heaved starboard, but when we looked for him, he was gone."

"Maybe you did ram him?"

Pavel shook his head. "There was no contact, no contact with anything. He simply vanished."

"Well that's quite a thing."

I returned to my cabin and made a list of things I would be requiring in the morning. I had the girl on the switchboard connect me to Irina Bok's voicemail, and I left her a detailed list.

Then I turned on the TV and started watching a program about whales, and how they swim all over the world, and eat, and I just couldn't get into it. I couldn't find any other English language stations, and for some reason, I couldn't fall asleep. I couldn't wrap my mind around Belov's attack. Something was off. Whoever attacked him was growling, crazed, according to Belov. Yet that crazed growler apparently had the foresight to disable the lights to make the hall by the elevator lobby dark. It made no sense. And why attack Belov? And while we're at it, why attack anyone just to knock him out?

According to my watch, it was just after two in the

morning. Early enough! I called Brice Laird.

"You're a bastard, Henry," he said. "It was you who told them about Darla, wasn't it?"

"It was me."

"Don't try to deny it."

"I didn't. It was me, I told them."

"Dedicating your life to making mine miserable, is that what this is?"

"Not at all, Leslie. I just need your help with something."

"What is it you could want from me, Henry? Some tips perhaps on how to talk to the ladies? And why should I help you at all? Thanks to you they're moving me in the morning. I'm to be relocated to the crew quarters. A bunk bed, Henry. Apparently my new roommate is a Russian busboy called Georgie. I'm sure we'll have much in common."

"He's Georgian, not Russian," I said, "but that's what I wanted to talk with you about."

CHAPTER TWELVE
DAY 2 - AT SEA - 5:00AM

I awoke just after five in the morning to find Irina Bok standing over my bed. "I knew it was just a matter of time," I told her, throwing aside the bedspread.

She shut her eyes. "Please put some clothes on, Mr. Grave. I need you to come with me."

"Geez, you'd think there was some crime in sleeping in the nude."

"We have had another attack," she said as I dressed. "It's the captain."

"What happened? I was talking with him on the bridge only a few hours ago."

"We don't know exactly. The watch officer came for him at four, but he wasn't in his suite. They called me. I initiated a search, and security found him in the Beluga Bar minutes later. He has lost a lot of blood."

"Is he going to be OK?"

"I don't know."

"You can open your eyes now," I told her. "I just need to pick out some pants."

She shut them again immediately. "Can you let me know when you're dressed?"

I did. "Why did the watch officer come for him at four?"

She consulted her notes. "He said he had instructions to wake the captain if anything unusual appeared on the radar."

I nodded. "I remember that. So what unusual thing

appeared?"

"Apparently a man in a canoe. I have not yet had the time to investigate what this means, really, but I . . ."

"Why was the captain in the Beluga Bar in the middle of the night? It should have been closed."

"It was closed. We think he went there to meet with someone."

"With who?"

"We don't know. I checked the phone records. A call was placed from the bar to the captain's suite. But we don't know who made the call."

"Are the calls recorded?"

"No."

Nuts. I followed Irina down to the ship's hospital, where I had been just a few hours ago.

The captain was lying on a bed covered in blood.

"How is he?" Irina asked.

"Not good," the doctor said. "He just died."

"Died?"

"Died. We tried to stop the bleeding but it was too extensive. He'd lost a great deal of blood. If we had been in an emergency room, maybe. But even then, I don't know."

I pulled aside the towels that had been wrapped around Captain Tolstoy's abdomen, but I wasn't prepared for what I was looking at. This was the work of an animal. This was about feeding. "Did he say anything?"

The doctor shook his head. "He never regained consciousness."

"And this happened in his cabin?"

"No, I just explained this to you." Irina was irritated. "It happened in the Beluga Bar."

"And that's the same place Rose was killed," I said, more to myself than to anyone else. "This isn't good."

"Agreed."

"We're going to need to tighten security," I told her "I

want the bridge secured, and I want the chief engineer armed. The engine room needs to be locked down. I want every deck patrolled at all times. As of now, the public rooms are shut down. No bars, no spa, no lounges, no pool. Only the dining room stays open."

"That is not your call," she said. "You are not in charge. We have a first officer. I will speak with him to review security protocol. But he is the acting captain now."

"Wrong," came a voice from the doorway.

We turned to find Belov standing there. "I am naval officer. I am authorized to take command of a ship if I see fit. I see fit. I am being acting captain now."

Irina nodded her head slightly. "Then I will wait for your instructions."

"You have them," he told her. "Do as he just said. And do it now before someone else is killed."

"This makes absolutely no sense," I told Belov after Irina had left. "It's as if it were random."

"No." Belov stared at the body. "They were lovers, you recall, he and Rose. Somebody remains angry."

"Doesn't feel like passion to me," I suggested. "It feels like rage."

"Passion and rage are not so far apart, maybe."

Maybe he was right. I had a hunch. I left Belov and headed back to my cabin to consult my paperwork. As luck would have it, the cabin I was looking for was just down the corridor from my own.

"Come back later," a woman called out in response to my knock. "It's too early."

"Ship's security," I called out, knocking again. "I need to talk with Mr. Lonagan."

"Doctor Lonagan," she said, opening the door. "And you're not with the ship's security."

"I kind of am." I checked my notes again. "You're Grace,

right?"

She tightened her robe before answering. "That's right. What do you want?"

"You're not outdoorsy-looking at all," I told her. "You're quite attractive. What are you, about 5' 5"?"

"What are you talking about?"

"Nothing. I need to talk to your hubby, is he in?"

"You know he's not my hubby, and he's asleep anyway, so come back later."

"No, no. We have an urgent situation. I need to talk to him."

"Best of luck." She opened the door and gestured for me to enter.

The cabin was a mess. Clothing lay strewn about the floor, and the table was a disaster – two comprehensive room service snacks had been picked at, and a pizza had been devoured.

I found Oscar Lonagan spread over much of the bed. I did some prodding but it wasn't going far. "What is with the thong?" I shook my head. "Men of this age and girth should not be wearing thong underwear." I poked Lonagan's belly, and when he didn't respond, I poked several more times, selecting several different abdominal targets.

"He drinks," Grace said. "He keeps it together most of the time, but then he goes off on a tear. He'll be down for a couple of hours and then you'll never know it even happened."

I stared at the room service trays. "That's a lot of cheese. How can someone not like cheese?"

"What?"

"You ordered the cheese but you didn't eat it. There's caviar here too. Why would your order caviar and not eat it?"

"I did eat it," she said. "But Oscar doesn't like caviar, and I wasn't going to eat it all. Is there a problem?"

"No." I counted two empty bottles of champagne and one empty liter of rum. "Does he get angry when he drinks?"

She chuckled. "Him? No. He gets happy. He starts singing botany ditties. It's not attractive."

"No, I'm sure it isn't. So listen, maybe you can help." I told her about the captain, and about the fact that both he and Rose DeSilva had been cannibalized.

The color drained from her face, which was not horsey at all. I saw no trace of a beard.

"What are you looking at?" She rubbed her chin.

"Nothing. I want to hear more about that kid in the kayak who ate his grandfather. Any theories on why that happened?"

She leaned back against the minibar and was silent for a moment as Lonagan snored. "That was like seventy years ago. I don't know what to tell you. Oscar is all into this shamanism thing. He thinks there's something supernatural going on."

"There isn't."

"He thinks something very old has come back to the world of humans, back to haunt us."

"That's nonsense."

"I know that. I'm just trying to answer your questions. You know, there are numerous pan-arctic myths about cannibalistic demons. You could read up on those."

"May I?" I grabbed a couple of cheese cubes as she spoke.

"Supposedly they captured one of the demons about seventy years ago out on the Pribilof islands. If you believe the stories, and I don't, they had him locked up for decades, but then he escaped."

"Is that right? This isn't cheddar. It looks like cheddar but it's not. Now assuming this demon isn't currently on board, what do you think is going on?"

"I don't know."

"Can I have some of the salami? I'll be honest with you, I'm still a little hungry."

She looked a little disgusted but she held her hands

wide which I took as an invitation.

"The thing about salami," I continued, "is that you don't want to eat it if it has been sitting around."

"It's cured meat," she said. "You can leave it sitting around for a week."

"Well for my own peace of mind then, how long exactly has it been sitting around? Do you remember about what time you ordered the snack trays?"

"I really don't know," she said. "It would have been around midnight."

I sampled some of the salami and the other smoked meats, which were really quite good. "So you and the big guy ate some snacks, drank a whole pile of liquor and then passed out?"

"We call it going to sleep."

"Did you go out afterward?"

"No."

"Did he? Maybe he went out for a nightcap."

"No, he's a sound sleeper, and I'm not. I would have noticed."

I watched the raindrops smacking onto the veranda. "It's raining. And you have a veranda. I don't have a veranda. I have one of those cabins that just has a window. I'm just down the hall from you, same side of the ship and all, but no veranda. It's sad really. Do you mind if I go have a look out there?"

"I would rather you didn't," she said. "It's cold out and raining, and I'm wearing a T-shirt."

"Another time."

"Fine."

"Hey, so how long have you and the big guy been together?"

She shook her head. "Too long. I really don't want to talk about it."

"I can understand that. Hey, would you mind if I used

your bathroom?"

"I do, yes. It's the middle of the night. You need to leave."

"One more question; would it be possible for an Eskimo guy in a canoe to be moving really fast, like ten knots?"

"Alright; first, they are Aleuts, not Eskimos, and it would be a baidarka, not a canoe. And no, that's too fast."

"So if a sailor told you he saw a guy in his baidarka out here moving at ten or twelve knots, he'd be lying."

"Yes. Well, maybe not. If there's a guy out here in the middle of the frigging deep blue in his baidarka, then he's here because he's got a harpoon set in a bowhead, and he's being towed around creation. And a bowhead can move at twelve to twenty knots."

"What's a bowhead?"

"It's a whale."

"So the guy in the baidarka is being towed around by a whale?"

"That's right."

"Like why? Why would you want to be towed around by a whale? Would that be fun?"

She stared at me. "You know what? I'm really tired. I would like to go back to bed for a little bit, and I'm not sure how this is helping."

"I understand," I told her. I switched on the overhead lights and she squinted.

"You're a drinker too, aren't you?"

"Can you turn those off, please?"

"Which was yours, the rum or the champagne? I'm going to guess the champagne."

"Not your business. Can you get out of my cabin?"

I scooped up the remaining cheese cubes. "I'm leaving," I told her. But as soon as I found myself out in the hall all alone, having eaten my cheese, I knocked on the door again.

"Go away," she called out.

"I'm going," I called back. "Just tell me why the guy wants to be towed around by a whale."

"He's waiting for it to die," she yelled from inside the room. "He's harpooned it, OK? It doesn't die right away. Sometimes it takes a couple of days to tire out. Now leave me alone."

Chapter Thirteen
Day 2 - at sea - 8:00am

Breakfast was already underway by the time I arrived at the dining room. I was moving against the herd. Everyone was sated and happy, their bellies engorged, except for me. "How is this possible?" I asked Vadeem. Outside, the sun was pushing its way through the storm clouds, making some headway here and there. "The light is getting confusing. What the hell time is it?"

"It is eight in the morning, Mr. Henry," he told me. "Can I get you the usual?"

"The usual?" I was impressed.

"We must have faith in patterns," he said. "A Bloody Mary and a table with girls?"

Nice. "That works."

"A beautiful woman is here," he confided as he led me deep into the dining room, "and today, she is here all alone. She is called Maud, and she has the voice of a summer fairy."

"What's a summer fairy?"

"It is a fairy of the summertime."

He led me to a table where I found a woman of incomparable beauty - pure cocoa unblemished skin, lips as red as the beets they use to make beet liquor. She held out a perfectly manicured hand when I introduced myself.

"Maud Munvez," she said, and I'll be goddamned if she didn't have the ethereal voice of a pixie, a sprite, or even a summer fairy. I could tell we were going to be close friends, and I told her so.

"Let me ask you a question, Maud." I scanned the menu looking for Belgian waffles. They didn't have Belgian waffles but they had Russian waffles, which were going to have to do. "If you were a cannibal looking to hide somewhere on the ship . . ."

I stopped when her mouth opened.

"No, no. That wasn't what I mean to ask. I meant to ask, if you were a single woman, and you were looking for a man, what sort of man would you be looking for?"

"That's a very forward question," she told me. "What makes you think I'm single?"

"No ring, no breakfast companion. No, you're a single woman."

"What makes you think I'm looking for a man? I'm not, you should know."

"I think you are. No doubt you've become dismayed by the selection, by the relative paucity of raw masculinity in its prime. But every now and again a man of true virtue comes along."

Vadeem returned with my drink. "A man so powerful and yet so kind, that you wonder if it might be worth taking a chance on love. Maud, you have to open the door, even just a little, to let someone in. I'm just putting it out there, that I might be that man."

I stood as another man took the seat next to this lovely woman. He was an older man. Fit, nice dresser, hair looked good. I worried for half a moment. A lesser man might have been intimidated by the competition, but I knew I could take him.

"Good to see you again, Henry." He shook my hand.

"Have we met?"

"Yes, just yesterday," he said, then he kissed Maud on the lips. "Murray Abramowitz, remember? We were out on deck having a conversation."

"That's right." I remembered. "We were admiring the . . ."

"The view," he said as he took his seat. "We were admiring the view."

"Yes, the view." I ordered the Russian waffles with a side of potatoes, some bacon, toast, and an egg-white omelet. "So do you two know each other?"

Murray chuckled. "Oh boy, do we."

Maud blushed. "I was having afternoon tea up in the lounge, and Murray just came up to me and told me I was the most beautiful woman in the whole Bering Sea."

"Is that right?"

"And then he took me dancing. So many men today don't know how to dance, but Murray is a true gentleman."

"Nearly seventy percent of seniors don't get enough exercise," Murray noted. "And dancing is the perfect way to bring that figure down."

"I dance the tango," I told Maud, pretending we were alone. "I have awards."

She smiled. "I love the tango. I think that it is the most intimate of dances. Would you agree, Henry?"

"Oh, yes."

"But it's not as popular," Murray suggested. "In fact, swing dances are the most commonly preferred of all the ballroom genres. After that, we're looking at foxtrot, and then, geez, then you're down into the single digits. The tango would be somewhere behind the cha-cha."

"Yeah, this is going to have to stop," Maud chided him. "The statistics, all evening, and now at breakfast too?"

Murray frowned. "Probability is the basis for all rational actions. I like to pay attention."

"Sure, but I don't need to hear it twenty-four hours a day."

"I'm not that bad."

"Really? Do I really need to know that there's a 65%

chance you'll be able to achieve a full erection?"

He grinned. "The odds were with me last night."

I grabbed a breadstick and prayed for an embolism.

"And if I hear any more statistics," she told him, "there's about a 99% chance you will be spending the rest of the cruise alone."

He frowned when she turned to me. "So Henry, have you noticed the security people everywhere?"

I smiled as the waiter approached with my breakfast. "I'm sure the chef is happy to be back at work," I told him. He shook his head.

"The chef, what is his name again?"

"Mr. Ember, our executive chef? Is this who you mean?"

"Yes, yes. They had him locked up, but they let him out."

He shook his head. "No, he is still in lockup."

I was going to have to talk to someone about that.

"Did you hear me, Henry?" Murray Abramowitz was going on about something. "All the security? Did you notice?"

"There do seem to be more officers on patrol." I had a look around the room and saw two security guys at the maître d' station. On most cruise ships, security is handled by Indian or Nepalese ex-military, but here it seemed to be mostly Russians. They were all openly armed too, which is a rarity. All ships have guns, but you rarely see them.

"Statistically," Murray Abramowitz began, ready to add his two percent, but I gave him my sternest look. Love is hard enough to negotiate, and it's easy to screw up by getting in your own way.

"Why are we stopped?" Maud stared out the window at the grey Bering Sea.

Russian waffles, as I learned, are essentially Belgian waffles, just as delicious. But my god, I don't know what kind of bacon they were serving but it was outstanding. Thick, like Canadian bacon, but still slab-like, not round, it was almost ham yet it retained that smoky bacon essence.

"We're turning," Maud continued. "It looks like we're turning around. Why would we turn around? Do you think someone went overboard?"

I shook my head. There would have been an alarm, I meant to say, but as soon as my mouth opened to say it, I put toast in instead. I grabbed three pats of butter from the dish, along with some extra rolls, and told my breakfast companions that I had to rush. Then I carried my waffles out of the dining room.

I meant to head up to the bridge, but I noticed the hallway was very cold, and when I got to Reception, I found the gangway door open. Rain was sheeting in, and several crewmembers in windbreakers were lowering the gangway.

"What's going on with this?" I asked the girl at Reception.

"Sir, I need you to step back. We need some room here. The crew is contacting another vessel that came up alongside."

"What other vessel?" I peered out the huge doorway but I didn't see any other boats. "Do you have any syrup?"

"What? No, we don't have syrup here at Reception. Sir, can I ask you to return to the dining room with your breakfast, please?"

I fished my ID from my wallet. "I think you'll find I am authorized to ask these questions."

"*Cat Fancy*? What does this have to do with cats?"

Nuts. "Give that back." I found my investigator's ID and handed it to her. "You can contact the captain or Officer Bok if you need confirmation. But I get to be here."

"Fine," she said, curtly. "Can you stand back, please? What is it you need?"

I held open my arms. "Syrup. I'm trying to eat my waffles, but if there is no syrup, can we get on with an explanation of what is happening here?"

She leaned in as passengers began gathering at the

doorway. "There's some guy in a canoe just sitting out there. He might be dead, so they're checking him out."

"Is that right?"

But it was right. I stood at the edge of the reception desk and ate my breakfast as I watched two crewmen in a Zodiak tow the canoe, the baidarka, back to our ship. They brought the man in and laid him out on a couch across from the reception desk. He was an old man, maybe as old as I am. A native man, and he wasn't moving.

The doctor examined him when they cut away his sealskin jacket. "He's alive."

CHAPTER FOURTEEN
DAY 2 - AT SEA - 9:00AM

He was an old fellow, very old, and by the time he regained consciousness, about forty-five minutes after he was brought on board, he was angry. He was strapped down to a bed in the ship's hospital and moaning. Irina Bok stood over him, her arms folded on her chest.

I found Belov talking on the phone near the entrance to the hospital. "I thought we agreed to let the chef out of the brig."

"What?" He covered the mouthpiece. "I did this thing already. I released the chef."

"No, no. I just checked on him. He's still up there."

"This is not true." Belov said something in Russian and then shut his phone. "You said to me to let the chef out of the brig, not the other man, so I am doing this. Chef Georgie Orbelani, I am ordering him to be released last night, just near eleven o'clock."

"No, no. Georgie is not the chef. He's a bartender. We wanted him to stay locked up. You were going to let the chef out."

Belov waved a finger up in my face. "Is not clear what you are saying then. You must be more clear when you speak to me. Who was the man we are speaking to in the crew bar yesterday? Was it not James Ember, the man who had the relations with the dead woman?"

I shook my head.

Belov let loose with a series of hard Russian words.

Howls came from the man strapped to the bed.

"Why is he tied down?"

"For his own protection," the doctor told me. "He's coming down off some kind of psychotropic event. He has taken something, some pharmaceutical. I don't know what it is yet, but his eyes aren't tracking."

"What are we going to do with him?"

"We are going to do nothing with him," Belov shouted. "We will be in Petropavlovsk tomorrow morning. We will let the maritime police handle it."

"Tomorrow morning? I thought we would be arriving this afternoon."

"I thought the same, but the storm grew in intensity and I did not wish to move through it."

"And the storm is over now?"

He shook his head. "No, still we are making no headway, but we should be able to make speed by about noon."

"So we have until tomorrow to figure this out." I held up the daily program that had been slipped under my door. "I thought we had agreed to lock down the open decks and shutter the public areas. But that didn't happen. And look, Oscar Lonagan is scheduled to give a morning lecture. This shouldn't happen. It's dangerous."

Belov stormed out of the room.

"He decided he didn't want to alarm the passengers," Irina Bok told me.

"The passengers should be alarmed," I told her. "There have been two murders on board, and a killer is at large. He could kill again."

"The maritime police will conduct an investigation."

"Won't that be swell," I told her. "They'll detain the passengers for a day or two, but that's all. You know that. Two hundred and ninety-two passengers; there's no way they're going to pay to fly everyone home."

"They might." She paused as another round of howling began. "They will fill the ship with politsiya, several squads I would imagine. They will ask if anybody knows what happened, if anybody would like to confess. Then when nobody knows anything and nobody confesses, they will turn the ship around. We'll sail back to Alaska."

"Unless someone else dies."

"Exactly. What is he screaming about?"

We asked the doctor the same question.

"I tried to give him a sedative," he said, "but he nearly chewed through the straps. I don't know what he is screaming about. He doesn't speak Russian or English. I don't know what he speaks. Do they even have a spoken language up here anymore?"

I had no idea. But I knew someone who did.

"I'm about to go on stage," Oscar Lonagan complained when I cornered him at the back of the theater. "What is this about?"

"I need your professional opinion about something," I told him. "Five minutes of your time."

"Five minutes," he said, and he followed me down to the ship's hospital.

"I need to know who this fellow is."

Lonagan approached the man and immediately began undoing the straps. He spoke softly and the man began to calm down immediately. "He's Aleut. He is speaking the Aleut language."

"Can you ask him his name?"

Lonagan turned. "No. I don't speak Aleut. Nobody does."

I hadn't noticed Belov standing behind the door. "What do you mean nobody does?" he demanded.

Lonagan frowned. "It's a dead language. Nearly so.

Maybe two hundred speakers survive, and most would be in their nineties, as this man certainly is."

"Ask him what he was doing out at sea alone."

Lonagan stared at him. "Once again, I cannot do that. He doesn't seem to speak any other languages, so it won't be possible for me to ask him questions. But he was almost certainly whale hunting. Where is his baidarka? Did you find rope?"

"The canoe has been lashed to the deck," Irina Bok told him. "There was rope found as well, high-quality, commercial grade marine rope."

Lonagan shook his head. "And let me guess, your men cut the rope when you brought the baidarka on board."

"How did you know?"

"It was heavy, there was something dragging at the little boat, and it was not easily maneuvered."

"That's right."

"It was a whale," I yelled out, suddenly figuring it out.

Lonagan nodded. "It was a whale."

"What is this we are discussing?" Belov insisted, as the Aleut sat up and swung his feet over the edge of the bed.

"Kiyt," the old man insisted. "Da. Da. Whale."

"He's speaking Russian." Belov moved closer. "Kiyt means whale in Russian. This man speaks Russian." He let off a volley of Russian but got nothing but stares.

"Whale?" the man repeated, then spread his arms, palms up and looked around the hospital.

"You're going to have some explaining to do," Lonagan said, but whatever he was about to say next got cut off when the Aleut twisted his arm around his shoulder, throwing him off balance.

And before anyone could do anything about it, Lonagan found himself twisted around again, now face to face with the old man, who then drove his fist into his stomach.

"Oof," came out of Lonagan's mouth. The Aleut got his

face in close, inhaling Lonagan's breath.

"Bolmoi," he said. "Bolmoi is man."

Lonagan pulled away. "What the hell was that?"

The Aleut shrugged, then shook a finger at him. "Bolmoi," he repeated.

"What the hell is bolmoi?" Lonagan demanded.

"Sick," Belov told him. "It is Russian. It means sick."

Lonagan frowned. "I'm not sick."

"You have been hitting the sauce kind of heavy," I suggested.

He frowned at me.

"I have an idea," I told Belov. "You have a satellite line on the bridge, right?"

"Of course."

"Bring this man to the bridge. I'll meet you in fifteen minutes. I have to find a friend."

It took me five minutes to track down Yoji Watanabe. I found him at Bingo where the girl at Reception said he'd be. It took me another ten minutes to convince him to come with me.

"You mentioned these two Alaskan fellows who you take care of," I told him as the Bingo caller pulled numbered balls from a cage.

"I do not take care of them," Yoji said as he marked his cards. "They are the grandsons of my friend who has since died. They are family to me."

"You mentioned that they still speak the native language."

He looked up at me and nodded.

It took about an hour for the ship's radioman to track down Benny and Short Lewis Tayagu aboard the *Nome Ranger*, a two-hundred foot pollock catcher/processor boat currently trolling about three hundred miles northeast of us.

Benny Tayagu had been drinking much of the morning,

being off duty, so was not favorably disposed to talking. But his brother Short Lewis came to the phone.

"My name is Lewis Tayagu," he began. "I'm southern Aleut, Bristol Clan. My father was Kimball Tayagu of Attu. I live in Dutch Harbor but I've spent time in Anchorage and Seattle."

It took another five minutes for Yoji Watanabe to impress upon his friend the nature of our request, but once we got clear of the maritime channels and secured a satellite connection, we were in business.

"He's a good man," Yoji told me as we listened to the strange conversation on the speakerphone. "He drinks too much, but he works hard. He cares for the elderly. His grandfather would be proud."

Short Lewis and the whale hunter were having a nice chat.

"His name in Unger," Short Lewis said over the phone. "He is from up by Savoonga. His people are northern Aleut, from the Norton Clan. He is ninety-two years old."

I whistled. Ninety-two was getting up there.

"I've met him," Short Lewis continued, "at the winter potlatches. He wants to know where his bowhead is."

"What is a bowhead?" Belov demanded.

"It's a whale," I told him.

"Tell him," Belov began, "tell him that when we rescued him, we had to cut . . ."

"Ah, ah, ah," Short Lewis complained on the other end of the line. "You did not cut the whale away, did you?"

Nobody said anything.

"He won't be happy," Short Lewis predicted, and he was right. The old Aleut howled and spat. Finally he pulled a document from his tunic and threw it at Belov. Then he unleashed a calm and reasonably low-volume tirade that continued for close to five minutes.

"He says you owe him $325,000," Short Lewis translated. "He says he just showed you his harvest license. He claims he can take one whale every two years, in accordance with Alaska Eskimo Whaling Commission Rules, and the season is now over. So he says you owe him for the whale."

Nobody said anything as the old man held his hand out.

"We were trying to help him," Belov said. "We were rescuing him."

We waited for the translation and the ensuing rant. "He said he was not in need of rescue. He was whale hunting, and he only wants his whale back."

Belov shook his head. "He was very much in need of rescue. Ask him why he could not move when we took him on board. Ask him why he made no motion, no sound for nearly an hour. Ask him why he appeared dead."

The line cackled with laughter. "That's just the drugs," Short Lewis told us. "Old Daddy Unger hunts his whales the old-fashioned way, with poison. He has a commercial grade harpoon tipped in poison from the aconite plant."

"What is this?" Belov demanded. "I know nothing of this aconite plant."

"It's an old poison. The plant grows on the islands. He makes a resin from the poison and dips his harpoon. And because he's an old-time whaler, Daddy Unger knows he has to keep the whale company once he's got him lined up. It takes a few days for the whale to die, so Daddy Unger takes a little bit of the poison himself, so that he can be in the same place as the whale, so he can sing to it, so he can thank it."

We stood there in silence as the old man started singing, presumably to his whale. It was a sad mournful song. I'd be sad and mournful too if I had just lost a $325,000 whale.

CHAPTER FIFTEEN
DAY 2 - AT SEA - NOON

Oscar Lonagan got a late start to his lecture, but I got an even later start getting there. Belov wasn't happy about our new passenger. We weren't moving too fast with our investigation, and on top of that, this Mr. Unger might have a legitimate claim under native rights laws to get some financial compensation. I didn't have any idea how that would work, and I really didn't care. I had a murderer to find. So we pointed Mr. Unger to the buffet, and he seemed to understand the gist of it.

Lonagan was winding down by the time I took my seat at the back of the Vitus Bering Theater. On screen was an image of a squat little palm tree, about the size of the fat white rabbit that foraged next to it.

"Imagine," Lonagan encouraged the crowd. "Imagine the lore transmitted by shaman to shaman, over the generations, insisting that this resource not be forgotten. A plant that only flowers once every sixty or seventy years could so easily be forgotten. But the Pribilof Sago is so much more than a plant. It is one of the most important ingredients of the Aleutian shaman's pharmacopeia."

The next slide showed an older woman shaving bark with an ivory knife. "Irina Prisigana learned the old ways from her grandfather, coming into her own as a shaman at the age of sixty." Lonagan's next slide was a close-up of the woman's face. "Here she is forty-five years later, a master of her trade."

Gasps from the audience caused Lonagan to pause. "Who here thinks she's too old?"

There were murmurs of laughter but nobody said anything.

"Notions of mortality are culturally-derived and culturally-manifested. But it has long been a central premise of certain coastal shamanic traditions that mortality is overrated." He slammed his fist on the podium to make a point.

"The lenticels," he continued, "part of the inner bark of the Pribilof Sago contain an enzyme unique in botany. When this enzyme is properly activated, and I should confess here that modern science cannot replicate this activation process, but when this enzyme is properly activated by the shaman, the resulting paste, when introduced into the nasal cavity, quite literally slows cellular aging to a standstill."

The audience was silent.

"I went seal hunting with Irina Prisigana last summer," Lonagan said, his voice nearly a whisper, "on her hundred and tenth birthday."

Now hands were raised throughout the theater, and the chatter was growing in volume.

"I'll address all your questions is due time," Lonagan told them. His next slide featured what looked like a little yellow pine cone. "It is the sago flower we are most interested in," he continued. "And here's where the Pribilof Sago differs from its tropical counterparts. Its buds are rich in alkaloids, which readily pass through the blood/brain barrier, producing powerful hallucinations and visions of the spirit world."

"I won't lie to you." Lonagan lowered his head. "We are talking about a poison, a poison so profound that were you to brew it into a tea, or even cook it into a cake, you would not last a minute before the stomach heaves began and you vomited it up."

"No, only by mixing it into a thick paste of seal fat,

and introducing it internally in suppository form, can this substance be tolerated by the body."

"What, now?" I couldn't help myself.

"I will address questions at the end," Lonagan reminded us, "but I do understand your surprise. Culture shock can be profound."

I started laughing.

"Is something funny?"

"I got to thinking about a joke," I told him from the back. I stood up so he could hear me. "So this guy goes to the doctor complaining about hemorrhoids, and the doctor gives him these suppositories."

Lonagan frowned. "I think our guests would be interested in hearing the rest of my lecture. Would you be so kind as to . . ."

"So the guy goes home, and a week later he calls the doctor, and says 'Doc, it's not working at all. For all the good these pills did, I could have shoved them up my ass.'"

Honestly, I don't know why that joke is still funny after all the long decades of my life, but it is. And the audience concurred, erupting in senior laughter.

"If I might continue," Lonagan suggested. "What is significant to our understanding of the sago is not how it is introduced, but what it produces. And for those of us who have huddled by a shaman's fire, let the smoke clear our minds, let hunger boil off both desire and toxins, the alkaloids in the sago flower allow nothing less than a manifestation of the flesh of the creator. A singularity, my friends. For a short time, we become one with the fabric of eternity. And when divinity recedes, it recedes not far, rebooting minds of men. Sadness is gone, mental illness no longer manifests, dementia is alleviated."

On screen, the flower was magnified until it looked like a dozen tiny suns.

"What that means for men like Edward Littlemore,"

Lonagan continued, as he showed the slide from the last lecture, of the man who ate his grandfather, "is that this arctic lunacy, this psychosis endured by native hunters, can be instantly cured. Edward Littlemore died in prison. Never again during the course of his life did the Pribilof bloom, but it bloomed this summer for the first time since 1943, all throughout the Aleutians. A plant that only flowers once every sixty or seventy years could so easily be forgotten. We must not let that happen."

I waited for the applause to die down. I couldn't hear the questions because the folks in front of me, who had probably been married for close to a century, argued loudly.

"I'm just saying it's something we could look into," the wife suggested. "Your memory . . ."

"I'm not shoving a cactus up my ass," the husband told her."

"It's not a cactus," she said weakly.

I left. I took a walk. I walked the length and breadth of the ship thinking about Rose DeSilva, and about Captain Tolstoy. I was pretty sure they didn't have anything to do with whale hunting or with arctic shamanism. I was getting nowhere. All I had were bodies. I thought about that for a moment more. Bodies were all I had. Except for an idea. I had an idea.

I found Mr. Unger, our whale hunter, sitting in the hot tub eating a Reuben. Behind him, Irina Bok was speaking to a security officer.

"Our new guest seems to be enjoying the digs," I offered.

"He is not wearing anything," Irina Bok told me. "He has been in there for half an hour, having stripped down in front of six Belgian women who were enjoying their morning soak. Two of the women left."

"And four stayed," I noted. "Hey, everybody loves a

Reuben." I motioned for Mr. Unger to get out of the hot tub but he shook his head and let loose with a tirade, his mouth half full.

"I'm going to need to borrow him," I told Irina. "Can you drain the hot tub and bring me a robe?"

She grinned at me.

"You're kind of pretty when you're not scowling," I told her, at which point she began scowling again.

Unger started to crab when the water level fell, and he shook his head when I held out the robe.

"I've got more time left than you do," I told him, though I wasn't certain that was true. We were getting some stares at this point. The hot tub was next to the pool, and the pool is the psychic heart of a cruise ship. Even if you don't swim, all passengers must pay their respects and join the congregation poolside. I counted nine gawks, sixteen guffaws, two 'Oh my's,' and a 'yowsah' during the five minutes that Mr. Unger sat naked in the empty tub eating his Reuben. I suspect he was getting cold. I told Irina Bok what I wanted, and she shut her eyes.

"I'm not going to do that," she said. "Absolutely not."

Pretty as she was, I was getting a little tired of her. "Yes you are. You need to help me, right? Because when we finish up, when I find your killer, I'm going to write a report that goes to a lot of people, including the owners of this ship. Including your bosses. Also maybe the Pope, I might carbon copy him. But in that report, I'm going to mention every time you got in my way."

Usually they back down at this point, but she didn't, and I was almost out of juice. "By the time I get through with you, you'll be a junior troll on the chum line of a halibut trawler."

"As if that would not be a step up in life?" She got in my face. "I have the authority to confine you to your stateroom," she said, then gave an involuntary squeak as Unger reached from the tub to pat her bottom.

She twisted his arm behind his back, which must have been painful but which made him laugh.

"Let me handle him," I told her. "I need his help."

She let go of his arm and stepped aside, her cheeks flushed. "Fine," she said. "Fine. Let's go."

Against my wishes, the Beluga Bar was open for business. Two dozen passengers sat reading or talking in the comfortable padded chairs. The view over the bow was expansive. It really felt like we were at the top of the world.

Unger spotted a pastry cart a second after I did, and we each took a momentary leave of Irina Bok to fill a plate with goodies.

"Ready?" She led us behind the bar and into the storeroom. If either of the bartenders was surprised, they didn't show it.

I had no idea how to prepare Mr. Unger for what I was about to show him, so I didn't.

"Open it," I said, as we watched as Irina Bok took down the yellow tape, unlocked the large padlock, and opened the beverage refrigerator. Inside, a stack of soda cans glistened in the frost. Unger whistled with delight and helped himself to a Dr. Pepper.

"They must have moved her down to the morgue," Irina said, so we left. We headed for the elevator and rode all the way down. Unger was munching from a bowl of trail mix that he had balanced on top of his plate of tarts.

"Where did you get that?" I demanded, but he said nothing. I moved in for a handful but he stepped out of reach. "I'm going to remember this," I told him. "One day you'll be starving, and you better not look to me to save you."

The hospital was closed, which was good. It wouldn't do to have any passengers around for this next part. Unger was at my side as I opened the two morgue drawers. And when I pulled aside the sheets, he didn't even stop chewing as he stared at the bodies.

Rose DeSilva was just as we left her, very dead, very brutally treated. Unger put his hand on her forehead, then opened her mouth and ran a finger over her teeth.

"What is he doing?" Irina Bok asked me. I had no idea.

Next he examined her hands. I've seen medical examiners work before, and if I didn't know better, I would have sworn this old guy was a medical examiner instead of a whale hunter. When he pulled the sheet down further and saw the stomach wounds, he just stared. Still holding his cherry tart in one hand, he reached the other inside her stomach and moved it around. Then he closed his eyes and sang softly as he chewed. When he finished the song, he pulled the sheet back up and stood. Then he moved on to Captain Tolstoy's body and did the same.

"Windigo," he said finally, moving on to his puff pastry. I had already eaten mine

CHAPTER SIXTEEN
DAY 2 - AT SEA - 2:00PM

"**M**rs. Connie Watanabe just checked out a book from the library," the woman at Reception told me. "The book is called *Sex and the Senior Woman*. It is due back in three days. At 224 pages, that's about eighty pages a day. But this was only ten minutes ago; she is perhaps not far from the library."

Everybody on this ship has an attitude, I mumbled as I headed up to the Beluga Deck. One thing I love about my traditional hunting grounds, the modern cruise ship, is that it takes next to no time at all to find someone. Purchases are centrally tracked, beverages are accounted for, the opening of a cabin door is recorded, and most public areas are monitored on video. In short, if you're on board, I can find you. Unless you're Yoji Watanabe, who hadn't made any purchases or sudden movements since lunch. So I decided to try my luck with the wife. I found Connie Watanabe playing poker in the card room with three other Oriental women, one of whom was smoking a pipe.

"I thought you played dominoes," I told Connie.

She frowned. "I play dominoes every day of my life. I would like to play dominoes today as well, but unfortunately there is only one box that does not have missing dominoes, and we got here about three minutes after Kitty Sekigawa grabbed it."

"That's unfortunate."

She pointed to a cluster of women by the window. "Look at her. Best table, best view. That pitcher of lemonade is provided by the staff, and is supposed to be on the table by the door where the cups are. And yet where do you see the pitcher of lemonade?"

The woman with the pipe looked at me appraisingly.

"The pitcher," Connie continued, "as you can see, is sitting right there in front of Kitty Sekigawa. How did it get there? Let me tell you how it got there. Mrs. Kitty Sekigawa thinks she is a princess, and therefore, she should have all the lemonade to herself, in addition to the best box of dominoes. I wouldn't be surprised if she claims the pool for her own princess self this afternoon."

I didn't know what to say.

"You're a strapping young fellow," the woman with the pipe told me. "You look like you work out."

"Cross-training," I told her. "I do a lot of martial arts. Listen," I turned back to Connie, "I'm trying to find your husband. Know where he is?"

"He's probably playing his Bingo. If you can't find him there, try the library. Or if there's any show on with dancing girls, you can probably find him there."

I thanked her and left before the pipe woman could get another word in.

I headed back to the Reception desk and stood in line while a skinny middle-aged couple dressed in identical tracksuits tried to book identical spa treatments.

"You must book such treatments at the spa," the woman behind the desk told them. "You cannot do this thing at Reception. Up at the Arctic Spa, there is a book in which your name can be written."

For reasons I could not understand, this response was unclear to the couple in need of spa treatments, and they pressed their inquiry for another five full minutes.

"Me again," I told the woman behind the desk. "I'm still looking for a passenger." I told her about Yoji Watanabe who liked dancing girls.

"There are currently no dancing girls dancing," she told me. "I'm sorry to disappoint. There are some lovely videos of ballet in the library you might enjoy."

"Still looking for Mr. Watanabe," I reminded her. "What time does Bingo start?"

She consulted her monitor. "Not until three. But Yoji Watanabe just ordered a gin & tonic at the pool bar."

"What's going on at the pool bar?"

"Women's shuffleboard tournament. He might be a spectator."

I thanked her and took the elevator up three decks. I found Yoji standing by the rail staring out at the water. Behind him, a dozen or so young ladies vied for shuffleboard greatness. I watched for a few minutes as one golden goddess, surely the youngest of the group, no more than seventy years old if she was a day, smacked a competitor's puck clear off the court.

"I like the cut of her jib," I thought. Then when she turned and smiled, I realized I had said it out loud.

"Hi Henry." She waved at me. I had never seen her before in my life so I wasn't sure how she knew my name. "It's me, Dot, remember, from the surfing class? Stick around and I'll share my winnings with you."

"That's a fine offer," I told her. "What do you stand to win?"

"Bottle of vintage port."

"I could partake. Also, my cabin is on the port side of the ship, so that's a good omen."

"Want to meet up later? We could talk about old times."

"We could."

"Or we could make some new ones."

"I like that idea. Hey, I have to go chat up an old friend

here. Good luck with your game."

She waved. I made my way over to the railing. "I didn't get a chance to thank you," I told Yoji. "I think Mr. Unger is enjoying his time on board, though he's likely still upset about the whale."

He nodded.

"You don't look so good," I told him. "You want to have a seat? Maybe we can go grab a bite to eat? How about some sushi? My treat. Sushi goes great with gin."

Yoji grinned. "I'm afraid I would disappoint. I am perhaps the only Japanese man you will ever meet who does not enjoy sushi. I do not eat fish of any kind."

"Then we'll order up some steaks," I said, "maybe a kebab or two, some burritos. What's going on with you? You look like you've seen a ghost."

"The old man in the canoe," he said quietly. "I remember such men. It was a long time ago."

"I wanted to follow up on what you mentioned yesterday; the demon."

"I spoke out of turn," he replied, "nothing more. It is not something worthy of discussion."

"Yoji, have you ever heard the term windigo?"

He paled instantly, his gaze locked on the sea. "It is not something I wish to discuss."

A couple of joggers approached, so we stood there quietly, waiting for them to pass. Then a group of teenagers burst through the doors and started harassing the bartender until he threatened to toss them over the rail.

I showed Yoji my investigator's license. "I'm looking into the murder of the young woman. I need to know what's going on here. What is a windigo?"

He took a breath and held it for a long time. He moved to leave but I grabbed his arm and held firmly.

"Help me," I told him. "I don't want to see any more dead girls." I let go. If he walked away, I wouldn't have followed him. But he didn't walk away.

"I saw one once," he said softly. "It was a long time ago, and yes, this is exactly what you are up against. I wish only to get off this ship when we make port. I will then fly to California and never give this part of the world another thought."

"Do you think a windigo killed Rose?"

He nodded again. "You must understand, this is an old thing, a thing that has been happening for thousands of years. It is extremely rare, but enduring."

"What is it?"

He took a drink of his beverage. "A demon of the north," he said quietly, "a malevolent entity with a craving for human flesh."

I stared at the shuffleboard court, watching as the women vied for position. "I don't believe in demons, Yoji. I've stared into countless pools of woe during the course of my long life. I've called out to anyone who might be listening. I've called out for help, for solace, for vengeance. And not once have I ever seen anything stare back at me. Not once have I ever heard an answer to my calls."

"You are a nonbeliever."

"You're goddamn right I am. There's nothing out there but ocean, my friend. Also, one very lucky whale."

"I saw one once, a windigo." He stared into his drink, then finished it. "It was the summer of 1943. It was the invasion, you see. We had already been on Attu for more than a year. You Americans tell the story about the Japanese never invading, as if Pearl Harbor was the worst insult of the war. But in fact, we occupied the Aleutian Islands for fourteen months."

"Go on."

"I was with my unit on Attu," he said, "one of the islands we controlled. If you read about this event, you might read that there were five hundred of us, five hundred soldiers holding Attu. But there were not, there were fewer than two hundred of us, perhaps only a hundred north of the villages. The Aleuts were already prisoners, and we had dug our positions deep into the mountains in preparation for the American counterattack."

"I remember hearing about that. The U.S. army used Aleuts as scouts."

"That's right. I have never felt such cold. I feel that cold again now just speaking if it."

"I could get you a coffee," I offered.

"I was manning a heavy gun," he continued, "a machine gun, one evening. We would soon surrender to the Americans, but up where I was, we were so alone. We didn't learn of the American counterattack until it was already almost completed. I remember thinking about my wife, my first wife, and how I missed her. I wondered if she had taken up with another man. Our unit was spread out. My nearest neighbors were two kilometers away on either side."

The ladies playing shuffleboard groaned, then started squabbling. Indications of foul play were evident. I had half a mind to investigate, but I needed to hear what Yoji was telling me.

"Another soldier, my lieutenant, was with me," Yoji continued. "But he was asleep when I saw it. I saw it in front of me, not twenty yards away. It was a man, but there should have been no man there. And it didn't move as a man did. I asked myself, is this a bear I am mistaking for a man?"

"You didn't shoot it?"

"I didn't think to. Perhaps I should have. Instead I punched my lieutenant awake and he immediately reached for his pistol and fired. But the . . . the thing kept coming nearer. At this point my lieutenant grabbed the machine gun, but the thing was gone."

"If it was shot, it would have left a trail of blood," I suggested.

"There was none."

"Could have been just a renegade, or someone escaped from confinement."

"It could have been," Yoji agreed, "but five nights later I awoke to find it had eaten my lieutenant."

"Eaten him?"

"Yes. His abdomen had been torn apart."

"Well I'll be goddamned. You didn't hear any screams?"

"I heard nothing. I was groggy from the cold. My lieutenant, his intestines, his stomach . . . I buried him the next day outside the cave. When I was asked, much later, what had happened, I reported that he had died in his sleep, perhaps from the cold. I was never questioned, and I never spoke of what I saw."

"That's a hell of a story."

"Not since I left the service have I shared it with anyone else."

"I'm glad you told me."

"That is what you are up against," Yoji said, "this windigo. He lives even still, and he has come here for one thing."

"What's that?" I asked.

"Me."

CHAPTER SEVENTEEN
DAY 2 - AT SEA - 3:00PM

I didn't know what to expect when I stepped into Tempo, but certainly not Mr. Unger sitting cross-legged on top of the ping pong table drinking beet liquor with the engine-room crew. Despite a near inability to communicate with anyone, he had quickly made the crew bar into his own. As I would later learn, most of the engine-room crew were Aleutian, and although they couldn't speak their ancestral language, they certainly seemed to recognize a kinsman.

Unger held out a bottle as I approached. It was one of many bottles on the table, but it was the only one not empty. I don't know what Aleut sounds like when slurred, but I suspect it sounds something like what was coming out of his mouth.

"He's like a god," one of the crewmen told me.

I smiled, and when I downed the shot, Unger clapped with the rest of them.

"How much has he had?"

"A lot." One of the crewman leaned over to talk in my ear. "He's got a shipboard account that seems to be unlimited. He's been buying us all drinks."

"That's very nice of him. Hey, are you Aleut too? Do you know him?"

"No, Daddy Unger is from up north. We are all from Umiak or Dutch Harbor."

"What is he singing about?"

"No idea. Nobody speaks that except him, and maybe a couple of old people back home. But we'll take care of him. He's one of us."

I stared at him. "This is taking care of him?"

He shrugged. "It is appropriate to show hospitality. Besides, he was getting frustrated earlier because he couldn't communicate. This seems to calm him down."

On top of the ping pong table, Unger rocked back and forth and started singing.

The crewman frowned. "That's a blessing," he said. "He's singing a blessing. My grandmother used to sing it when someone was about to die."

Around him, drinks half raised were lowered. And the expressions on the assembled faces conveyed a deep sadness. Nobody said a word when Unger pointed a finger at me. It was a big knobby finger with a cracked nail, I noticed. But it left me soon enough, moving from one crewmember to the next. One man began to weep openly.

"What is this?" I asked.

"He's suggesting, I think," a crewman told me, "that we're all going to die."

"Windigo," Unger announced. He clapped his hands on the table. "Windigo baidarka." He kept repeating the same thing. There was another word after baidarka, something nasal, but I didn't recognize it.

"It sounds like the word for gigantic," the crewman told me. "My grandmother used to call me a gigantic pain in the ass. I'm pretty sure that's the word for gigantic. So a windigo is on the gigantic baidarka, on the gigantic boat. I think he means the ship."

"And this windigo is a monster, right?" I had to ask.

He looked down at the floor. "We don't discuss it."

This wasn't good. At that moment, I was glad that Unger wasn't able to communicate more. We might have a mutiny on our hands, I remember thinking, not knowing just how close to the truth I had come.

I took the bottle from Unger's hand and helped him down from the table. "There are no windigos," I told the men. "It's just an old story. Now, somebody take this gentleman somewhere where he can get some rest."

I didn't leave until Unger did. He left singing. Two men carried him as he sang about how we were all going to die. I hoped he was wrong. I had one more generous tot from that bottle of Tuz, and then I went to find Brice Laird.

Georgie opened the door.

"Housekeeping," I told him as I stepped into the cabin. I took a look around. "This is awful."

A tiny porthole provided the only light in the closet-sized room. Although the bunk beds suggested this cabin was designed for double occupancy, I had a hard time seeing how that would work out. Two built-in wardrobes flanked a desk large enough to support two, maybe three postcards.

"Do you remember me, Georgie?"

"You're one of the detectives."

"I am. Hey, aren't you supposed to be locked up? You're a suspect."

"Mr. Belov said I was no longer a suspect." He stared at his watch. "I have to be on duty in ten minutes. Is there something I can help you with?"

"The good thing about living in a space this small," I began, taking a seat on the bottom bunk, "is that there's only so messy it can get."

He didn't say anything.

"When did they let you out of the brig, Georgie?"

"I think about midnight. I'm not sure. I was exhausted. I came right back here and went to sleep."

"No, you didn't. You assaulted Belov and then you killed the captain."

He frowned. "Why would I want to do that?"

"Because Rose dumped you for the captain. She was sleeping with both of you, but she liked him better. You were jealous. I don't know why you attacked Belov. You tell me. You're the psychopath."

He checked his watch again. "I don't have to listen to this."

"You do, Georgie. You do. You're a killer. I can't see you as a cannibal but I'll figure that part out later. For now, I'm going to bet that if you open that bathroom door, I'm going to see a lot of blood."

He opened the door and I saw no blood. Nuts. "Hey, so I hear you have a new roommate." I picked up a pillow to get more comfortable, and I found two porn magazines. "*Tik-Tak*? I don't know this one. And this other is what? *Cebu Honey*. I don't know any of these." I leafed through images of naked and half-naked Filipinas. "I'm going to go out on a limb here and guess the bottom bunk is yours."

He stared again at his watch. "It's just reading material, OK? From the Philippines. I got it from one of the guys working in the laundry. It has a lot of good stuff in it. They do interviews with people about interesting hobbies."

"Look at the bosoms on her." I held one of the magazines vertically and let the pages unfold. "Lulu enjoys watercolors, and ballroom dancing." I turned to Georgie. "I didn't know this about her. Hey, did you know that swing dances are the most popular ballroom dances?"

He looked down at the floor.

"How is the new roommate working out? Are you and Brice getting along?"

"I only met him once, this morning. He didn't have much to say. I think he's not happy to be down here."

"Nonsense, I'm sure he's delighted. I'm going to make a prediction here. I think you and he are going to be close pals. Two killers." I saw a flash of irritation cross his eyes, and I wanted to cultivate that. "He's quite the ladies man, Brice is.

I'll bet he could teach you a lesson or two about how to score with women."

"I do all right."

"Yes you do, Georgie. You do. I have to say, judging by the photos I've seen, that Rose was a good looking girl. I might cheat on my wife too if a girl like that came along, or if I had a wife."

"It was just a thing, OK?" He picked up a pencil from the desk and started fiddling with it. "I feel guilty enough. I'm going to tell my wife as soon as my tour is over."

"No you won't," I told him. I wanted to see what he would do with the pencil.

He shifted it from one hand to the other. I don't think he was aware of it. "What do you mean, no I won't? I will."

"Guys like you never do. I read your employment profile, Georgie. You have an exemplary record."

"What of it?"

"It fails to mention the fact that you were incarcerated."

His mouth opened just a bit, then closed before the denial came. "What are you talking about? I have never been in prison."

"Your left eye quivers when you lie."

"What are you . . ."

"The pencil is a weapon, isn't it? I was in a prison camp myself many years ago. You get to thinking about everything in creation as either food or a weapon. Like that plastic bag in the corner there by the chair." I pointed. "I've been thinking about it since I stepped in here. It's either chips or something else, but I can't help thinking it might be chips."

"I don't know what you're talking about."

I turned the page in the magazine. "Rosalinda enjoys barbeque," I read. "I hope she puts some clothes on for that."

I looked up at him. "You can't eat a pencil, Georgie. I lined up on you and you grabbed a weapon. It's a thing we convicts do to stay alive. So come clean or I'll violate your contract. I'll send you packing back to the Philippines."

"I'm from Tblisi. It's in the Republic of Georgia."

"Whatever. I'll still send you home. And it would make me sad to have to do that. I like you."

He put down the pencil. "I was a kid," he said. "I got to spending time with these other kids. We got into some minor trouble. I spent the summer in a detention facility for youths. It was unpleasant."

"How was the food?"

He shook his head. "Unimaginable."

"You lied on your employment application."

"Wouldn't you?"

"Oh, yes."

"And technically I didn't lie. I was a juvenile."

"And you learned a little about violence, didn't you?"

He picked up the pencil again. "I didn't kill Rose."

"You did, and I understand why. A girl like that comes along once every six lifetimes. What I can't understand is why you would carve her up and eat her." I leafed through the magazine. "This Gigi is adorable. Look at that skin. She's perfect. And she likes to make Halo Halo. Just looking at her, I want to make Halo Halo too, all night long. Or maybe for just a little while. I get tired."

"It's dessert," he said.

"No, she's more than that. She's a three-course meal."

"No, Halo Halo; it's a dessert. They have it in the crew mess. It's like a banana split."

I frowned. "I was imagining something else. Hey, do you ever watch Spicy Bombay? That's my favorite channel."

"I don't think I've seen it."

"It's kind of like the Playboy channel only it has Indian ladies on it. I was watching this one series, I can't remember what it was called. Forbidden something. Most of the shows, they're called Forbidden this or that. Anyway, there's this rich man and he has this wife but he's a little tired of her, you can tell. Anyway, he wants this other girl for his wife, young girl, and she's a looker, but of course he can't do that because he's already married. Unless . . ." I stared up at Georgie.

He shrugged. "Fine. Unless he kills the first wife; I get it."

I frowned. "Georgie, why is it always killing with you? There are other ways to resolve disputes. You don't always have to rush to kill. Like in this TV show I've been telling you about, OK? So the rich guy, he has a talk with the wife, he lays it out for her, and then he brings in the girl to meet the wife. And she's gorgeous, great big bosoms. And you would think the wife would be upset, so the rich man told them that they have to spend twenty-four hours together, just those two women, so they could get to know each other. Then the rich man leaves, and guess what happens next?"

"Let me guess, the girls start . . ."

"And don't say killing, Georgie, because there was no killing. In fact, the girls started liking each other very much. Very much."

"That's fascinating," he told me. "I didn't kill Rose. And I didn't kill the captain or Belov."

"Belov isn't dead."

"I mean I didn't attack him."

I shoved the magazine back under his pillow. "You did, Georgie. You did."

CHAPTER EIGHTEEN
DAY 2- AT SEA - 5:00PM

I slept.

After leaving Georgie's cabin I spent some time wandering. I walked the decks and I walked the hallways. I had a gimlet at the Beluga Bar and then I went back to my cabin and I slept. I slept for hours and I dreamed.

I don't know if it was the rocking of the ship, or the weather outside my window that had taken a bad turn, but I dreamed of stormy seas and memories.

The year was 1990. George Bush was in the White House. Gas cost $1.16 a gallon. The Berlin Wall came down, and I was a handsome young man. A dapper sixty-five years of age; I had my whole life in front of me.

I wore a grey fedora and a corduroy jacket and I had a gorgeous lady on either arm. The *Concordia Sapphire* had just crossed the international date line north of Tonga and I was a day younger. I had not a care in the world. But that's not true. I had a murder to solve. An aspiring actress by the name of Halene Delacroix went over the railing one starlit night about fifty miles south of Vanuatu. She was from Metarie, Louisiana, and she was twenty-three years old.

It was sheeting rain that night, not a good night for Halene to be out on deck. She had been drinking. She had very likely been doing a little something else too, but I was never able to prove that. She had been having a physical sort of argument with her husband, one that ship's security had been called to break up. By midnight the husband was back in the cabin but Halene went dancing, made a friend, then made another friend.

We put together a timeline after the fact. Halene and her new beau went off radar for about an hour and a half. But by two in the morning she was drinking again in the smokers' bar. She ordered a Gin Ricky at 2:15 in the morning from a bartender named Aldo Klegg. It was the last drink she would ever order.

Fifteen minutes later, when Aldo Klegg cut her off for being intoxicated, Halene wandered up top. We know this because it was captured on tape by one of the security cameras. I've watched that tape so many times that I can replay it now in my mind. Halene got herself to the railing, stumbling from the drinks. She stood there staring, as people do at railings late at night. She was crying I think. I'm not sure. She wiped her eyes a couple of times and her chest convulsed in what looked to me like a sob. Then someone came up behind her, lifted her clean over the railing and dropped her. He stood there long enough. Long enough. Watching. He had his back to the camera the whole time. Even when he backed out of the frame. No shot of his face.

Every now and again, when I'm at sea, I find myself looking over the railing, down into the depths of the ocean, squinting to see if just maybe I can catch a glimpse of Halene down there. I never have.

And I let her down. I didn't bring her killer in. Oh, I found him alright. I questioned Halene's new friend for hours. I questioned her other new friend for hours. I questioned Aldo Klegg for hours more, and I questioned the husband. Bullshit he was asleep. I could see it in his eyes. He was a stone killer; I had him down, but he was a cool, cool man. He tried to tell me a joke. 'What did the man say to his portly wife when hiking in bear country?' But I was having none of it. I drew my gun, stuck it in his ear and pulled back the hammer. "I'll shoot you dead, you fucker," I told him. But he just laughed.

Five days later he walked down the gangplank in Sydney, Australia, and my case was cold. He had a swing in his step. He was fifty years old. His name was Brice Laird.

The ringing of the phone brought an end to my dream. I let it ring as I moved my mind back to the present. I sat up, got some fresh socks from the drawer, then poured myself a nice tot of vodka from the minibar. The phone rang again.

It was Irina Bok. "I have been looking all over for you."

"You don't need to apologize," I assured her. "Yes, you were rude. Yes, you were insubordinate. But the important thing is that we are working on the same team. Water under the bridge."

Silence on the line, I was pretty sure her eyes were closed.

"Mr. Grave, would you have a sense of why our ship is not currently in motion?"

I sat up and looked out the window. I saw nothing but storm clouds. "I hadn't noticed."

"Would you please meet me in the engine room?"

"Now?" I checked my watch. "I was just thinking about dinner. They're having lamb."

"Now."

On most cruise ships, the engine room is not the most comfortable place to be. It's messy, it smells, and there is a lot of grease. You might not see the grease, but just lean up against anything and it's on you. But on this ship, the engine room was immaculate. It smelled horrible, like burnt oil, but it was immaculate. Occupying half of the lowest deck, below the crew quarters, the engine room was dominated by two massive twelve-cylinder marine diesel engines, each capable of producing more than 18,000 horsepower to propel the ship.

Behind each of these behemoths was a smaller six-cylinder engine whose output was converted to electricity to power the lights, the elevators, the TV, the washers and dryers, the navigation systems, and basically anything requiring electricity.

Chained to one of these smaller engines was the chief engineer, a portly Canadian named Benson Holder. Belov was screaming at him.

"There was nothing I could do," Holder pleaded as I followed Irina Bok down the central walkway. "There were six of them."

"I am not believing you," Belov spat. "You have alarms on each wall. You have a weapon in your office. You allowed the ship to be taken over by foreign miscreants. I will have you jailed."

"There was nothing I could do," Holder repeated. "I'm as mad as you are, believe me. These guys, some of these guys I've worked with for years. I trusted them. But they came at me. They chained me, and then they jammed a bunch of life jackets into the air cleaners."

"Into the air cleaners?"

"That's right."

"Of all four engines?"

"Yes, all four."

"How bad?"

"How do I know how bad? I'm chained here. You want to think about getting me loose? At least then I could have a look. The turbochargers are probably shot, possibly the intake valves too. I don't know how bad."

"What happened?" I asked.

"Mutiny," Belov spat. "Mutiny. Our engineering staff has deserted, having disabled the engines."

"Why? Hey, this whole place smells like Pine-Sol. I know because I use it back home. It gets out tough stains."

"Why? Why is the question of this day." Belov turned back to the chief engineer. "Why? Why are my engines disabled? And where is my engineering crew? Did they share that information with you? How long do they think they can hide onboard?"

"No way," I began. My thoughts were racing. Mutiny? You can't mutiny and stay on board. You either have to take the bridge or you have to leave the ship.

I was already out the door by the time Belov finished his thought, but he caught up with me at the elevator, being a little younger and faster. Maybe on a massive liner, you could hide six people for couple of hours, but not on this ship, which left only one option – they had no intention of remaining on board.

Belov's radio chirped as we raced to the elevator. I heard the first officer's voice. "Captain, we're showing an initiation sequence for lifeboat number two. We don't have a drilled scheduled at this time. Is this something . . ."

"Which lifeboat?" Belov yelled into the mouthpiece.

"Ah, number two, starboard. Sir, she's being dropped as we speak. The waters are unsafe at this . . ."

We lost contact for probably thirty seconds as we rode the elevator, but it seemed like an hour or more.

"Open the hatch." Belov screamed at the Reception staff as soon as the elevator door opened. And they did. It took about three minutes to pull that massive door open. The cold air and the rain poured in as we stared out just in time to see the lifeboat cast off its lines.

"Put a team together and follow them," Below spat, yelling at Irina Bok who was standing an inch behind him. "This is desertion. Arm every man and follow in a Zodiac. If you have to kill them, kill them."

I shook my head.

"What is it you are shaking your head for?" he demanded.

"You have to let them go."

"I have to let them go? Are you an insane man? These

men are mutineers. They will be punished."

"You have to let them go."

"He is right," Irina told him. "We cannot afford to lose any more crew. And we cannot have the security team go after them. If you recall, we still have a killer on board."

"I will go myself," Belov roared. "Prepare a Zodiac."

"That is irrational," Irina told him. "One man against six in a larger boat? They would repel you."

"Mr. Grave will come with me."

I was surprised to hear that. I didn't like the look of the chop out there.

"No." Irina shook her head. "No, this is not acceptable. A captain's place is on the ship. No."

"You cannot stop me. I am making a decision."

"No," she said again. "If you insist on this course of action, I will relieve you of duty for your irrational behavior. Furthermore . . ."

Something big hit the water, drenching us in ice-cold brine.

"What is this?" Belov demanded as a baidarka bobbed up from under the surface. Mr. Unger howled with pleasure, wiping the seawater from his face.

"Get back on this ship," Belov screamed, but the old Aleut laughed and then paddled after the lifeboat. We watched him go. Before long, he caught up with the lifeboat and threw them a line.

Chapter Nineteen
Day 2- at sea - 9:00pm

"I am relieving you from duty," Belov told Benson Holder, the chief engineer. "You are a disgrace. But you are still required to answer all my questions."

"We're on the same side here," Holder told him. We were seated in the captain's office. A tray of sandwiches sat untouched in the middle of the table, cruelly mocking me with their promise of unattainable savory promise. I could take it no longer.

"Nothing wrong with tuna," I announced, an icebreaker to cut the tension, as well as a claim to the only tuna on a croissant that I could see. I grabbed a ham sandwich too in case the meeting ran long, and some cheese cubes.

"You said these guys, the engine room crew - you've worked with them for a long time."

"Yeah, five of them, that's Alex, Big Pete, Little Pete, Pecker Pete, and Warren, they came on the same contract. They're cousins or something from Dutch Harbor. They all came onboard about three years ago, together. The other guy, Random Redmond, he came about six months later, but I think he might be a cousin too."

"Why do you call him Random Redmond?"

"That's his name. Like Random is his first name and Redmond is his last name."

"Is that right?" I ate another cheese cube. "I thought

maybe it was because you would ask him a question and he'd give you a random answer. Like you'd say, 'how was your day, Redmond?' and he'd say, 'I'd like a sponge bath' or something like that."

Holder shook his head. "No, nothing like that. Like I said, it was his name."

Belov cleared his throat. "And you are never having any problems with these men before?"

"No way." Holder shook his head. "No way. These guys are family guys, straight shooters. They have like eight kids each. They drink a little, but that's it. No fooling around, no gambling. They do good work, they keep to themselves, and their pay gets wired home to their wives."

"So what happened?" I asked.

He shrugged. "Like I told you before, they got spooked. They had been drinking with the old man, the whale hunter. They were Aleut too, these guys, like I said. And somehow the old man convinced them that there was a demon onboard."

Irina Bok gave me a sideways glance.

"A demon?" Belov scowled. "Why would they think that?"

"It's a myth. Some kind of cannibalistic demon."

Holder looked over at my sandwich so I pulled my plate closer. "I'm telling you, I've never seen grown men so afraid. A wibilo, that's what they called it."

"Windigo," Irina and I simultaneously corrected.

Belov turned to us.

"Demon of the north," I shared. "It turns people into cannibals."

"And what would give Mr. Unger the notion that we had one on our ship?"

I took a bite of my sandwich to avoid having to answer. Irina took that as her opportunity to inform on me.

"Mr. Grave suspected that the old man might have some insights into our crime scene. We brought him to see the bodies, to see Rose's body, and the captain's."

Belov buried his face in his hands. "What you are telling me is that this man was taken to see the bodies, became convinced that a demon was responsible, and then convinced the engine crew to disable our ship before stealing a lifeboat to abscond."

That sounded about right.

"Look, they're not bad guys," Holder said. "You know, it took me a minute or so to realize what was going on. They grabbed my arms and all, and they chained me up, but honestly, I thought they were kidding. Once I saw what they were doing, messing with the engines, I got pissed."

"And yet you let them." Belov moved into his space. "Perhaps your friendship with these men clouded your judgement and you let them disable the engines."

"Yeah, that was it." Holder was angry now. "They had just chained me to a pipe but I was so overcome with loyalty to my friends that I told them exactly what to do."

"So you admit it," Belov screamed.

"Gentlemen," I said, "this is not helpful. And this ham isn't good, right here in this sandwich. I don't think it's real ham. It may be goat ham or some ham substitute, but it's not real ham. But that's neither here nor there. I have very little interest in motivation at this point. Only results. Where are they going, Mr. Holder. Where are they going in that lifeboat, did they say?"

"Yeah. They're going east. They said they were going to find a shaman."

Belov couldn't keep out of it. "Where is this shaman?"

"They didn't say. Like I said, they were going east. I'd say they're headed back to Gurbka. It's the closest island. At full speed, they could be there tomorrow."

"They have shamans on Gurbka?" I asked.

He shook his head. "I have no idea. They just said they needed a shaman. They said they couldn't risk us bringing the windigo to the mainland where it would be free to hunt for eternity. This way, since the windigo was confined to the ship, and the ship was disabled, then only the people onboard could be killed."

"That is a comfort," Belov yelled. "Do you know why that is a comfort? Look at this." He pulled a tablet computer from the sideboard. "Do you understand this weather pattern?"

Holder frowned. "This can't be right. We've already moved north of the storm system. Where did this other storm come from?"

"It is coming tonight," Belov said. "Where it comes from, I do not know. Perhaps your webugo brought it."

"Windigo," I corrected him between bites.

"We cannot be facing a squall this big without engine power." Belov told him. "We need to be able to turn the ship. Without our main engines, that will be difficult."

"I think I can get the smaller engines back on line. The mains, I don't know, but the little guys, I think we can fix."

Belov shook his head. "Can you shunt power from them to propulsion?"

"Yeah, I can do that."

"How long will they take to repair?"

"Give me a couple of hours."

"And I will be able to bring the ship back under power?"

"Yes. I could give you a cruising speed of six knots, that would be sailing dark, no navigation, no heaters, no elevators."

Belov shook his head. "You can have the elevators only. I need the rest of my electrical systems."

"Three knots," Holder told him. "For a few hours, I could give you four."

Belov scowled. "I could walk faster."

"I could almost swim faster."

Belov looked down at his tablet and drew several lines with his fingertip. "At four knots, I can't move us out of the squall. By 11:00 tonight, the sea will be rough. By midnight, it will be uncomfortable."

"We should put the crew on alert," Irina said. "We'll shut the fire doors between bulkheads. We'll close the outside decks. All staff to report to emergency duty stations by midnight."

"Half staff," Belov said without looking up. "Do all that you said, but half staff. I can keep the ship safe. But we still need a functioning staff and crew. Mr. Holder, please return to your station and make the arrangements we discussed."

The engineer nodded. "So I'm not relieved of duty."

"Apparently not. Can you accomplish your task without an engine crew?"

Holder shook his head. "We'll be wringing every last bit of power from these engines. I need someone to monitor. Can't afford to overheat."

"Who was the duty commander of the lifeboat we just lost?" Belov asked.

Irina shook her head. "I will find out."

"Good. Whoever that person is, he is now the new assistant engineer."

"We can, of course, radio for assistance," Irina noted.

"You have already done so," Belov reminded her. "They sent me."

When all else fails, you almost have to dance. Top hats and tails were on display in the Vitus Bering Lounge as a four-piece Filipino orchestra serenaded us with the silky, seductive sounds of big-band music. Although a memo had gone out to all the passengers urging caution, informing everyone of the engine problems, and explaining that one of the lifeboats had been dispatched to fetch some necessary supplies (which was actually true), none of the passengers seemed overly concerned.

The weather was holding. True to his word, Belov kept the ship mostly out of the squall. He had even sacrificed some of our power to keep the stabilizers running. Without them, the pitch and roll would have been much more pronounced.

Passengers get sick at that point, and it's not what people look for when they sign up for a cruise. Bad enough we had already had a cannibalistic murder on board which they hadn't even been told about, on top of a dead and partially-eaten captain which they also hadn't been told about.

No, the last thing anyone needed was to get sick.

Although Brice Laird was not officially on duty, he was there anyway, whooping it up with the ladies, every last one of whom seemed to be enjoying his attentions.

I was keeping an eye out for Oscar Lonagan, but I hadn't yet spotted him, so I took a perch at the bar and had some champagne. The thing about free unlimited champagne is that it can sneak up on you. One minute it's free, and the next, it's unlimited. I was thinking about that when I felt a gentle hand on my shoulder.

"I was wondering where you had gone off to."

I turned and looked into the eyes of one of the most beautiful women I had ever seen. Young and tender like a spring lamb; she couldn't have been more than fifty years old. She was everything I had always been looking for.

"Remember me?"

"Of course," I lied, certain I had never set eyes on her before.

"Maud Munvez," she reminded me. "We had breakfast together this morning. You left me in the care of Murray, which I did not appreciate. It was just a small thing for me, you understand. We have no future together, Murray and I. I'm looking for someone a bit more spry."

What Maud Munvez didn't know was that I am a champion tango dancer, having won awards at retirement communities both in the US and Canada.

"I know," she said when I told her. "You told me so this morning."

It didn't matter. I led her out onto the floor and spun her like a golden angelic top. At one point, a man wearing a top hat tried to cut in, but I told him no. I saw Oscar Lonagan sitting at the bar with his girl, and I knew I had to talk with him, but I've always found it difficult to turn my back on a tango.

When the music changed, morphing seamlessly into something slower and more intimate, Maud moved in closer and held me tight. "I get scared at night," she said. "Do you?"

I shook my head. "I don't." I saw Murray Abramowitz at the entrance to the room, and I tried to maneuver Maud out of his line of vision.

"There's just so much that has gone wrong already," she said, her mouth nearly pressed to my ear. "First a murder, and now we have a partially disabled ship. What's next, monsters?"

"Bet on it."

"What?" She pulled back a bit but I held her tight.

"Nothing. I won't let anything happen to you," I promised.

"But I'm scared. What if something happens during the night and I'm all alone?"

She was a forward lass, I'll give her that. But I have decades of experience in this kind of thing. I am nothing if not smooth. "You can call me anytime, day or night."

She drew back and looked me in the eye. "That was hardly the response I was looking for."

"I'm just teasing you," I told her. "My cabin is your cabin. I'll warn you in advance though, the minibar is empty."

"Don't they fill it?"

"Not often enough."

Murray Abramowitz tapped me on the shoulder.

"May I?"

Maud squeezed my hand and wouldn't let go. I was having a predicament: on one hand, a woman who had already provided a good faith guarantee of a romantic encounter, something I was quite keen to participate in, and on the other hand stood a new friend, a man who cared for her deeply, possibly more than I did.

Murray didn't wait for an answer, and I have to give him credit for that. "I figured there was a 75% probability I would find you here," he told her as he put his arm around her. She gave me a sad glance, and I watched her head grow smaller and smaller as she danced away from me, following her new partner's lead.

I would reacquire her later, I told myself. But in the meantime, I would get some work done. I looked around for Lonagan but he had disappeared. I spotted Connie Watanabe sitting at a cocktail table with several members of her posse but I really didn't want to talk with them so I headed for the corridor, where I bumped into Brice Laird.

He had a woman on each arm, each draped in more jewels than the other, and he was leading them to the dance floor. I needed to speak with him but this wasn't the time.

"Henry," he said loudly. "Ruth and Marnie want to dance. Why don't you join us? Aren't you quite the dancer?"

"Rain check," I told him. "I have work. Hey, why don't you tell them about the time you played that Mexican zombie. That was outstanding. Hey, how do say 'brains' in Spanish? I can't remember."

"I can't either," he whispered, leaning in, "but it was a good role. We filmed on location in Mazatlan for two short weeks, and in that time I made love to six different women."

"My good god, that's impressive."

"Yes I was." He leaned in even closer. "Henry, you would pass up a night with two beautiful ladies just to chase down a whore's killer? You're a sad old man."

He was right. He was right about everything. I leaned in too. "I'm still going to shoot you dead," I told him, but he had already moved on.

CHAPTER TWENTY
DAY 2- AT SEA - MIDNIGHT

Rose DeSilva was not a whore. Let's just agree on that before we go any further. I had stared into her eyes. And I know, I know, I know, she was already dead. But something of a person's soul is vested in that person's physical form. I've known women who are so beautiful that they can barely get through the day without the incoming nonsense - women who refuse to shop in the evening when men become more common in stores.

These women are sick to death of the comments, the attention, the derision they get from other women, the relentless yearning of men. But they're still mostly gentle kind people just moving through their day.

I've known some prostitutes too. But I've been working in this industry for many years, long enough to understand that cruise ship prostitution is nearly nonexistent. I'm not saying that there isn't a lot of sex transpiring within the steel confines of any cruise ship, because there is. But actual organized prostitution where passengers could, for the right price, get a little something on their pillow at night other than a mint? No way.

Don't get me wrong, I have no illusions that the cruise environment is anything other than a near collision of haves and have-nots. Where else would a twenty-year-old Nicaraguan chambermaid come in such close and sustained contact with a wealthy seventy-year-old Buick dealer from

Akron? Where else would a twenty-two-year-old Dominican father of three find himself kneading the aching flesh of sixty-year-old widow from Palm Beach? Ekatrina, the nineteen year-old Romanian librarian couldn't possibly be lovelier, and she very likely might enjoy your attentions.

When haves and have-nots collide, predictable results ensue. Crushes are about as common onboard as deck chairs or cocktail cherries. That widow from Palm Beach will as likely as not fall in love with her masseuse, and the Buick dealer will daydream about his chambermaid. She'll return the favor, imagining briefly, the life she might have with him, Buick and all, food and safety too. And that masseuse will hazard a thought to the new shirts he could buy, a car perhaps, good wine and enough rice to send home, if he smiled back at that older, yet still handsome woman.

Don't even get me started on Ekatrina. She's half imagining her new life with me back at Rolling Pines. I made her up of course, but if she existed, she'd be envisioning herself ensconced in my La-Z-Boy listening to my Perry Como albums while drinking a gimlet. Hey, it beats eating turnips back in Bulbburg, Romania.

So I'm not going to tell you that romance doesn't happen. It does. But no prostitution.

Here's why: every last cruise ship afloat prohibits staff and crew from sexual or amorous relationships with passengers. They're not even allowed in passenger cabins unless explicitly involved in ship's business. And they are not going to break those rules lightly. Their pay is uncommonly bad, but a portion of their pay is withheld until they have successfully completed a contract, usually three months. Get caught sneaking into someone's cabin, and you don't get your bonus. Furthermore, you won't get invited back. And you want to get invited back.

No matter how bad that pay is, it still beats what you could pull down back in Managua or Santo Domingo or

Bulbburg. So no prostitution; the risks are too high. Unless you had the whole ship wired, the whole crew paid off, and some major onboard muscle to keep security out of the way. Unless you were willing to take some extraordinary risks. Unless you were so self-confident that you could nearly guarantee you wouldn't leave a customer so dissatisfied that they would have a word with the captain.

I called Michelle Parker from a courtesy phone but she wasn't in. I left a message asking her to meet with me, and to let me know if she and Rose were prostitutes. I didn't have time to sugarcoat things. In the end, she never got back to me.

I had some thinking to do.

By one in the morning, most cruise ships are winding down their evenings. Buffets are cleared and waiters take some deep relaxing breaths. Oboes are stowed and Filipino troubadours dressed like Sinatra sit heavily on barstools for well-deserved nightcaps. Discos will still be open for another hour. Why? Because nervous single men in their twenties who got the bad advice to take a cruise to meet young women are confronting the mother of all demographic nightmares: yes, cruise ships are full of single women, but most of them fondly remember voting for Herbert Hoover. He was a good man, Hoover was, but he never got a break.

A bar or two will still be open. They have to be. A cruise is a vacation, after all, and only the most temperate among us can resist the call of the late-night tot. Listen closely to the sound that gin makes when it hits the glass. It's different after midnight, softer. Some folks take a cruise to celebrate. Others are dragged reluctantly by more adventurous spouses. And still others cruise to get away for a small time, from the grind, from the kids, from the divorce papers. And none of these folks are interested in heading back to the cabin just yet. It's too early.

I needed to have a look around the Beluga Bar, because

that's where Rose DeSilva was killed, and that's where Captain Tolstoy was killed. The Beluga Bar was somebody's hunting ground.

One of the conditions of my employment is that I can move around the ship freely, unaccompanied, and wherever I choose. Back in the day that meant I got a master key, but mostly these days I get a keycard that will open anything. Yes, that means I can get into your cabin. But no, I probably won't unless I really need to.

The Beluga Bar was closed when I got there, but not to me. I kept the lights off and stepped inside. It was all grey as I remembered, but I had never seen it so dark. Notwithstanding the midnight sun, a storm was raging outside. I could see it clearly through the floor-to-ceiling windows at the bow. I moved closer until I stood at the glass. Bad night to be out in a little baidarka, I found myself thinking. I wondered what Mr. Unger was up to right about now.

I made my way over to the bar and ran my hands over the surface. Who did this, Rose? Behind the bar, a metal grate kept the liquor bottles safe from thieving passengers and crew. I checked the beer taps but they had been turned off. I moved behind the bar and tried the door to the storeroom, where the big fridge was, but it was locked with an actual lock, so I wasn't getting in. Then I walked the room moving from table to table. Walking is important. Most people don't realize how important until they get old. You see stuff.

Someone had left a paperback on one of the chairs. *Sex and the Senior Woman*, it was called. I hadn't read it, and after confirming that there were no illustrations, I made a decision never to read it. I found a silver earring. I would have missed it but a crack of lightning made it shine for a moment. And I found a wallet wedged in the cushions of a banquette. There's really no need to carry a wallet on a cruise. All you need is your keycard, but apparently nobody told that to Wilton Mayer of Bald Knob, Arkansas. Bald Knob - I shook my head. In truth, you can learn a lot about a man by looking through his wallet; it's all part of the training.

Wilton carried two credit cards, a library card, a photograph of someone who looked like Ethel Merman, and a folded up obituary column about Mrs. Nettie Mayer, also of Bald Knob, who also looked like Ethel Merman. Wilton was also carrying a AAA membership, four hundred and thirty dollars, and a condom. He was 83. Good for you, Wilton.

I put the wallet on the bar, along with the earring and the book, and then I moved back to the windows. Just outside, a narrow ledge ran the length of the room. Maybe it was for the window cleaners, I didn't know. Below it, I could just make out the stateroom verandas a deck below. There had to be a way to get out onto that ledge. And if there was a way out, there was a way in.

I saw something out of the corner of my eye; movement. I wasn't alone in the room.

"Who's there?" I called out, but I got no answer. I didn't know how to turn the lights on, so I waited for the next crack of lightning but I still didn't see anyone. I took my gun out, and just as I did so, the door opened and a man walked in.

He was about my height though thinner; that's about all I could see from the silhouette of him. Still, my eyes had adjusted to the darkness, so I could probably see him better than he could see me. I watched him. He came forward, moving slowly but confidently. He might not be able to see in the dark but he knew the layout of the room. He avoided a couch that he couldn't have seen. He works here, I told myself. The lightning flashed. It was green. It was a kind of lightning I hadn't seen before. I think it was that aurora thing but it lit the man up, lit me up too. He started walking towards me, smiling a bit. The lightning again. And the closer he got, the smile faded bit by bit until it was replaced by a frown, something like a look of disgust.

"That's close enough," I told him. I put my gun on him

and I told him about it. "Close enough. On the ground now."

He seemed startled but he dropped.

"Who are you?"

The lightning again. I got a look at his face but I didn't know him. He got a look at mine too but I don't think he knew me either.

"Sasha," he said. "I'm Sasha. Please do not shoot at me."

"Sasha, why are you walking around this closed bar in the dark? Want to tell me right now? Right now?"

"Yes, yes." He groaned. "I came to meet you. You called me. You told me to come. I came to meet you."

"What, now?"

"I said I came to meet you."

"You know who I am?"

"No, sir. I came to meet you."

"Now Sasha, this is not making any sense to me. You're going to need to do much better. You're telling me you don't know me but you came to meet me because I called you."

He nodded. "Yes. That is it. You called me and told me to meet you here."

"Stop saying that. Sasha, have you ever met me before?"

"No, sir. I am a bartender. I am good with faces. I have not seen yours. You have not been in my bar. I work at the piano bar."

"There's a piano bar?"

"Sir, there is. It is lovely."

"Walk me through this, Sasha. What makes you think I called you?"

"I got a call, on the telephone. I was at the piano bar and I got a call on the telephone to come to this place now to meet you."

"To meet me, who you do not know? Come on."

"To meet someone. I don't know who. To meet someone. Someone told me to meet him here for a surprise."

"What kind of surprise?"

He blushed. I know that because the green lightning lit up his red face making a horrible brown."

"Let me get this . . ." I started but Sasha moved his head all of a sudden as if to look past me. I spun and I saw him. Someone was back there, moving quietly, using the chairs and the banquettes as a cover.

"Sasha," I said calmly, "do you know who is in this room with us?"

"No, sir."

I was hoping for a little more lightning at that moment but it wasn't forthcoming. "Sasha, I need you to do something for me."

"Yes, sir."

"I need you to turn the lights on."

"I can stand up, sir?"

"Yes, please."

He did, and I heard him move toward the door. I kept my eyes on the back of the room, looking for movement between the chairs.

"They're not going on," Sasha reported a moment later. "The power is off. I can't put the lights on."

Nuts. "Sasha, I need you to go outside and call ship's security. Tell them to come here right now."

"Yes, sir. I should do this now? I am to leave now?"

"Yes, please. And lock the doors on your way out."

I waited until I was confident I heard the internal mechanism of two locks being set. The lightning came again but I saw nothing.

"Just you and me now, sport," I called out. I pulled back the hammer of my gun. "You think I'm afraid? I'm eighty-five goddamn years old. I've gone up against nitwits, nazis, and every manner of nutcase. I've hunted sinners and sickos and more shitbags than you ever imagined. So here's the plan, my hidden friend: you stand up right now, walk over here and lay down on this dance floor, right here under the disco ball, and I'll let you live. I'll count to two, and then I start shooting. I'd count to ten but I don't have a lot of time. The security people are on their way and I like to get a little shooting done every time I go to sea."

I got nothing in response. A clap of thunder seemed to come before the lightning this time. I didn't know that could happen, but who knows what's possible with that aurora thing.

"One," I said as loud as I could.

Nothing.

Not nothing. I was about to say 'two' when I heard a crash. Something from across the room, but I wasn't born any kind of yesterday. I didn't turn. That's when I saw him. He was closer than I thought. I fired my gun. I did so again and again and again. I don't like to use all the bullets because it takes me a long time to reload, and I had all my other bullets in the cabin.

Then quiet, all quiet, except for the deafening ring, the familiar aftermath of a handgun being fired repeatedly in relatively close proximity to my ear. "Is that all you got, sport?" I called out. "I got two more. One of them has your name."

He showed himself then, popping up. He threw something at me. It was a vase, I would later learn, and it hit me in the face. It was a good shot. So was mine. I shot him. I heard that 'oof,' that sudden exhalation of breath a man makes when you shoot him. He went down. I figured he was down for the count, but a moment later, he was gone. He went out through the door.

Chapter Twenty-One
Day 3- at sea - 2:00am

"Your head is bleeding," Irina told me. "It is very bad. You will have permanent scarring. This scarring will not go away in time. It will be permanent."

"I'll be even sexier."

She looked away.

"No stitches," I said.

"Yes stitches," the doctor told me. "If I put a butterfly on it, it could open up. You could bleed out while you're asleep."

"Then I won't sleep." I sent Irina on a mission to find my bullets. "I'm almost certain I hit him. What I can't figure out is how he got out of the room. I had Sasha lock the doors."

The lights were on now. The doctor pointed to the doors. "You need a keycard from the outside, but from the inside, just turn the knob."

Nuts.

Belov frowned at me. "And you say you didn't see him?"

"That's what I said." The lightning snapped again. "Hey, Belov, what ever happened to keeping us out of that storm?"

"I am doing my best," he said evenly. "Why are you being here in the first place?"

"Investigating," I told him as the doctor applied a butterfly bandage to my forehead. "It's what I do."

"And you told nobody you were coming here."

I told him about Sasha. "He says he was meeting

someone here."

Belov spun around to Sasha. "Who? Who? Tell me."

Sasha shrugged. "I was locking down the room, the piano bar."

"Alone? You were alone at this time, in the piano bar, which you say you were locking down?"

"Yes. No, well, Kathryn was there. Kathryn Tsaryov, the bar manager. She was finishing the stock inventory, but she was in the back when the phone rang. One bottle was missing, I remember this much. One bottle of Tequila; we were thinking where it might have gone to, and we did not know. And then the phone rang. I answered and I spoke to a man. He didn't say who he was, just to meet him up here."

"He said to come to the Beluga Bar, that is all?"

"That's right."

"In the middle of the night?"

"Yes."

"And you didn't know who it was?" Belov started at Sasha as if all of creation's lunacy had set up shop in his head.

"No. I did not know who it was. He was whispering."

"And it was a man? You are certain of that?"

Sasha lowered his head. "Yes."

Belov looked about ready to explode. "Then why would you come?" he screamed. "What kind of demented, turnip-shitting imbecile would be doing such a stupid thing? It is a senseless thing."

Sasha shrugged meekly.

"I think you are lying," Belov spat. "I think you know who it was you were meeting. I think you may be a killer yourself."

"I don't. I am not."

"Then why?"

Sasha shrugged again. "To see."

"To see what?"

"To see who wanted me."

Belov moved in slowly until his face was an inch from Sasha's. "To see who wanted you?"

"Yes."

"Why would someone want to meet you in the middle of the night in a bar that is closed? Why would you want to meet that person? Are you a very stupid man?"

Irina Bok put her hand on my shoulder. "You shot three banquettes and one chair," she said. "That is four bullets. Show me your weapon."

I did, and she checked. "You fired five rounds."

"I hit the fucker."

She laughed. "Yes, you hit the fucker."

"You are so pretty when you laugh," I told her. "It's as if all the gloom in you just suddenly evaporated. No wait, it's back."

She turned to Belov. "Sasha Khabalov is a bisexual man," she said. "He came here, I am guessing, thinking that someone was interested in him, perhaps wanting to meet him for, for some . . . for some conversation."

Sasha nodded. "What she said. Yes, it is what she said."

Belov shut his eyes. "So we have no idea who this man is, and no way to find him. Is that what we are all saying?"

"No, we'll find him." I stood up. I got dizzy for a moment but it passed. "We'll find it because I shot him. So sooner or later, that's going to narrow down our list of suspects. Because whoever is walking around with my bullet in him, that's our killer."

I was feeling a little unsteady but I wasn't ready to call it a night. At two in the morning, I learned, only the Vitus Bering Lounge was still open, doling out nightcaps to the lonely, the dejected, the rejected, and the downright disrespected.

I counted about thirty people as I made my way to the bar. Oscar Lonagan and the girl were among them.

I didn't know the bartender, and he didn't know me,

so I showed him my ID. "I need to know how long he's been here," I said, pointing to Lonagan. "And hey, make me a vodka martini. Shake it, stir it, leave it alone, I don't care, just make it and make it fast."

"Are you OK, sir? You're bleeding a little. Did you hurt yourself?"

"I fell in the shower."

"*Cat Fancy*?" He held up my ID. "What does *Cat Fancy* have to do with anything?" He was a young guy, red hair, looked like he was about eleven years old.

"Nothing." I switched IDs and pointed at Lonagan. "He looks drunk."

"He is," the bartender told me. "They've been here for hours. Both of them."

"Is he doing OK?"

"He's tanked. Now and again passengers go over to chat but he's mostly too far gone to deal with it."

Oscar Lonagan was half out of the chair, his feet crossed in front of him on the cocktail table.

"You said he'd been here for hours. Are you sure? He hasn't been out of your sight? Not even to go to the bathroom?" I didn't have any idea why Oscar Lonagan would want to attack Sasha, but I was anxious to suspect someone.

"No, he's been here the whole time?"

"What makes you so certain?"

He grinned. "I have been onboard for three months. And in that time, not one single woman has given me the time of day. Not Rose, bless her lovely soul, not Michelle, not Kathryn from the bar, not any last one of them." He handed me my drink. "I am a lonely man, sir."

"You and me both."

"But that girl," he said, pointing, "that girl sitting there with that old man, she's just something lovely. She doesn't belong with that old guy."

"You know, I pretty much think they have a lot in

common," I began. "And they're in the same field of work. So when it comes to love and amore and all that, I'm not certain that age is really a . . ."

"He's too old for her."

"Love recognizes no . . ."

"He's too old for her. But who am I, right? I just like looking at her. I've been looking at her for a bit now."

"Is she drunk too?"

"Probably. She has a nice laugh."

I walked over and took a seat at their table. "Hey Lonagan," I said, "have you ever propositioned a male piano player?"

"What are you asking me?" He was slurring his words.

"Have you recently been shot? Would you remember something like that?"

He turned to his lovely girlfriend/assistant. "What is he going on about?"

She shook her head. "What happened to your forehead?"

"Cut myself shaving," I told her. "You look very nice, by the way."

She laughed, but there wasn't much call for it. Nothing was funny.

"Hey Lonagan, you ever hear of a windigo?"

"Windigo," Lonagan slurred, as he refilled his glass from a bottle of vodka next to his foot. "Not a word you hear much in these parts, it's an Athabaskan thing."

"My mother's people were Anabaptists," I told him. "There was a lot of quilting, a lot of repenting. Holidays were grim."

He stared at me. "What are we are talking about?"

I couldn't remember. "How about a dram of your vodka for an old man?"

Grace poured me a glass. "You were asking about windigos. They're Athabascan, not Anabaptist. They comprise a supernatural theme of arctic mythology."

"And they can turn people into cannibals?"

"A windigo," Lonagan began, "is a mythological demon that possesses a hunter, instilling in him an insatiable desire for human flesh."

I was having a hard time concentrating as I spied a hostess moving through the room with a tray of something, they looked like mini- quiches.

"So it's just a story, just a myth."

Lonagan stared at his drink. "Now that is a deep philosophical question. Let me put it this way, if a windigo is a myth, then so is the Christian god as well as our conceptions of heaven and hell."

"Works for me," I told him. "I just want to make sure we're talking about something not real."

"Oh, it's real, all right," he said. "Just because it's a myth doesn't mean it isn't real. Christianity is very real, even if god is not. Just as surely, a belief in windigos is very real."

"Explain," I said as the hostess came within grasping range. "One for me, one for the pretty girl, one for Lonagan. That makes four." I piled them up on a napkin and then doled them out.

"Crab cakes," I proclaimed, as the first one went down. I was halfway through the second when Lonagan coughed his up.

He spent the better part of a minute gurgling, fussing, and washing the taste out of his mouth. "I cannot abide seafood," he explained. "I'm allergic, perhaps. I don't know. But I can't stand the taste."

"I know what you're saying." I nodded sagely. "I bought these off-brand fish sticks once at the 7-11. They were on sale, but it turned out they were no bargain, no sir. I had a rash all over my chest, my stomach, and my buttocks. It wasn't pretty."

Grace stared at me, then put her crab cake back on the table.

"Do you mind?" I finished that one off too.

"As I was saying," Lonagan continued, his words slurring considerably, "windigo psychosis is another culture-bound psychosis, like Amok, or anorexia. In this case, the only culturally-acceptable role for a man living in the cold, cold north of our world is to be a hunter. Yet a small percentage of men in any society cannot stand the thought of killing."

"That's a good thing."

"Yes," he said. "In most cultures, an aversion to killing is not a problem. Simply do something else with your life. Yet for the Athabascan man, this is not an option. He must hunt, and if he finds it deplorable, he might begin to feel such insatiable guilt that he becomes an agent of vengeance. He might turn on his fellow hunters."

"And this actually happens?"

"It has been documented through the centuries."

I had a follow-up question but it was eluding me. But by the time it caught up with me, Lonagan had nodded off.

"He gets like that some time," Grace told me. "Just smack him in the head and he'll wake up."

"I'll let him sleep for now." I moved in closer to her. "Let me ask you a question. Are you having fun?"

She laughed again, kind of nervously. Then she made a point of refilling her glass. "Good friends, free drinks, what's not to like?"

"You look miserable," I told her.

"Excuse me?"

"No, you're gorgeous, but you look like you haven't had a day of fun in your life."

She bristled but she didn't make a sound.

"You're a big drinker," I said. "I get that. And he's a good companion for that sort of thing. He's right there with you. But he's not the guy for you."

She nodded softly. "He's too old."

"Well, no." I shook my head. "No, no. History is full of successful, enduring, loving relationships between mature men and younger women. So no, I don't think he's too old. He's just kind of a dick."

She nodded. "He has his moments."

"Grace, is there a windigo onboard this ship? And I don't mean a demon, I mean a disenchanted hunter or whatever the hell he was talking about?"

She drank deeply, but comfortably, displaying more familiarity with the vodka than she should have at her age.

"Listen to me." I leaned in. "I am a very old man, and that means that I have been alive for a long time. In that time I've picked up some skills here and there, like how to tell when someone is lying or trying to hide something. And Grace, you're lying."

"I didn't even say anything."

"Then you're trying to hide something."

She looked into her drink.

"Is the good biologist here killing people?"

She shook her head. "He's a botanist, not a biologist, and no."

"Tell me what is going on here?"

"I don't know."

"I think you do. Is there a windigo on board this ship?"

"I don't think so," she said. "I think you have a garden-variety psychopath dressing up his kills."

"That doesn't get me far. A man attacked me. I need to find out who he is."

"It wasn't me."

I refilled my drink. "It probably wasn't," I told her.

CHAPTER TWENTY-TWO
DAY 3- AT SEA - 9:00AM

I slept through breakfast. The phone woke me up. It was Belov. "Where have you been?"

"Sleeping."

"It is late. Have you looked outside?"

I got up and almost fell back into the bed as the ship rolled. "It's getting a little choppy in here," I said into the phone. Outside, the sky was almost black.

"I am having to shut down the stabilizers. I am trying to outrun a storm system but it is not easy with such limited power."

"The storm looks like it's worsening."

"It is. Have you worked as a ship's captain?"

"No, no I haven't."

"Do you have any nautical skills?"

"I can row. What do you need, Belov?"

"I need help," he bellowed.

I got myself together as quickly as I could.

Up on the bridge, Ben Holder, the chief engineer was getting yelled at again.

"So you clean out the engines," Belov howled. "You are chief engineer, and you are telling me you cannot do this? I do not want to go over this with you again. You fix the engines."

"What I'm telling you," Holder began, "is that our mutineers knew what they were doing. And because we don't have an engine shop onboard, we cannot undo what was done. Like I said, they pulled the air filters off the engines and shoved a bunch of life jackets inside. It was pretty clever actually."

"Clever?" Belov stared at him. "I have sent men to very bad prisons for even thinking thoughts half as clever."

Holder looked confused. "Look, all I'm saying is that if you wanted to disable the engines, this was not a bad way to go about doing it."

"So the life jackets gummed up the engines?" I asked.

"Yeah, kind of. The two little engines, the six-cylinders - the intake valves are narrow, so when the life jacket went inside the air cleaner, all the clips and the plastic and metal got caught on the flanges. Everything else got sucked in and chewed up."

I stared at the diagram Holder was drawing on a sheet of notepaper. "What is that thing there?"

"That is the turbocharger," he said. "The life jackets got jammed up in the turbochargers, so we cleaned them out."

Belov frowned "And when will the main engines be up and running again?"

"Well, that's the problem. With the mains, the intakes are wider and the life jackets went in, clips, plastic, metal and all. And the metal and the plastic parts shot through and screwed up the intake valves like I suspected. So that's our real problem."

"They cannot be repaired?"

"They're a mess," Holder said. "I put some guys on it, but with what we've got on hand, I don't know if it would amount to anything. Best shot now - I might be able to scavenge parts from one of the mains to get the other one up."

Belov did some cursing in Russian. If it wasn't cursing, it sure sounded like it.

"Settle down," I told him. "Gentlemen, whatever problems we have are minor in the great scheme of things. Why don't we all just settle down, have a nice tot of beet bourbon, and see where that takes us."

Belov looked down at his computer tablet and shook his head. "Broken," he whispered, "yet one more thing is broken." Then he threw it against the wall, dislodging bits of black plastic. He shouted at Holder in Russian.

"I don't speak Russian," Holder answered.

"OK. OK." Belov was calming himself down. "Then go do as you say. Go savage the engine. Do whatever. I do not care any more."

My counsel, laden with wisdom, moved Belov to the sideboard, where he poured himself a generous tot of something from a crystal decanter.

"Getting a little parched myself," I noted, and he poured me a drink. "So hey, what's going on? You seem even angrier this morning than you did last night. You need to watch the blood pressure. Do you take statins?"

"Of course. Also, every day, I have an aspirin meant for a baby."

"Prudent. Hey, so what happened here? Why all the fussing?"

He took a deep breath and then drank his beverage. "Lightning strike. We have lost all communications. SatNav is down, GPS. We have no geographical reference points to work with, and I cannot get a star sight due to clouds."

"So we're lost?"

"I cannot fix a position." He ran his finger across the chart on the table. "I drove her north under what minimal power I could draw from our backup engines."

"Why north?" I stared down at the charts. "I thought we would be out of the storm by now."

"So did I." He pointed to a radar scope mounted on the desk. "It is still raging, but we are out of its range now. Yet we have another problem."

I nodded. "A murderer on board, and perhaps a cannibalistic demon."

"Da." He smiled, and pointed back at the radar screen. "And look at this."

I squinted but it didn't look any different from the storm we had just emerged from. I told him as much.

"Correct," he said. "We have another storm coming in from the west. High winds, choppy seas, warm air from the Pacific meeting the cold Siberian air, brutal and unforgiving."

I moved over to the scope. "It looks even bigger than the last storm."

Belov nodded. "Yes, and to avoid it, we must sail east, away from Russia, not towards it as we have been trying to do. We must sail nearly true east at whatever maximum power we can derive," he said, shaking his head. "And I can barely determine which way is east."

"Are we going to sink?"

He turned and stared at me. "No. We are not going to sink. We are just in for a rough ride. I have to turn off the stabilizers to pull as much power as I can. Already I am turning the elevators off for the night, but I cannot do that during the day with a ship full of very old people. No offense."

"None taken. You're older than me."

He clapped me on the back without looking up from his charts. "Not by a very long nautical mile."

"But we're not going to sink, right?"

"We are not going to sink," he repeated.

"Then my work here is done," I told him. "I'm going to go try to find our murderer. Hey, let me get another tot for the road."

Instead of refilling my glass as courtesy would dictate, he handed me a curled up sheet of computer paper. "This is the last communication we received from the ship's owners. They have decided that we will end the cruise in Petropavlovsk. The passengers will disembark and be flown to Anchorage. The ship will remain in port for another week until all this is resolved."

"That's assuming we can even get there."
"Da," he said.

I don't know if it was getting choppier out there, or if I was starting to feel the combined effects of the pain pills and whatever Volgan distillate Belov was pouring, but I nearly fell down twice on the way to my cabin.

By profession, I am a hunter of men. By temperament, I am a bulldog. Once I get a scent, I will follow a trail until the end of time or space. Once I set my jaw, my jaw remains set. But nothing in my experience led me to understand what was going on onboard this ship.

Ordinary men kill. It happens every day. And half of them will be driven to the grave or to the drink by what they have become. The other half make their peace. But ordinary men do not carve up and eat women. That is the language, the grammar of a psychopath. And a psychopath who can tolerate the rigor, confined spaces, regulations, rigid hierarchy, and strict choreography of cruise ship life is one truly exceptional individual.

Someone summoned Sasha to the Beluga Bar to kill him. Of that I was certain. Had I not been there, Sasha would be dead. But who would want him dead? Georgie Orbelani was almost certainly a killer. And Brice Laird definitely was. Oscar Lonagan could wring a man's neck over breakfast and still be hungry at lunch, but where was the motive? I was still thinking this through when I get back to my cabin and found a man waiting for me.

"Just sit," he told me. His accent was Russian, thicker even than Belov's.

I put my folders on the bed and grabbed a beer from the minibar. "You being who?"

"My name is Rurik Lebedev," he said. He pulled a wallet from his jacket pocket and flashed an ID badge. "I am security consultant, officiated by the Russian government."

"That's grand. Is this a social call, Mr. Lebedev? I have work to do. If you're here to kill me, get on with it. Otherwise, I like to use the toilet at this time each and every day."

"Courtesy call," he said. "Maybe we can help each other."

"How is that?" I popped the cap off the beer and handed it to him. "I don't like people in my cabin unless I invite them in. So that means I'm really pissed off. I don't know if I can even express to you how pissed off I am, but I'm going to try."

He chuckled. "I am not here to play games. I am armed, as I know you are."

"Are you the man I shot last night?"

He shook his head. "No. I was not shot last night, nor any recent night."

I opened the minibar and found another beer in the back. I pulled it out along with my backup gun which I pointed at him. "Turn around," I told him. "Hands on the TV, on the edges. Don't get fingerprints all over it."

"This is a mistake," he said.

"Maybe. But it's my mistake. Do it now. I usually shoot two people per cruise, so I'm good for one more. Stop messing around and do what I told you to do or I'll shoot you dead."

He shook his head, but he did what I told him to. I found a razor in his jacket pocket next to a .22 automatic. I also found a pack of cigarettes, a cell phone, a wallet, and a little cellophane bag of cocaine.

"Rurik Lebedev." I read his drivers license. "Now I know your real name."

"It is same name I told you."

"Quiet. You are a security consultant, are you? What on earth is a security consultant? This is expired anyway."

"I have an arrangement with the captain," he said. "It is private."

"Sucks for you," I told him. "The captain is dead. No

more arrangement. What are you doing onboard?"

"Bodyguard."

"For who?"

"Michelle Parker, American girl."

"Not ringing a bell."

"You interviewed her. I was there. Then you called her last night and left a message accusing her of being a prostitute."

I snapped my fingers. "That's the one. Hey, so you're the guy with the steel teeth?" I let him up. I put my gun away.

He grinned in a not too friendly sort of way, but I got to see the teeth. "Courtesy of Russian federal prison system."

"Cool," I told him. "So why does she need a bodyguard? Wait, did you say bodyguard or pimp?"

"Bodyguard," he repeated. "The girl's real name is Michelle Krilov. She is daughter of Sergei Krilov."

"Who?"

"You know who he is."

"I don't. Who are we talking about?"

"Sergei Krilov; he is famous."

"Say more."

"Russian emigrant, he started big computer company in Oregon? Ringing bells now, is this?"

I shook my head.

"KrilovBioCom, they make circuit boards out of algae. Not on the market yet, but it will be revolution in computers."

I shook my head again.

"It does not matter. Sergei Krilov is worth billions. This is his only daughter. She wants to roam the world dangerously, so what can her father do? He can make sure she is not all alone."

"And that's where you come in?"

"That is where I come in."

"And when I talk to Irina Bok and Captain Belov, they'll tell me the same story?"

He looked down at the desk, then down at his cigarettes.

"May I pick them up?"

"Have at it."

"Michelle is very beautiful," he said. "You have noticed?"

"I have."

"And very much trouble. Drugs, adventure, three visits to rehab after three visits to jail, and still she will not sit still."

"So you're a babysitter, I get it. But why the secrecy?"

"She is worth a billion dollars and she has had four credible threats against her this year alone. So if we can't keep her locked up, then we change her name and let her loose, but we keep a close watch. That is my job."

"That's quite a story. So why the cocaine, which I'm keeping by the way?"

He shook his head. "I don't like it any more than you do. But if I do not get it for her, then she will get it somewhere else. I do not want to sit by hospital bed in Barbados again because she bought heroin by mistake."

"Is that right? Hey, so as long as we're being honest, she's a prostitute, right?"

He shook his head sadly. "She doesn't even need the money, of course."

"Well now we're getting somewhere. How does she identify clients? Or is that your job?"

"No. It was something they just began to do; they liked the rawness of it."

"Who is they?"

"Michelle and the dead girl."

"And you helped identify clients. You were the pimp, weren't you?"

He shook his head. "No. Never. I care about this girl. She is kinship to me. I would never."

"Then who? Who found clients for them?"

"You would not believe it if I told you."

"Rurik, my buddy, by the time you and me finish this cruise, we're going to be the best of friends. We'll probably buy a timeshare together. So tell me what I want to know or I'm going to put your ass in the brig."

"That would not be good," he said.

"No."

"The man in charge – you already have him in the brig."

I stared at him. "Is that right?"

"The chef, Mr. Ember."

"Is that right?"

"It is."

"Hey, Rurik, who attacked me last night?"

"I have no idea. My only care, my only job is to keep Michelle Krilov safe. So I want you to walk away from her. Leave her alone. She is crazy bitch, but she is not a killer."

I nodded. "OK, but I'm keeping the gun, and the cocaine. If I need to talk with you, I'll find you."

CHAPTER TWENTY-THREE
DAY 3- AT SEA - 11:00AM

I found Chef James Ember where I left him, languishing in a cell, or at least as languishing as is humanly possible while dining on a nice trout, scalloped potatoes, baby carrots, and what looked to be a dollop of horseradish sauce next to a Caesar salad.

"How about that," I told him, pointing at his meal. "That's a nice lunch."

"It's garbage," he said between bites. "Goddamn Pang knows how I like it, but do you see any anchovies in this salad? I do not."

"That could be one there," I said, moving in close.

"No, that's a caper. It's not even close. There should be anchovies. I've already dealt with this - that bulbous oaf of a lecturer, that Lonagan guy, he gets all in my face the very first night. Not expecting fish in his Caesar salad, he lectures me. But he's full of it. A good Caesar salad will always have anchovies. Always, and Pang knows that. But he's just messing with me."

"Hey, they gave you a knife," I noted. "Aren't they afraid you're going to off yourself?"

"I guess not," he said, between mouthfuls. "What can I do for you? Have you come to steal more of my crackers?"

"Don't mind if I do." I reached through the bars for a package of Sunshine Krispys.

"Why am I still here? You don't even suspect me.

Neither does the new captain, so what's the skinny here?"

I opened my folder. "Mr. Ember, one of the things I like to do before I come out on a job is to pull as much paper as I can. I like to know all about the senior staff – officers, the captain even, the chef even."

He shrugged, then ate a bite of potato.

"I have an assistant who does this all for me. She's in DC. Her name is Beth. Really cute girl. But that's neither here nor there. Mr. Ember, you have quite the arrest record."

He nearly coughed up his potato. "I do not."

I turned the page. "Two counts of aggravated assault, you were also arrested and released nine times on the charge of sodomy."

"Excuse me?"

"Sodomy," I repeated, "which is illegal in your home country of Bangladesh. And last year, you stole a donkey."

"What are you talking about?"

"A donkey."

His shoulders dropped, and he wiped his mouth with a cloth napkin. "I never stole a donkey, and I'm not from Bangladesh. Try again."

I looked back at my notes. Some of the pages appeared to be out of order, so I did a little organizing. "James Ember," I read, starting again. "Manchester Police has quite a file on you."

"They do not."

"Quite a file." There wasn't much there. "I'm seeing a lot of disrespect for the law here. Quite the outlaw, Mr. Ember, do you think you can just go ahead and park anywhere?"

"Two parking tickets." He raised his middle finger. "Two."

Nuts. He was pretty clean. "So tell me about the prostitution thing," I said. "How did you wind up becoming the pimp daddy of the North Atlantic? The whoremaster of the arctic?"

"Are you finished?"

"The Big Sea Lion of the Bering Sea? That's all I've got."

He ate another bite of potato and then wiped his mouth. "It's not what you think."

"Did you get freebies?"

"I wish. Look, it's not what you think, really. This girl comes on board a few months ago and everything goes to hell. She's crazy, a thrill-seeker, and instead of hating her, guess what? Everybody loves her."

"Who are we talking about?"

"Who do you think we're talking about -- Rose. Remember her? The girl who got herself killed."

I rarely touch another man, but I shot my hand out between the bars and smacked him in the head.

"What the hell?"

"She didn't get herself killed," I told him. "Someone killed her. You'll treat her with some respect now, or I'll make your life miserable. And that's something I'm good at."

"OK, OK, fine."

I worked on calming myself down. "So we're kind of coming around to the fact that Rose was a prostitute, right?"

"No. Not really. She was friendly. Maybe eager. Then this other one comes onboard, this Michelle, little Russian girl who pretends she isn't Russian. She was like this sexy bottle of accelerant. When she and Rose got together, it was like sitting in the core of the sun. They fell into each other; kindred spirits, both of them living life dumb stupid minute by dumb stupid minute."

"Girls gone wild," I suggested. It was a program I had seen on the TV.

"You have no idea. They moved from man to man, and do you think those men minded?"

"Yes," I said, interrupting what promised to be an interesting story. "Yes, I think some of those men minded. I know how men's minds work. Someone would have minded."

He nodded. "Most men don't mind. These girls were equal opportunity service providers. They moved from one guy to the next. Sooner or later they finished with the crew, the staff, even the captain."

"You too?"

He shook his head, then patted his belly. "Too portly I was told. Rose promised that if I lost fifty pounds, she would make it worth my while."

"And."

"I tried dieting."

"Doesn't look like it." I pointed to his lavish meal.

"Well, no sense now, right? She's dead."

That was cold. "You know what," I told him, "I have a gun, and some of the lawyers at the place where I work think I shouldn't have a gun. They tell me I'm too old, too much of a risk, too much of an insurance risk. And I sat down with one of these guys once. I ran into him at a bar in DC and I bought him a vodka martini. He said he didn't drink vodka martinis and I told him he did today. I told him I'd shoot him if he didn't drink it. What do you think that lawyer told me, Mr. Ember?"

He sighed. "I think he told you that his estimation of you was probably correct. You're probably dangerous. Also old."

I clapped my hands. "That's it. I'm an actuarial liability. If I shoot someone, there could be some lawsuits. They almost fired me."

"But they didn't."

I was making conversation because otherwise I was going to shoot James Ember. "They didn't. They didn't because I'm effective. And four vodka martinis into this conversation I had with this lawyer, the truth came out. If I lost control and shot someone it would be ruled an accident, a horrible thing, a mistake, but not murder, never murder. Do you want to guess why?"

"Because you're senile?"

I have to watch the blood pressure. I almost lost sight of the blood pressure at that moment. "Not yet," I told him. "Not yet. Maybe it will start tonight or tomorrow or ten years from now. But if I shoot you, Mr. Ember, I promise you, they'll go easy on me. I'll get nice pillows. I'll get better cable TV and I won't ever have to microwave my food again. And I'll smile each day knowing that I killed a man who treated women like trash."

"Fine, fine, fine." He stood. "OK, I get that you're angry, but I'm not that guy you're making me out to be. I'm a good guy. Look, I didn't do anything, OK?"

"Not OK. How did you wind up hustling for Rose and Michelle?"

He sat back down. He picked at his fish, then found a pudding cup that I hadn't noticed. "It didn't start out like that. It was a bet the girls had, just to see if they could do it. I think it was Michelle's idea. She was the crazier of the two, but Rose was no slouch. She was excited. We all got drunk one night. It was a party, and the girls made it a contest – whoever found them a guy willing to pay $2,000 would win the contest."

"What was the prize?"

He chuckled, cleaning out the pudding cup and pulled another from the cot beside him. "Michelle or Rose."

"How many puddings do you have?"

"Just the two. So the contest; it was me verses Sasha. He's a guy works at the piano bar. Whoever found a willing client first would win, so we both started mentioning pretty girls whenever we found a single wealthy looking guy. I'd show him a picture of Michelle, and Sasha had a picture of Rose."

"Who won?"

"Sasha did."

"Wait, Sasha from the piano bar? The guy who almost got killed?"

Ember looked up from his pudding. "Did he almost get killed? I don't know about that. I've been in here. Who tried to kill him?"

"I don't know. Tell me the rest of the story."

"That's all there is to it, really. Sasha chatted up this guy at the bar, old fellow from California. I thought he was a dandy but evidently he was not. He took one look at Rose and he forked over the money. Forked it over the next night too."

"So did Sasha collect?"

"You bet. But that's as far as it went. If you heard otherwise, you heard wrong. These girls weren't prostitutes. They were just thrill-seekers."

"And you never procured clients for Rose or Michelle?"

He shook his head. "It was just that one time."

"When was this?"

"I don't know, about a week ago."

"A week ago? You mean it was during this cruise?"

Ember looked up. "Yeah, why?"

"It was during this cruise?"

"Yeah, like I said. That guy from California, he's still on board. Why not go talk with him?"

"Why not?"

"Strange old cat, goes by the name of Brice."

CHAPTER TWENTY-FOUR
DAY 3- AT SEA - NOON

I went looking for Lonagan. I couldn't get him out of my craw. The bartender at the Vitus Bering Lounge hadn't seen him. "I'm positive," he said. "I've been pining over that girl. If she was here, I would have been paying attention. Seriously, she's like something out of this world. She's smart, you can tell that just by looking at her. I want that in a girl. Are you going to arrest the old guy?"

"Not sure." I ordered a gimlet. "And he's not old; prime of his life."

"Whatever, because if you do arrest him, I want to be around to comfort the girl."

"That would be kind. She would be in need of some kindness."

He nodded as he made my drink. A small crowd had assembled up front by one of the larger tables, and the crowd seemed fascinated by one fellow's wisdom.

"What's all this?"

"That started about half an hour ago. The guy claims to be a psychic. He's guessing people's weight."

"Is he staff or a passenger?"

"Passenger, but he's handing out business cards. Says he works parties in and around Los Angeles."

"Good to know," I said, taking my drink. "Guessing weight is easy, you just have to lie if you're talking to a woman."

"How much do you think I weigh?" the bartender asked.

"A hundred and fifty pounds, if you were soaking wet. What are you, about five foot two?"

He shrugged. "What's that in meters, in kilos?"

"I have no idea." I wandered over to the crowd by the window. There were seven of them, mostly younger folks sitting around a cocktail table laden with beer bottles. I got a few nods but they were engrossed by what they were hearing.

"My point is that I already know what card you will pick," the man said, fanning half a deck of cards. He was a young fellow, about forty, and he wore a tuxedo, which was never required this early in the day.

A woman leaned forward, knocking over her beer in the process of snatching a card from his hand. "Ha," she said, slurring even that short word.

"Jack of Diamonds," the man told her, returning the deck to his pocket.

The woman gasped in elaborate appreciation when she threw the Jack of Diamonds down on the table. "No way," she said. She shouldn't have been impressed. I told her as much.

"But of course it's a trick," tuxedo told me. "I'm a magician. And I'll bet I can make a believer out of you too."

"I don't think we have that kind of time," I told him, but he insisted.

"The entire deck would have to be Jack of Diamonds," I suggested. "Mind if I have a look in your pockets?"

He giggled knowingly then shook his head. "We all have our secrets. How about I tell you five things you have in your pockets?"

"Have at it." By this point, the assembled drunks were watching attentively.

"Let me see." My magical new friend rubbed his chin. "You're American, a man of a certain age. You have an extra hearing aid battery in your jacket pocket just in case."

I bowed in acknowledgement, then produced the item in question. "But you can plainly see that I'm wearing a hearing aid. So it's not that big a leap of faith."

"A comb and some gel or wax for your hair."

"Once again, this is obvious." I produced my comb and my pomade. "I could do the same for you. You have some trick coins in your pocket and more than one pom-pom. You're nowhere near Europe but I'll bet you have a wallet full of euros. What say we up the ante?"

"Tough customer, but OK." He closed one eye and stared at me through the other. "Life savers or breath mints."

I shook my head as I pulled out my breath mints.

He rubbed his temples. "OK, this time I'll go out on a limb. I'll say you have a St, Christopher's medal, a star of David, or some religious symbol."

"Nope." I shook my head. "Nope, you're out of luck. From this point on, I'm unpredictable. I have a pocket full of stuff – I have five things left in my jacket pocket. Take ten guesses and you won't get one right. If I win, I get all the euros in your wallet. If you win, I'll redeem you in front of your audience." That got everyone's attention.

He laughed but he wasn't amused. "Ten guesses. I can do that. Fountain pen, magnifying glass, or blood pressure medicine."

"No, no, and no," I told him. I pulled out six diabetic candies, but he wasn't able to convince anyone at the table that this counted as medicine.

"A key, an expired credit card, and an AA token."

"No, no, and heavens no. Four more."

He took a deep breath, growing more concerned. "Flash drive, flashlight, pocket knife."

That was a little close for comfort. I always carry a pocket knife, but for some reason it was in my suitcase, and I lost my flashlight some cruises back. I shook my head and smiled. He had only one more guess.

"Then I'm going to have to go with a snack," he said, staring triumphantly at my bulging coat pocket. "You have some candy bar or granola bar or cookies in there."

"I hate to disappoint," I said, equally triumphantly, "but I eat as I go. I rarely prepare. I enjoy the surprise. So let's have it – give us your euros."

He squinted for a moment. "Not so fast. I need to be sure you're telling the truth. Empty the pockets."

I hadn't thought this through. I was inclined to walk away, but the crowd was compelling, and it's never a good idea to disappoint a crowd. "If you must know," I began, transferring my possessions to the table, "I am a man of many talents." The roll of quarters got a few chuckles, as did my strip of condoms. "You never know," I confessed, as I plunked down a little bottle of Viagra. "I think that's about it."

"I don't think so. Still looks pretty full to me."

There was no getting around it. The little .22 automatic I took off the bodyguard went into the middle of the table, as did the bag of cocaine. "It's a bag of cocaine," I explained to the consternation of the crowd as I gathered my belongings. "I'm complex."

I walked away with fifty euros, but I didn't walk far. "Let me have a gimlet," I told the bartender. "I have some thinking to do."

Maybe I hadn't been thorough. The ship was filled with people I hadn't even considered as suspects. Maybe it was time I started. I opened up my folder and started on the passenger manifest. "Some nuts would not be unappreciated," I called out. But in truth, those nuts never came.

I read.

Bernice Adams, age 85, of Boca Raton, Florida was a retired public school librarian who enjoyed wine, the outdoors, macramé, travel, and lighthouses. Bernice was allergic to avocados, which was not currently a huge issue since avocados were about as numerous on the average arctic cruise as spider monkeys. Bernice was traveling alone, and had paid a $300 single supplement to ensure that she would not have to share a cabin with anyone else.

Eleanor Andrews, age 67, of Key West, Florida was a retired real estate broker who enjoyed fine wines, travel, and reading about nature. She was a diabetic.

Tyler Appleton, age 74, of Miami was a veterinarian. Recently widowed, he was interested in nature, travel, and meeting new friends and possibly 'someone special.' I wondered if he had met Bernice or Eleanor. They had a lot in common. If Tyler played his cards just right, and uncorked enough of the good stuff, he might be able to talk them into making a Tyler sandwich.

Ernestine Aronsky, age 86 of Akron, Ohio, liked someone or other, and I think she might have enjoyed lighthouses, or long walks somewhere or another, but I have to admit, she wasn't doing anything for me.

"Can I get another gimlet?" I asked.

"Make it two."

I turned and found Murray Abramowitz on the stool next to me.

"So I'm having a bit of a problem."

"You and me both."

"Maud is a complex woman, Henry. In addition to great beauty, she also possesses a fine intellect."

"Is that right?"

"She wants to know if we have a future together."

"Well good for you. That's a grand thing."

"No, she wants me to move in with her."

"Is that right?"

"And?"

"And it's kind of sudden, don't you think?"

I closed my eyes. "Murray, we are both unimaginably old men. If, during the next ten seconds, we both stroked out, it wouldn't make the papers. It wouldn't even make the shipboard newsletter."

"But it's still a big step."

"You don't want to move in with her?"

"I would follow her to the end of the earth."

"Great, well we're already here," I told him. "We'll probably sail over the edge by morning. Where exactly does she want you to follow her to?"

"Coral Gables. She has a condo."

"Hard to see the downside."

"There's one thing."

I waited.

"Cats. She loves them. I don't. America's favorite pet, we keep seventy-eight million of the wretched things, giving them dominion over our homes. The only pure carnivore ever domesticated by humans, an animal with no evolutionary history of dominance hierarchy, and therefore with no natural inclination to do anything for the pleasure of another being, the cat is statistically the most useless animal on the planet."

"The purring is nice."

"Yet it serves no purpose. A cat has a modified reptilian brain with no capacity for empathy or compassion. This isn't symbiosis, Henry, it's nothing less than humanity's most persistent and expensive parasite."

"Jeez, Murray, did a cat eat your mother or something? What's the big deal?"

"I just don't like them, but that's not the point. What do you know about toxoplasmosis, Henry?"

"Nothing."

"That's what I thought, yet up to a third of the human population is infected with the toxoplasma gondi."

"A what gonad?"

"Toxoplasma gondi, it's a paramecium. Its primary host is the cat. Change a littler box and you will be infected. This is dangerous, Henry. Toxoplasmosis can cause neurological diseases, even schizophrenia."

"Is that right? So every cat owner is insane?"

"Maybe. No, though some of them will experience neurological disorders. Is the purring worth that?"

That was a tough one. "Let me ask you a question, Murray. Could some infection like that turn you into a cannibal?"

"You're just making fun of me now, but I'm . . ."

"I'm serious too. Could a parmesan infection turn someone into a cannibal?"

"Paramecium, and no. Probably not. What are you talking about?"

I told him about the windigo, and about the cactus. I ordered a drink for Murray to help him think, and one for myself as well.

"It is a near statistical impossibility that a cactus could thrive this far north."

"You know, it might not have been a cactus, some kind of pine cone or pine nut or pineapple. We have to move on. Could eating something like that turn you into a cannibal?"

"I'm not sure why you think . . ."

I told him about Rose DeSilva and about Captain Tolstoy, and about the cannibalism. He looked ashen. He took a moment to consider.

"OK, so if the condition only arises every seven decades as does the plant flowering, then the two factors are linked. That is a statistical certainty. On the other hand, the rarity of the condition could be explained by differential loads, such as massive ingestion on behalf of some individuals, but that would be rare, even . . ."

"I have no idea what you are saying," I told him. The waiter arrived with my drinks. "Beverages," I told Murray, "are my null hypotheses."

"That doesn't mean anything"

"Just drink and help me solve my crime."

He did. In the end, he did both. "What I mean, Henry, is that it doesn't make a lot of sense. If this plant was neurologically active, it is unlikely to be eaten. Neurotoxins are toxins, right. They're poisonous. Unless the plant was used specifically to induce hallucinations . . ."

I told him about the shamans.

"Is there more?"

I shook my head.

"If it's prepared," he said after a moment, "then it is likely to be inactive in its native form. A tangential analogy is poppy seeds – you can ingest them in their native form with no pharmacological outcome. But properly prepared, they can be rendered into opium, which is a drug. So, unless the shamans are dealing this substance for recreational use, which is inconsistent with everything I've ever read about shamanism . . ."

"So what's going on here, Murray? Explain it to me statistically."

He nodded. "I remember reading once about the Chamorro people of the Marianna islands. Consumption of fruit bats was linked to a neurological disorder. It seems the bats themselves consumed large quantities of cycad seeds, which the bats tolerated but humans do not."

"And what happened to the people?"

"Those who ate the bats developed dementia over time."

"So that could be going on here? Maybe that's what we're talking about. Except it's unlikely that there are bats up here in the arctic."

Murray shook his head. "It wouldn't be bats. Look at fish or rabbits or birds."

"Fish or rabbits or birds," I repeated. Light bulbs were flashing in my head but I wasn't sure why.

"You look hot, Henry. Are you feeling OK?"

"I am." I needed to leave. "Murray, I think you're going to have to get over your fear of cats."

"It's not a fear, it's . . ."

"It's the trapezoidal gonads, I get it, but you can live with those. That's my point."

He frowned. "What is your point?"

"My point is almost nobody goes crazy. You can live with the gonads." I slapped him on the shoulder. "Live with the gonads, Murray, am I right?"

"I'm not sure what . . ."

"Murray, it's a damn cat. If Maud's cat climbs up on your lap, then push it off, then go back to thinking about this lovely woman. What is the biggie?"

"She has eleven of them."

"Then play through. Kick those eleven cats off the bed and get on with it. Maud is a beautiful woman. You have to get over it. Just keep an eye open. But if you even start thinking about cannibalism, I'd run."

CHAPTER TWENTY-FIVE
DAY 3- AT SEA - 5:00PM

Four years and three months after shoving Halene Delacroix over the railing of the Concordia Sapphire, Leslie Wayne Humholz, aka Brice Laird, married Henrietta Mayer, the angry illegitimate daughter of one of Hollywood's fading players. Seventeen years older than Brice, she was a monster in her own right, raving at the new moon in a manner that even Brice, to his horror, had to appreciate.

I read about it in the newspapers. And I read about her death a year later, drowning in her own pool under suspicious circumstances. She had already filed for divorce.

I bought a ticket on my own dime, and I sat quietly in the back of that courtroom for nine days. On day one, it looked like Brice was going down. But by day five, his lawyers, paid for with his dead wife's money, had established Henrietta's troubled history; the drugs, the affairs, and yes, a prior suicide attempt. I knew by day six how it was going to end.

Day nine, I followed him up the steps. He was there with his lawyer in his dumb suit, and I followed him up the steps as he headed back in to hear the verdict. I had been quiet all this time but I couldn't let it go. I followed him, and just as his lawyer opened the door to the courtroom, hand on his back and all, I had to take a moment.

"Hey, Leslie," I said, grabbing his hand for a shake. "Remember me? Blast from the past, you stone cold murdering bastard. You thought you had seen the last of me?"

He just stared.

"Every time I look into the deep blue sea," I told him, "I see Halene's face. It haunts me, Leslie. It haunts me."

I was escorted out of the building by two bailiffs, one of whom was a woman named Mindy who was gorgeous. But the upshot is that I walked away, and so did Brice.

But he wasn't going to be so lucky this time.

It was time I paid him a visit.

The crew deck was pulsing with activity. On the crew deck, it's never too early for partying, never too late for breakfast. You can meet a new friend any time, day or night, and when you slip out quietly into the hallways to sneak back to your room, everyone will understand. By five in the evening, you should be just waking up for your shift, or drinking with your pals.

Regulations ensure that the music is kept to a minimum. Steel conducts sounds easily. And the passengers need not be reminded that the minions who keep the ship afloat, who change their sheets and ball their melons, are in fact people too. Crew culture is vibrant, electric, highly sensual, and just underfoot. It's another world down here, and I like it.

About half of the cabin doors were open. I went inside one and joined a small group of Russian girls clustered around a computer, staring through a haze of cigarette smoke at a dancing man. "That's a nice song," I said, trying to break the ice, as I refreshed my beverage from their gallon of vodka.

That got me nothing but stares, so I left. I wandered briefly into another cabin that had been furnished as a TV lounge. Two couches and a flat-screen TV did effectively make a party, especially given the alarmingly large number of beer liters making use of all the available floor space.

"I'm looking for Rose DeSilva's killer," I announced to the room, but it got me nothing but shushing. And looking up at the screen, where Oriental vampires made quick work of half-dressed Oriental girls, I could see why. "This is outstanding," I told a Filipino engine room tech. "Make room for one more."

I watched for about fifteen minutes and then I left. Without any more pit stops, I found myself in front of Brice Laird's door. "Open up," I called out, knocking. I only had about half a liter of someone's beer left, so I hoped Brice wasn't thirsty. "Rise and shine, Brice." I knocked again. "I don't have a lot of time left."

A moment later, Georgie Orbelani opened the door. "My shift starts in three hours," he said angrily. "Can you not let me sleep?"

"Where is Brice?" I moved past him into the room but there was no Brice to be found.

"I haven't seen him."

"So where is he?"

"How would I know. We're not friends."

"I thought by now you would be. Two killers; you probably have a lot in common. Hey Georgie, have you been shot lately?"

"What? No."

"You ever proposition men for sex?"

"Can you leave me now, please?"

"I guess. Do you want some beer?"

He helped me out into the hall and closed the door behind me.

The reception lobby was empty and I quickly saw why – Oscar Lonagan's third and final lecture was underway. I crept inside and took a seat in the back.

"And that is how a man becomes an immortal god," he said as the audience applauded. "Thank you very much for coming. If you have any questions, please consider acquiring one or more of my books, which are available in the shipboard store."

Nuts. I waited for the crowd to disperse. A few passengers hung back, asking questions of their own, so I waited for them to leave. "You had a full-house," I noted.

"Yes," he said. "Although I could attribute that to the fact that the ship is adrift, the outer decks have been locked down due to the presence of a murderer, and the passengers are scared, I choose instead to attribute it to my oratorical skills."

"I have some questions about the pine cone," I told him. "You said that the shamans use it to live forever and to experience what it's like to be a god."

He stared at me, as did the girl. "It's not a pine cone," he said. "It's a palm."

"Is that right? So here's my question, Oscar. Have you tried it?"

His grin widened. "What do you think?"

"I think you have some packed along with you."

"Why do you ask? Do you want to try it?"

"Is it safe?"

"Is it safe to want to become as one with eternity, to peer into the soul of our creator? I don't know. It might be enough to drive you over the edge."

"Will it interfere with my diabetes medicine? I also take a little something for blood pressure. Not to mention, have a look at this." I rolled up my sleeve and showed him my elbow, which had swollen to the size of a small orange. "What do you make of that?"

Lonagan frowned. "What happened to you?"

"I don't know. The last couple of days, I don't know. It might be the weather. It feels kind of strange too, kind of leathery. Feel right here."

"I would rather not." He backed away. "And for your information, I do not have any of the Pribilof powder with me. But yes, I have tried it."

"Yeah, what was that like? Did you get chummy with

the big guy?"

"Make fun if you must, but that won't make it not real."

"So what was it like?"

"Transformative. I began to let go, to understand that I am but a filament in the fabric of eternity. And though nothing more than a filament, I am fully heaven and time and you and me." He touched my chest as he made that last point.

"That's grand. You know, if it was me, I'd want to be doing that filament thing every night after drinks. You told me you and Greta here were out on that island for months studying this cactus."

"Grace," the girl called out. "My name is Grace. We've met, we've talked. You can remember my name."

"Grace and you," I said turning back to Lonagan, "all alone on that island staring at this cactus all the damn day long, tell me you didn't crush up a little bit and make your own batch."

"Never." He slammed his fist on the podium "First of all, and you are angering me now . . ."

"Remember the filament thing," I suggested. "You're part of eternity, one with monotony. Deep breaths."

"First of all, it's a palm flower, not a cactus. And second, the Pribilof powder is an entheogen. Are you familiar with that term?"

"Am not."

"An entheogen is a drug used in a spiritual context."

"Is that right? So it's kind of like a drug."

He scowled. "It is a drug used in a spiritual context."

"But it's still a drug right? I'm a big drug user myself. Heroin, mostly. Can't get enough of the stuff."

"I doubt that very much."

"Don't be too quick to judge." I pulled the little bag of cocaine from my pocket and set it down on his laptop. "This was just to get me through the afternoon. Cocaine. They call it the Devil's catnip."

He stared at the bag. "I don't think they call it that."

"In any case, it's yours to keep. So is it a drug or the other thing? I'm not seeing the difference."

"An entheogen; if one partakes of an entheogen, one cannot partake of drugs. What I mean, is that if you hold tobacco sacred, which I personally do not, then I would never smoke recreationally, which I do. And because I hold the Pribilof sacred, I would never prepare it or use it in a non-sacred context. Only under the direction of a shaman would I ever indulge."

I turned to Grace. "Does that go for you too?"

"Of course. That's kind of a sacrament in our line of work."

Nuts. That wasn't what I was hoping to hear. "Because if you had been ingesting a ton of this stuff, it might actually cause you to go crazy, right? I mean in really high doses, you could be stark raving mad. You did mention hallucinations."

"Potentially, yes," Lonagan said. "And that is one reason why the substance is controlled, and only used under very specific circumstances."

"How crazy could you get? I mean, crazy enough to eat people?"

Grace looked over at me all of a sudden.

"What?" I asked her.

"Nothing. And no, it wouldn't happen."

"It would," I insisted.

She shook her head again but Lonagan gave her a warning look.

"He's right, of course," he said, turning back to me. "You're right, of course. If you did ingest enough, you would lose anything resembling a tether to waking consciousness, and you would become emotionally uninhibited, free to act on your baser animal instincts."

"You might even eat someone."

He took a deep breath. "If you're suggesting that the

windigo myth is related to the Pribilof, I would caution you that the links are tenuous. The powder is not easy to prepare. It is made only by shamans under controlled circumstances. And there would be no way to get a hold of concentrations high enough to induce that kind of behavior. You should recall that the sago only blooms every six or seven decades."

"That's what I'm thinking," I told him. "And the last reported windigo walked out onto the tundra on Attu back in 1943. I think he ate some bad cactus."

Lonagan stared at me. "It's not a cactus."

CHAPTER TWENTY-SIX
DAY 3- AT SEA - 6:00PM

I had a bit of time before dinner, and it was high time I had a chat with my old friend Brice. I stopped back at the cabin for a moment and found Irina Bok sitting on my bed.

"I knew this day would come," I told her. "There's a magnetism about me that women find hard to deny."

"Empty your pockets, please."

"What, now?"

"Empty your pockets. We discussed the issue of guns when you first boarded. But you are not going to bring drugs onto my ship."

"I don't know what you're talking about."

"Please empty your pockets," she repeated, so I did.

"Why would you need a roll of quarters?"

"You never know."

"That's a lot of condoms."

"I had twice as many yesterday," I said, but she ignored me.

"Where is the cocaine? I received several reports today mentioning an old man stumbling around the ship with a bag of cocaine."

"I could help you find him."

"You don't know what I'm talking about?"

"I don't," I told her. "Listen, I need you to back off. You're starting to get in the way of my groove."

"I have noticed no groove."

"It's subtle." I sat next to her on the bed. "Assuming you don't have a crush on me, which may or may not be a safe bet, do you have a reason for being here unrelated to unfounded rumors and drugs?"

She looked up at the window. "How is your investigation progressing?"

"I'm learning a lot. There's more going on here than meets the eye."

She nodded.

"You have a private bodyguard working on staff protecting a crazy Russian heiress who is also a prostitute. You needed to have told me this."

She nodded again. "I was under Captain Tolstoy's orders not to. He believed, as I did, that Michelle Krilov is unrelated to this investigation."

"You did? You mean you no longer believe that?"

She took a deep breath. "I think something went too far. She and Rose, they . . . they alienated someone. I was concerned that this someone would come for Michelle as well, so we tried to protect her as best we could, keep her away from the investigation."

"Did you know Rose was a prostitute?"

"Stop using that word," she said. It was almost a sob. "She was not a prostitute. She was not."

I gave her a minute to pull it together. I checked the minibar, thinking she might could do with a beverage, but it was empty save for a tube of nuts. "Nuts?" I suggested.

"Rose was my friend," she said. "She was free with herself, mind and body, and that's not a crime, not something she should die for."

"You're right about that. So who killed her?"

She pulled herself together. "I have been thinking about that a lot. I think it was Georgie Orbelani."

"I do too. He knew about Rose and the captain. He

knew about Rose and Sasha. He was going after anyone who got between him and Rose. I just need some evidence."

She turned to me. "He has a powerful family; they have kept him out of trouble, paid to make some mistakes go away."

"Really? Powerful family? He's a bartender on a third-rate cruise ship."

"That is insulting."

"I'm sorry. I should have said second-rate cruise ship. My point is that I'm not afraid of his dumb family connections."

"Then be afraid of him. He is smart, you know. He is careful. He does not make mistakes."

Everybody thinks that about killers; that they are these machines, careful and methodical, somehow more efficient, more intelligent than most people. But they're not. Most killers are not very bright. If they were, they'd have come up with more effective solutions to their problems. Sure, some killers are sociopaths who don't care about anyone but themselves. But that doesn't make them smart.

"Everybody makes mistakes," I told Irina. "And it's just about time for me to help Georgie make his next one."

"What do you mean 'just about?'"

I held up my watch. "Dinner time. Hey, I need you to set something up for me." I told her what I had in mind.

"A table with girls, Mr. Henry?" Vadeem greeted me with a smile. I was purposefully ten minutes late because I wanted to be at the tail end of the dinner swarm.

"Not tonight, my Slavic friend," I told him. "I'm on duty. Listen, have someone bring me a gimlet, OK?"

I found Brice Laird sitting at a two-seater by the window. He had a split of Proseco on ice.

"Don't mind if I do," I told him, grabbing the bottle and pouring myself a glass as I sat across from him.

"This is not acceptable, Henry." He stood and threw down his napkin. "Not at all acceptable. I am a working man.

It is my job to entertain ladies, and I have a dinner date tonight with a lovely widow named . . ."

"Vivienne LePont," I interrupted. "Originally from Rouen, France, she now makes her home in Berlin where she owns a travel agency. Sit down."

"And she will be along any minute, so why don't you go crawl back to whatever retirement home you live in and give me some peace."

"It's a community of active seniors," I told him. "Now sit or I'll have you jailed. No joke. I need to talk to you."

Brice shook his head but he sat down.

"Vivienne will not be able to join you tonight, unfortunately. She has had the good fortune of winning one of the lottery drawings – dinner with the captain and $100. She's up there with Belov right now. And hey, just between you and me, Leslie, I'm not sure that's going to be a whole pile of fun for her."

"And I'm sure you had nothing to do with this?"

"Me? No, of course not. I'm not the kind of man who would ask the head of ship's security set something up for me. And don't bother looking around for the waiter. He isn't coming. I've prepared something special for us tonight."

"What are you talking about?"

"Shrimp cocktail, Greek salad with croutons, filet mignon, and asparagus. Do I have a memory or what?"

"Henry, I have no earthly idea what you're talking about."

I frowned. "Come on, that's what you and Halene had the night you pushed her overboard. It was her last supper."

He stood again. "I have had enough of you," he said, "enough of you for the rest of my life."

"Sit, Brice. I'm not going to say it again. Sit, or I'll have you taken into custody for interfering with my investigation. I'm not kidding around here. You sit now, or you get incarcerated."

"I have done nothing."

"You told me you had nothing to do with Rose. You said you had never even had a conversation with her. But that's not true, is it?"

He stood there for a moment behind his chair.

"You paid money to spend the night with her, Brice."

He looked away, looked over at the folks at the next table. "So you found out about our little game. What of it, Henry? It was innocent fun, nothing more."

"Sit. I have some questions for you."

"And why should I help you?"

"Because some time in the next day or so, we are going to sail into a Russian port. And I can guarantee you priority disembarkation. You'll walk off in chains on your way to a dank Soviet prison."

He sat. "There is no Soviet Union anymore. You should know that by now."

"Maybe, but there are Soviet prisons, Brice. They're stinking places and the guards are underpaid. And I'm willing to cash in my last IRA to give away to the guard who can deliver the most misery on to you. I'll bet the competition will be fierce."

"I think you're all talk." He tucked his napkin back into his collar, and when the soup came, he was ready for it.

"Pass me the rolls, please."

He did. "You're a sad old man, Henry."

"I am, but that's not really germane to our conversation. I asked you to do something for me, remember?"

"Yes, and I refused, remember?"

"I asked you to keep an eye on your new roommate. How is that going by the way? Are you guys getting tight? You have a lot in common."

He gestured with his knife. "When I think of you at all, I think of you as a minor nuisance, but this time, taking away my cabin, you got under my skin."

"Thank you for saying so."

"I remember you, do you know that? I remember when you came to my trial, after Henrietta took her own life. You shook my hand, do you remember that?"

"I do." I tried my soup, then moved on to the salad.

"You said it was good to see me again. You thought it was something of a cute thing to say, but I didn't remember you, do you understand that? You told me I had gone and done it again. You thought it was something ironic, but I didn't know who the hell you were. Only years later did I realize that you were the same ineffective, impotent man who hassled me all those years ago when Halene was pushed overboard."

"Not impotent," I noted. "Far from it."

"You're not memorable. And you would do well to stop threatening me, Henry. I could just as easily pay someone to beat you to death. And I'll bet I have a lot more money than you."

I shook my head. "I doubt that. I'm a saver."

"Really, how much have you saved?"

"When you add it all up, bank accounts, that IRA I mentioned, cash, stamps, we're probably talking close to six grand. Also, I have a gold coin somewhere but I can't find it. I think it might be under the couch."

"Henry, I have two million dollars left just from Henrietta's money, not to mention my own film residuals."

I looked up. "Film residuals, that has to add up fast, peso after peso."

"Henry . . ."

"But even so, two million dollars, man, you've got me beat. That's a lot more than I have, a lot more. Do you get social security as well?"

"Every month."

"Wow, you're making a killing. Get it, a killing? Now tell me about your new roommate."

He shook his head. "He's a bore. He spends the bulk

of his free time reading these very tame, very adolescent pornography magazines. They're terrible."

"I saw them. Knock-Knock or something like that. I've seen dirtier pictures on cereal boxes."

"My point exactly. Quality pornography is not hard to come by."

"It's not. And a subscription is usually a good value. Tell me more. What does Georgie talk about? What does he do when nobody's looking?"

"I can't imagine."

"He killed Rose, didn't he? Come on, help me out here. You'd be helping yourself out too. If you don't help me, I'll keep talking to you. Help me out, and I'll get you your own cabin back."

He set down his knife and fork. "I hate the thought of helping you, Henry."

"I get that. But think about it; your own cabin. You could have that cute woman I met come back over and spend the night. What was her name, the one I met in your cabin, the one with the bosoms?"

"Darla."

"Darla, right. Hey, can you pass the butter?"

He did. "OK, I'll accept your arrangement. Yes, I believe Georgie killed Rose. I believe he killed the captain too. He's a spiteful jealous man. Rose spurned him and he killed her."

"You mean like how Halene spurned you and you threw her over the railing?"

I was getting to him.

"Careful, Henry."

I leaned in. "Let me ask you a question, Leslie. Sorry, I mean Brice. Just you and me here, and I'll never tell another soul; you killed Halene, didn't you? Just like you killed the other one, Helmonica."

"Henrietta. Her name was Henrietta. Helmonica isn't a name."

"It should be. Now tell me why you think Georgie killed Rose. What did you see? What did you hear?"

Brice leaned in too. "You'll keep your end of the deal? I get my cabin back tonight, agreed?"

"Agreed."

"I didn't see anything. I didn't hear anything. Georgie is not an idiot. He's not going to confess in the middle of the night. We're not cellmates who confide in each other. I don't want to be living in the same room as him any more than he wants to be living with me, so there's nothing to report."

"So you're wasting my time."

"No, I'm not. I'm telling you that he is a brutal man. Anyone paying attention, anyone who lives down there, down among the swine, knows he killed that girl. And the captain."

"And they're not afraid?"

"Yeah, they probably are. They're going to be careful around him, but why should they be afraid really? He's only going after Rose's lovers. Poor girl hadn't been on board that long, or there would likely be others."

"That's not much to go on, Brice. That's all you have for me?"

He shrugged. "I just solved your case for you, Henry. Don't be an ingrate. You asked me who the killer was and I told you. What more do you want?"

"Evidence, maybe. Some proof?"

"I can't prove anything, Henry. I know he did it, but if there's any actual evidence to be found, well, I can't help you there. Now, please have the girl refill my minibar. I intend to celebrate in my cabin tonight." He stood up. He didn't even finish his food. "Perhaps I'll give Darla a phone call."

"Perhaps." I moved his plate over next to mine. "Thanks for your help, Brice. You've given me everything I need."

"Always happy to help a friend."

"Goodnight, Brice. Hey, be sure to lock your door tonight; you might be in danger."

He stared at me. "Henry?"

"Georgie doesn't know about you and Rose, does he?"

"What are you talking about?"

"He doesn't know that you paid her money to spend the night with her, disrespecting her that way. Disrespecting him, because she was his after all, wasn't she."

"Henry, if you're suggesting . . ."

"I'm suggesting I'm going to tell him. Yes, Brice. That's exactly what I'm suggesting. I think it will make him mad. Mad enough to kill again. Maybe I'll catch him in time, maybe I won't. Hey, you didn't even touch your asparagus."

CHAPTER TWENTY-SEVEN
DAY 3- AT SEA - 10:00PM

I was halfway through desert by the time I figured it all out. And by that time, the storm had mostly cleared. Even though it was late in the evening, I could see sunlight outside. I used the house phone to call Irina Bok and tell her to take Georgie Orbelani into custody. I told her to have him cuffed and chained to the table in the staff dining room. Then I finished desert and went down for a little nap.

By the time I showed up, he'd been sitting there for two hours.

"You've been harassing me ever since you got on board," he told me when I sat across from him. "And for what? I haven't done anything."

"When we reach port, I'm going to have you charged for the murders of Rose DeSilva and Boris Tolstoy," I told him. "And for assaulting me."

"You've got nothing on me."

"I've got more than you think. You have a temper."

Belov came in as I had requested. "You are sure it is him?"

"Pretty sure," I said.

Belov walked over and smacked him in the mouth. I had half a mind to restrain him, but another half of my mind wanted to watch it play out.

Georgie was furious. If he wasn't handcuffed to the

chair, he'd be up in Belov's face. "Old man," he said, "you just violated my rights. I'll be speaking to the union about you. Pretty certain you won't be doing another tour."

"Love the accent." Belov simmered. "You're Georgian."

"You already know that from my file."

"I was down there once in Tiblisi," Belov continued. "Only for a half an hour or so, thankfully. We were on the way to Tehran but we were hungry, so we ventured into that fetid city to see if we could find some mongrel to cook us up something."

"We could not find one, of course. They were all eating offal from pails. At one point, I am wandering into a bathroom and do you know what I am seeing there? A wretch, a man so poor of health and temperament that he was confined in a wheelchair with one wheel broken. And this man, he wore a diaper, the kind very old men and most Georgians of any age wear. A moment later, he began to speak, and I realized that he was demented, feeble in mind as well as body, crippled, incontinent, and insane."

"And do you know what I did at that moment? I dropped to my knees in that fetid sewer of a restroom and I gave a prayer of thanks. 'Thank you,' I prayed to our lord. 'Thank you, lord. I am so grateful to not be Georgian.'"

Georgie jumped against his restraints and tried to spit at Belov but it didn't work out, dripping instead from his chin. "I'm going to have you fired. You have no idea who I know. Do you know who my uncle is?"

"You have a temper," I told him. "Do you know what I just learned, Georgie? I just learned that you have an uncle, which I don't care about. But I also just learned that your new roommate also had a thing with Rose."

He shook his head slowly. "You are inventing things to distress me, both of you."

I hated what I was about to say. It wasn't true, but I had to say it. "That's right, Brice had a relationship with Rose. Ask around. People might be afraid of you, but they won't lie to you. Ask around. You know they will tell you the truth."

He didn't say anything, but he was listening.

"I hear that she really liked him. I'm a detective, so I listen to what people tell me. And they tell me that Brice gave her something that no other man could."

He laughed at that. "Be serious. That's just an old man you're talking about. She would never be interested in him."

"Oh, he had to pay. See, that's the thing. He had to pay $2,000 because Georgie, I have to tell you, I've been wanting this not to be true, but every way I come at it, I have to conclude that Rose did a little sleeping around for pin money."

He kept shaking his head, but he didn't say anything.

"And she wasn't going to turn down $2,000."

"You're lying."

"She was a prostitute. Ask around if you don't believe me. You could ask Brice too but I'm moving him back to his cabin. A little bonus, you could say, for his help in pointing me in your direction and keeping an eye on you."

He stared at me. "You're lying. You just made this all up."

"I did." I held up my hands. "You got me. I was hoping for a confession, but you got me. You're right, I was fishing. I've got nothing."

Belov's mouth hung open.

"Let him go," I said. I opened the door and had a security guard come in and un-cuff our prisoner.

"What are you doing?" Belov howled. "You told me it was him. You were certain. You said you had concrete evidence."

"I was bluffing," I said. "He's free to go. Now, please send someone down to take Oscar Lonagan into custody."

Belov did some yammering, which was followed by a long tirade in Russian. But he agreed to send someone after Lonagan. I was pouring myself a stiff Scotch from the sideboard when the first officer came in.

"Captain, sir," he began, holding out a tablet, "you will want to see this."

"What?" Belov frowned as he looked at the screen. "This is not right. What is her heading?"

"She is heading straight toward us."

"Who is she?"

"She's ours, sir. She's our number two lifeboat."

Belov made some haste toward the bridge. I followed him, making somewhat less haste. By the time I got to the bridge, he was shouting at his officers. I learned a number of Russian profanities during the war, and I was learning more here. ". . . incarcerated for a long time, a very long time," he said, switching to English. "They have put all our lives at risk."

"Sir?" The first officer was not pleased. "Do we really need the weapons?"

"We will take them into custody as soon as they board," Belov spat. "If anybody resists, you are to shoot them. Do you understand?"

The first officer nodded and took a pistol from the cabinet behind the helm.

"Can I know what's going on?" I asked.

"Apparently our mutineers are returning."

"Is that right?"

Belov searched the nearest drawer for a pair of binoculars which he trained out the window. "I have her just there." He handed me the binoculars. "You can just see her out there in the spray. I do not know why they are coming back. If it was me, I would flee to some hole at the edge of the earth to hide from men like me."

A series of high-pitched beeps punctuated his remark. "Hey, Belov, I think you just won the lottery or something."

"What is this you are saying?"

The beeps again.

"You've got something beeping here," I told him. "Not sure what it is. Small craft advisory? Or maybe your check just cleared. Have you ordered anything online recently?"

"What is this?" He came toward me. "You are beeping."

"Not me," I said, but I spoke too soon. I opened my jacket and found my satellite phone ringing. "Hey, I didn't even know it was turned on."

"You have a satellite phone?" Belov frowned.

"Yeah, but I didn't know it could accept incoming calls. Usually I have to set up the antenna, you know, get a clear signal."

The first officer pointed out the window. "This far north, you don't even have to be above deck. Most of the satellites are south of us. They're hitting your antenna through the window."

"Well I'll be goddamned."

"You have a satellite phone?" Belov repeated. "I told you that we had lost all communications, that we are adrift at sea. I told you that a lightning strike had taken out our antenna, disabling our radio. And you never thought to tell me you had a satellite phone?"

"Slipped my mind." I took the call. "Hello?"

"Yes, yes. I'm looking for the captain of the *Nikolai Gorodish*. I was informed by a cruise ship accreditation firm in Washington, DC that this phone number might reach the captain."

I shared this information with those in the room. The first officer approached carrying a cable. "May I?" He plugged my phone into the ship's communication system.

"Hello," came the voice again.

"Who is speaking, please?" The first officer asked.

"Yes, this is Captain Gambell of the *Nome Ranger* up in Norton Sound. We're a pollock boat."

"What is this about?" Belov demanded.

"Is this Captain Tolstoy?"

"Tolstoy is dead," Belov said.

"Dead?"

"Yes, dead. Someone ate him. This is Captain Belov, of Russian Maritime Authority. What is nature of your communication?"

"Ah, condolences, Captain. Our line is a little unclear. I thought you said someone ate him. Captain, I have a seaman by the name of Short Lewis Tayagu. You, I mean, Captain Tolstoy had recently asked him to assist in a translation, you might recall."

"Yes, yes, and so what?"

"Well, Short Lewis is no longer onboard. He took a leave to help out with some friends. And, well, for some reason, Captain, he has asked me to help communicate with you. He says he's been trying to reach your ship but cannot get through."

"Yes, we have damage to communications. It is due to lightening. Now what is this you are telling me?"

"Captain, I have Short Lewis on the line. I'd like to patch him through."

"Yes, fine."

We heard nothing but static for most of a minute, but the line cleared.

"Hello?"

"Yes," Belov answered. "What is it?"

"Is Yoji there?"

"Is what? What is Yoji?"

"Yoji Wantanabe. He was my grandfather's friend from the war. He's my friend too. We are very close. Can I say hi?"

"What," Belov yelled. "No. We are busy here. What is it you want? I shall be hanging up if you do not say."

"OK. Hi. My name is Lewis Tayagu. I'm southern Aleut, Bristol Clan. My father was . . ."

"Enough with this," Belov shouted. "What is it you want?"

We all stared at the speaker for a moment or so, as if that would help.

"Are you still being there?" Belov demanded.

"Yes."

I picked up the binoculars and watched as the lifeboat approached.

"What is it you want?"

The speaker crackled with static. "Do you remember Mr. Unger?"

"No, who is this?"

"Daddy Unger, the whale hunter from the baidarka."

"Yes, yes. What of him?"

"He has a message for you."

Belov howled at the ceiling or the moon or something. "What is this message?"

"He said to tell you that you owe him $325,000 for his bowhead."

"His bowhead?"

"Yes, it was his whale, which you cut loose."

Belov closed his eyes.

"And also said to tell you that he's coming to take the wolf back with him."

"What is this, what wolf?"

"He says only to tell you that the wolf, who is also the man who eats the people, will be taken care of. Daddy Unger is bringing with him a medicine package for the wolf, and a medicine provider."

"What are you saying to me?" Belov demanded. "This is no business of Unger. We will not pay for his whale, and certainly we will not be giving you a wolf we do not have. We have no wolf on this ship."

"Daddy Unger is onboard the lifeboat coming toward you," Short Lewis continued. "As am I. I agreed to come along to translate. We are bringing with us a medicine provider. Her name is Agnes Nujalik. She is an Umaquiut shaman who has kinship with the windigo. She will take the wolf home and release the windigo."

"It's a demon of the north," I explained to Belov. "They think someone on board is possessed."

"There is a payment to be made," Short Lewis went on. "Mrs. Nujalik will need to be paid $4,000, and would like also to be provided with a banana crème pie for her own consumption."

"Why not?" Belov said incredulously. "Two pies we will have ready."

"One pie is all that is required. And Daddy Unger asked me to remind you to have his $325,000 ready."

Belov switched off the channel. "This is lunacy," he said, but it wasn't.

CHAPTER TWENTY-EIGHT
DAY 4- AT SEA - 1:00AM

I rina Bok was waiting for me in my cabin. She had changed out of her uniform and was wearing slacks and a V-neck.

I flashed her a smile. "Young lady, you are now officially stalking me."

"You told me to meet you here."

I sat on the bed and motioned her to take a seat next to me, which she declined. "I might have said something yesterday or the day before, but tonight? No tonight, you came on your own. I have a certain magnetism, I'll admit. It's pheromones and all, my natural aroma augmented by talc and Bengay. Musky, I've been called. Women are drawn to me."

She closed her eyes. "Thirty minutes ago, as we were leaving the bridge, you told me to meet you at your cabin. You told me your trap had been set. You told me to change into something sexy, and that we would catch our murderer."

I remembered. "I did, yes. That's right. Hey, I figured out this whole thing. I just need your help to put it all together."

"What do you need me to do?"

"Grace Redfield, Lonagan's assistant – I want you to sit on her. Question her or talk with her. Do whatever you have to. But I'm going to line up hard on Lonagan and I need her to be otherwise occupied."

"You think Lonagan did this?"

I do." I grabbed a soda from the minibar. I needed my

wits about me. I drank a little and then added some bourbon. "Lonagan is our man."

"Not Georgie?"

"It's complicated. Right now I'm focussed on Lonagan."

"And all you want me to do is keep his girlfriend away from him?"

"For now."

"So why did I need to dress sexy?"

I shrugged. "You're always so buttoned up. I thought it would be nice to see you in a different light. You look lovely, by the way."

She looked away. "How long do you need?"

"Give me an hour, then come meet me at the brig."

"Why the brig?"

I frowned. "Because that's where I'll be questioning Lonagan. You guys picked him up, right?"

"We detained him, yes. But the brig is still occupied, remember?"

"So where the hell is Lonagan?"

"We confined him to his quarters."

My heart froze. "We need to go now."

Irina ran, and I did my best to keep up. I worked on catching my breath as she pounded on Lonagan's door. There was no answer.

"Open it," I said, and she did, finding her master keycard before I found mine.

The lights were off but someone was sitting by the veranda door. The shades had been drawn. I took out my gun as Irina tried to turn the lights on. She flipped the switches but nothing happened. I opened the bathroom door and turned on the vanity light. It didn't do much, but it allowed us to see Grace Redfield.

"Where is he?" Irina demanded.

I was right behind her as she approached. Grace stared

straight ahead but she didn't say anything. She was drunk, I could tell immediately. A nearly empty bottle of vodka sat just within reach.

"Where is Lonagan?" Irina lifted up the girl's face and snapped her fingers. "Hey?"

There was nowhere to hide in the bathroom, so I checked the closets, and even peeked under the bed. "Get back," I told Irina as I moved toward to veranda. "Listen, he's not going to be rational. I'll probably have to shoot him, so whatever you do, don't try to talk him down. It won't work, not in his state."

"What are you talking about?" Irina asked.

I opened the drapes, half expecting to see an enraged Oscar Lonagan rush toward me like zombie. That I could have dealt with. Instead, I saw nothing but an empty veranda, and that scared me. "He climbed up," I told Irina. "That's how he does it. He climbs up from the veranda. You know what's just overhead, right?"

"Oh, god, we are right below the Beluga Bar."

"And there's a ledge just overhead."

She nodded. "Yes, a maintenance access. So he has been doing this? Killing people?"

"Eating people."

"Why?"

"Because he's insane. Get some of your men upstairs and lock down the Beluga Bar. I need you to stay here with her. You need to keep her safe." I checked the sliding glass door lock. "You're armed, right?"

"Of course."

"If he comes back, you don't let him in, understand? Even if he looks fine, even if he acts fine, he's not. If he gets in, you'll have to kill him."

She nodded.

Grace lifted her head. "He's not a bad man," she slurred. "It isn't him that's doing this."

"Then who is doing this?" I asked.

"The demon. The windigo."

I left.

It was only one floor, and I was in a hurry, so I ran up the stairs rather than wait for the elevator. The lobby was dark, the night lights making sure that nobody would slip or fall, but still relatively dark. And the Beluga Bar was locked. I took a few moments to catch my breath and considered waiting for security.

I didn't want to go up against him alone, but I couldn't take the chance he would get away, maybe roam the ship.

I went inside and locked the door behind me. The lights were off but there was still enough outside light filtering in. My eyes took a moment to adjust.

I saw Lonagan standing at the window, staring out over the bow. His chest was heaving up and down with rapid breaths. He was making noise too; part growling, part moaning, I had never heard anything like it. He raked his fingers along the glass as if he were trying to crawl through. But there was nothing out there, nothing but the sea and the clouds.

I moved quietly. I wasn't going to let him out of the room, of that I was certain. This was his hunting ground, but I wasn't certain he wouldn't move on to another one if he had to flee. Even so, I didn't want to kill him. Grace was right. He wasn't a bad man, and it wasn't him that was doing this, not exactly.

He froze. His hands on the window, he looked up and started sniffing – short quick breaths. He turned. The growling and the moaning got even louder.

I couldn't see his face until he took a step forward into a shaft of light. And it wasn't a human face. I don't mean that he had changed into something else. He wasn't a werewolf or anything like that. But he wasn't human either. I've seen madness and I've seen evil. This was something else. Lonagan's mouth was wide open in what could only be described as pain. Trails of mucous ran from his nose, and his eyes were black.

He came at me slowly, his steps almost dainty.

"You still in there, Lonagan?" I asked. "One with the pine cone, remember? Deep breaths." I didn't want to shoot him. There was something of an animal to him, that's the only way I can put it. I knew if I ran, or even if I backed up, he would rush me, so I held my ground even as he came closer.

He moved slowly, cautiously. I took a deep breath and tried to make myself as big as I could, unsure if that would help or not. I'd never read any books or pamphlets on this sort of thing. "Oscar," I said softly. "Oscar, let's go back and find Grace. Remember Grace? She's your wife. Or, no, maybe. I can't remember, but she loves you, Oscar. And she's a nice girl. She has been taking care of you. Let me help you. I'm your friend."

He was drooling pretty badly, and his breath was ragged and guttural. He looked like he was going to say something, but only that low growl came out. And he was still coming forward, tentatively, but he was closing the distance. I wasn't going to be able to stand there too much longer.

"Settle down," I told him, louder this time. I took a little step forward, thinking maybe I could bluff him. And he stopped for a moment, but just a moment. "Don't make me shoot you, Oscar. I'm a bad shot on a good day, and so far, this has not been a good day."

I heard the doors open, and I heard footsteps behind me, several people, but they were moving slowly, which was good.

"It's going to be OK, Oscar." I said it a little bit louder, hoping that Irina Bok would follow my lead. "You're not going to jump at me. You're not going to hurt me, are you? You're going to be OK."

But he rushed me all the same. I don't know if he got

spooked, or if he caught sight of the security team, but he came at me. I heard a series of pneumatic pops and electronic crackling as Oscar Lonagan found himself on the receiving end of several intertwined taser electrodes.

He howled and he writhed, but he fell.

Irina Bok put her hand on mine, and I lowered my gun. "How did you know?" she asked. "How did you know it was him?"

I watched as the security team strapped him in plastic restraints. By then he had fallen silent. And he wasn't an animal anymore. Whatever was in him was gone.

"He doesn't eat fish," I told her.

CHAPTER TWENTY-NINE
DAY 4- AT SEA - 9:00AM

I slept. I slept for hours. Belov's screaming voice on the phone woke me up. He was asking me to do something and I told him I would be right there. But I slept for another hour until the girl from housekeeping woke me with her shrieking.

"Nudity is a natural thing," I called out as she ran into the hall. I dialed room service to order a massive breakfast and then I hopped in the shower. I could hear the phone ringing but I had my hygiene to take care of, so I let it ring. Besides, my work here was done. Almost.

I dressed and went over my paperwork as I ate my breakfast. When the phone rang again, Belov howled something about the lifeboat arriving, something about how he was planning to conduct summary executions, and something about the old man gone missing again. He demanded I meet him at the captain's suite immediately, so I promised him I was on my way. Then I headed down to the crew bar.

By the time I arrived at Tempo, the tempo was severely depressing. The four mutinous Aleut engine room crewmembers were back on board. Apparently they had not been shot, nor incarcerated. Instead, they sat sullenly at a tiki table drinking cans of Pepsi as Daddy Unger slammed shots of beet liquor at the bar. He seemed to be in a good mood, upbeat, cleaner too, as if he had taken a bath sometime recently. Next to him was a man I didn't know. He was Aleut too but he wore the heavy all-weather synthetic clothes of a fisherman. He was matching the old man shot for shot.

Unger beamed when he saw me. He poured me a shot of Tuz and slapped me hard on the back when I took it. Then he let loose with a string of Aleutian that lasted for the better part of four minutes.

"Daddy Unger says you're a friend and a wise man," the other man told me. "He says if not for you, by now a monster would already be consuming the entirety of the earth. The whole world would be dim and dying."

"I have been known to liven up a party," I said.

"Daddy Unger says if not for you, the windigo would by now be in Russia, hunting by night, village after village, town after town, until the wind blows the moon from the skies."

"Is that right? And who might you be?"

He held out a hand. "Lewis Tayagu. I'm southern Aleut, Bristol Clan. My father was Kimball Tayagu of Attu. I live in Dutch Harbor but I've spent time in Anchorage and Seattle and Bakersfield. I am mindful of the honor I receive in meeting you."

"Well that's a fine thing." I told him my name. "I'm from the Rolling Pines clan of eastern Pennsylvania. Originally from Albany, I have lived for periods of time in Washington, DC, Los Angeles, and Stalag 7A in Moosburg, Germany."

"Ha, ha. You did good. That is how a man introduces himself to another man."

"You like that? Oh yeah, and my father was Winston Grave. He worked in steel."

I tossed back another shot of Tuz as Short Lewis translated.

"He wants to know how you knew; how you knew the windigo was Oscar Lonagan."

I stared at Unger. "It's the rabbits, isn't it?"

"Yes, yes," Short Lewis said. He translated. Daddy Unger smiled. Then he grabbed the bottle and took it over to the tiki table to join his illicit crew.

"I arrived on a helicopter," I said. "The pilot told me that every few generations, nobody eats the rabbits. Something happens to the rabbits every seventy years or so, doesn't it?"

Short Lewis nodded. "Daddy was right; you are a wise man. It is the rabbits, yes. Every day the wolf eats the rabbit, every day of the whole world. But every one hundred rabbit generations, a rabbit like no other is born. This rabbit travels to the sky to confront the spirit of the wolf. 'We give so much,' this rabbit says, 'for one summer, you must let us live in peace.' And the wolf, not an unkind spirit agrees. 'For one summer then, you will live without fear of man or wolf.'"

"That's a nice story," I told Short Lewis. We stood there in silence for a few moments, just two men enjoying their beverages talking about cannibals. "Here's how my story goes," I began. "Every seventy years or so, the Pribilof Sago blooms. The rabbits eat the seeds and multiply. But something in the seeds builds up in their tissue, making them toxic to humans. Your legends keep people safe, as many of the world's legends do. Because if someone eats a rabbit who has been dining on those seeds, he'll be ingesting a massive dose of a powerful psychotropic drug."

Short Lewis shook his head gently.

"Oscar Lonagan probably would have respected the legend," I continued, "except he can't eat fish. So he and the girl were out there, month after month. She ate fish, but Lonagan hunted rabbits. He ate rabbits and he went mad."

"If you say so," Short Lewis told me. He shook his head as if I were being foolish. "Lonagan knew not to eat the rabbits. He knew the story. But he did it anyway, and the spirit of the wolf came to him and took him. The wolf turned him against his fellow man so that he would eat them and not the rabbit. Why? Because this is the summer that the wolf promised the rabbits they could live in peace."

I motioned for the bartender to refill my glass. "Your

story isn't so bad," I told Short Lewis. "So what's going to happen to Lonagan?"

"He's upstairs in the captain's bedroom. We brought a medicine woman. She will speak with the wolf. She will use a medicine package to bring back the man. He will survive. He will have no memory of any of this because it was not himself who was acting. It was the wolf after all."

"Is that right?"

He nodded. "I have seen it before."

"About that," I said, as a bowl of potato chips was placed at the end of the bar. They were the first potato chips I had seen since coming on board, and I was anxious not to lose sight of them. "About that, I seem to recall another man who doesn't eat fish. Rare in an Oriental fellow, I remember thinking. He's your uncle or something like that, isn't he?"

Short Lewis looked down at the floor. "Yoji Watanabe became friends with my grandfather during the war. Yoji was stationed up here on Attu for over a year."

"World War II," I said, as the bartender set out bowl after bowl of gorgeous potato chips, finally handing me mine. "I remember it fondly. I wore blue and the Germans wore frowns. In these parts, I don't know what they wore. But in the summer of 1943, I'll bet you a case of Tuz that the Pribilof was in bloom."

He bowed his head. "It is a bet you would win."

"Lot of rabbits up here that year."

"Yes."

"Would have been about the only food available to a man who didn't eat fish."

"That's right."

I looked him in the eye. "Does Yoji know he was a windigo?"

Short Lewis sighed. "Maybe some part of his mind knows. But remember, it wasn't him. The wolf took him, so he would have no memory of it."

"But you knew, didn't you?"

He nodded. "My grandfather told me. He told me to take care of him always. And we always have. We travel to him every year. We sing the old songs. We burn the sacred incense. We talk to the wolf and remind him that Yoji Watanabe is ours again, and that he can't have him back. We take care of him."

"That's a fine thing," I told Short Lewis. "A fine thing."

CHAPTER THIRTY
DAY 4- AT SEA - 11:00AM

T he captain's suite was locked. Irina Bok answered my knock. "You're missing all the fun," she said as a sweet-smelling blue cloud swelled out into the hall.

"Is that patchouli?" I asked. "Irina, it's not for you. First, you don't have an ounce of hippie in you, and second, you know, a dab will do ya. You don't need to bathe in the stuff. Could you please go shower off? Then we'll talk."

She ignored me as she led me into the room. Oscar Lonagan had been laid out on Belov's bed. A thick towel covered him from the waist down. He groaned softly as an older woman rubbed him with a mixture of poplar ash, seal blubber, and sawdust. He looked like he was doing some light exfoliating.

"This is Mrs. Nujalik," Irina whispered. "She's a shaman from Gurbka."

"Drink, drink, drink," the woman said. She raised Lonagan's head and ladled something into his mouth from a tin camping cup.

"What is she giving him?" I asked Irina, but the old woman heard me.

"Tang," she said, as Lonagan coughed. "It has more vitamin C than orange juice."

"Is he going to be OK?"

The old woman frowned. "Am I going to get my $4,000

and my pie?"

Irina pointed to Belov's dining table. "Your pie is right there. And we have authorization from our corporate offices to pay your requested fee. An officer is preparing the cash as we speak."

"Small bills," the woman said, "non-sequential serial numbers."

"Why?"

The woman frowned. "I don't know. I heard it a bunch of times on the TV."

"That's only if you're stealing," I suggested, "or maybe if you're demanding a ransom."

"Oh." She looked back at Irina. "Still, small bills. My children are always whining for money, and I don't want to give them hundred dollar bills. My children are all in their sixties, so it's a disgrace anyhow."

"I'll make sure they're all small bills," Irina promised.

"Then I'll make sure Mr. Oscar will be fine. I tell him last summer, I tell him when he plans to go sit out on that island with all them special little plants. I tell him, Mr. Oscar, you know I don't want to come back and hear you did something stupid, you understand me? I don't want someone whispering in my ear that Mr. Oscar has gone and melted ice from the lee side of an outcrop for his drinking water. That's for the spirits. I don't want to hear that Mr. Oscar has been making happy wakeup boom-boom with his fine woman before the first bird calls, no matter how much horny he has. And I don't want to hear that Mr. Oscar has been eating rabbits. Not this summer when the rabbits have their time. So what happens? Fuck, here we are."

"What will happen to him?" I had to press the point.

Lonagan groaned and Mrs. Nujalik gave him some more Tang. "He's going to have a bad day, is what's going to happen. But I'll guide him through. More ash, more wood to draw out the toxins. Then in about an hour, we'll give him some NyQuil."

"NyQuil?"

"That stuff can cure anything."

"Will he remember any of this?"

She turned and stared at him for awhile. "Maybe not, but maybe. I've seen it drive a man mad. But most men," she gave Lonagan a smack on the shoulder, "most men can shrug off a little madness here and there and get on with their day."

I was glad to hear it.

I found Belov on the bridge. He gave me a short wave but he was deep in conversation with one of his officers, so I took at seat at the helm. I stared at the knobs and the video screens. I pressed a few buttons. I even sounded the ship's horn which got me some uncomfortable stares. I closed my eyes for just a moment.

"What, now?" I felt a rumbling in my dreams, and then it felt like the entire ship coughed. "What was that?"

"Look who is coming awake," Belov said. "It has been nearly seven hours since you are sitting in that chair."

"You lie."

Belov roared with laughter. "You are sleeping almost an hour, my friend, but it is a rest you earned."

"Did something just explode?"

"Possibly the heads of our mutineers. I ordered my chief engineer to have them repair the engines they disabled. I gave him permission to detach their heads to shove inside the air cleaners to remove any lingering residue. Perhaps that is the noise you heard."

"Perhaps, but seriously, did something explode?"

"No."

"Then what was the noise?"

"One of the main engines is just now coming back online. We'll make it to port this evening. Finally."

"That's a grand thing."

He smiled, and it was nice to see. Belov had been working hard. He had sailed the ship through some nasty weather with very little resources. "Also, the replacement antenna has been installed. We are back in radio contact with the rest of the world."

"Full speed ahead," I shouted as I pressed the button for the horn. "We should celebrate. Free liquor for everyone!" But it turned out to be the wrong button. I heard shouts and clapping in the distance.

"You just turned on the shipboard microphone," Belov told me, but he still had a smile on his face. "You have made our passengers very happy."

"And the sun is finally out." I stared out the window. "So tell me the news from the home office.'"

"I am to receive a promotion, I am told." Belov stood straight. "But I do not care for it. I wish to go home."

"And what will you do? Drink whiskey in Moscow?"

"No," he said. "I'll return to St. Petersburg, find a new dacha, and again woo Sarah Ivanova, perhaps reminding her of the pleasures we once shared."

"Good plan. Hey, I came here to talk to you about something."

"What is it?"

"I can't remember. Hey, do you have any food around here?"

He came toward me and swiveled my chair around. Behind me, the sideboard had been laid out with cold cuts, breads, sausages, and an assortment of treats.

"I've had dreams that weren't half as pleasant," I told him.

"As have I."

I filled a large plate with blinis and blintzes, sausage and sauce, liverwurst and more liverwurst. "Pass me that liverwurst over there," I told an officer by the door, and he did.

Lunch was wonderful. "Oh yeah." I spun toward Belov.

"The mutineers, I think you should cut them some slack. They were doing what they thought was right, and you know, in the end it was the right thing to do."

Belov frowned. "If it were up to me, I would have them shot. But of course it is not up to me. My superiors have instructed me to do as you say. They are not at all interested in this becoming a newspaper story."

"That's wise."

"What is more, they are prepared to honor the whale hunter's claim. Apparently there is a ministry relating to indigenous affairs, and that ministry has money for the settlement of legal disputes."

"You don't say."

"They cannot be saying for sure just yet, but I believe that Mr. Unger will be paid the outrageous sum he claims to be owed for his whale."

"$325,000," I said.

"That is the sum."

"He'll be pleased. Also rich. So how soon until we reach port?"

Belov consulted his tablet. "Nine hours. We'll be there this evening. There is one more thing you should be aware of." He paused. "Georgie Orbelani has an uncle who is an attache at the highest levels of Russian government."

"How nice for him."

"Yes. And he has prevailed upon this uncle to expedite a lawsuit against you for harassment, for defamation of character, for belligerence, and for creating a hostile work environment."

I frowned. "I was never belligerent."

Belov looked down. "This is a serious issue. He could make your life difficult."

"Look," I said. "Two days from now I'll be back in Rolling Pines listening to my records. No offense, Belov, but I really don't think a Russian lawsuit is going to ruffle my feathers."

Belov shook his head. "He is petitioning that you be remanded into custody in Petropavlovsk pending resolution of this action."

"What, now?"

"It could take the better part of the year."

I couldn't believe what I was hearing. "Georgie is a thug and a murderer."

"A thug yes, but a murderer?" Belov looked down at the floor. "Look, I like this no more than you do, but we are all interested in concluding this business. I have a request to be making of you, and you won't like it."

I didn't like the sound of this.

"If you were to issue a sincere apology, I'm certain that he could be convinced to let the matter drop."

"Is that right?"

"I like this no more than you do."

"You said that. You really want me to apologize to that piece of crap?"

Belov came in close. "If it were up to me, I'd have him shot. But it is not up to me. So I am having an idea. We will have lunch together, you and me. We will drink some fine Chilean wine because it is cheap, and because it is said to be as good as European wine. Then we will send for him. We will drink with him to calmer skies and gentler seas."

I was in a foul mood when I left the bridge. My work was almost done but not quite. I stopped back at the room to get my case, and headed out. I needed a cocktail.

The Beluga Bar was brimming with guests. Something about free beverages for the remainder of the cruise, a woman told me. Then she winked and linked her arm in mine. "Let's get drunk together," she said, "see where it goes."

"That sounds like a fine idea," I told her. "But I need some time to get my affairs in order."

She gave me a coy look. "Young man, if you play your cards right, I might become one of your affairs."

I introduced myself.

"Dot," she said. "We were surfing buddies if you recall."

I didn't. I told her I'd meet her later. I needed some relative quiet.

The Lido Cafe met my needs. Several couples read several paperbacks as a lone waiter made little in the way of tips. I made my way to the bar and ordered a gimlet.

"I've been hearing rumors," Michelle Parker told me as she mixed my drink. "Is Oscar Lonagan really a cannibal?"

"Something like that." I needed about half an hour to write my notes. And I spent that half an hour writing my notes. I have a little computer that my organization set me up with. It has all the regular internet webs, all the fancy applets, and the resolution is sharp enough to bring a bosom into focus in seconds. But it also connects to my satellite phone. I typed up my report and sent it back to Washington DC. I told them what had happened with Lonagan. Then I told them who the killer was.

"Are you just going to stare at me?" Michelle Parker asked. "You want me to spin around so you can get a better look?"

I shook my head. "You know what I want most of all right now, little girl?"

She batter her eyelashes. "I can guess."

"A cheese plate," I told her. "Maybe a little bowl of pretzels."

She pouted.

"Do you golf?"

She feigned yawning as she finished making my drink. "Boring beyond belief."

"I couldn't agree with you more. I've got this friend back in Pennsylvania. Charlie Quinn. He used to sell Mazdas. Charlie insisted I come golfing with him one time. It was about the third time in my life I'd ever golfed. We finally get to the end, and I'm thankful to head back to the clubhouse. And you know what Charlie says to me?"

"I don't."

"He says, 'We're just now getting to the back nine.'"

"Because you were only half finished."

"That's right." I thanked her for the gimlet. It was delicious. "You're just getting to your back nine, Michelle."

She chuckled. "I'm just getting started."

"No, you're already halfway."

"I'll be breathtakingly gorgeous for another twenty years."

"You'll be breathtakingly gorgeous for another fifty, if you survive, but nobody will take you seriously. You'll be someone's trophy, then someone else's trophy. That's all. Cocaine, alcohol, and casual sex, that's all you'll have left for kicks."

She smiled. "I'm hard pressed to see the downside."

She had me there. "You played a really dangerous game here. Your friend died and you came this close to getting yourself killed." I held my finger and my thumb close together.

"This close." She held her finger and thumb even closer. "Come on, you really think you can get me to change my ways? I'm a bad girl."

I was too tired to come up with a retort. I stared at my drink as one of the ice cubes dropped. "I don't want to open up the newspaper one day and read a sad story about a stupid girl who had it all."

She laughed. "Then stop reading the newspaper."

CHAPTER THIRTY-ONE
DAY 4- AT SEA - 1:00PM

I was intentionally late for my farewell lunch with Belov. We were five hours from Petropavlovsk and I was looking forward to the end of this cruise. There was something I had to do before dinner.

"Interesting times," I said to Yoji Watanabe. We were standing outside at the pool bar under a heat lamp.

"I had a conversation this afternoon with Short Lewis," he said. "He told me that a shaman had come to tend to Mr. Lonagan."

"A lovely woman, that shaman - one of the finer shamans I've met."

Yoji frowned. "Have there been many?"

"Women? Oh, my yes. I have quite the reputation back at Rolling Pines, they call me Henry the . . ."

"Shamans. Have you met many shamans? That was my question."

"Oh. No, no. I think this was the first."

"I've been told that Mr. Lonagan would recover fully. Short Lewis believes that he was possessed by the windigo spirit. What would you say to that?"

I stared out at the water. "What do I know, Yoji? What's important is that we were able to do something here. We were able to stop something and save a man, and that's a fine thing."

He didn't look at me. "Short Lewis also tells me that

none of this was Mr. Lonagan's fault, mostly."

"Mostly?"

"Mostly. He should have known better than to eat the rabbits. There were . . . there were warnings."

"Easy." I knew he was struggling to keep it together.

"Lonagan assumed this was mere superstition. But there was something in the rabbits, was there not?" He turned to me now.

I kept my eyes on the water as I spoke. "I'm thinking that every few generations, there is a plant that blooms, a plant whose seeds are toxic in high doses. The rabbits eat the seeds but are somehow able to metabolize the toxin. Yet it remains present in their meat."

He nodded. "And a man who ate this meat might . . ."

"Might not be responsible for his actions," I told him, "might never know what actually happened, might have succumbed to one of war's innumerable indignities, maladies, or madnesses. Such a man might be forgiven, might even forgive himself."

We stood there in silence for the better part of ten minutes before Yoji turned to me. "Did you do things in war, things that trouble you still, things that haunt your nights?"

I thought about Mikhail Palacek, the young Russian boy in the prison camp who stole our food. My friend, who I killed with my own hands. "Yes," I said. "I did things."

"And have you forgiven yourself?"

I stared out at the purest blue sky I had ever seen. "No."

"As you are late, you will have no soup." Belov consulted his watch as I took my seat.

Vadim had my beverage ready. "And have the waiter bring me some soup," I told him. "I'm famished."

"I almost thought you would not come," Belov said.

"Crossed my mind. What are you having?"

"Medallions of venison with sausage dumplings, a

salad of warm beets, and glazed turnips."

"I'll have the same," I told him. I slapped the menu shut. Our waiter came and I told him of my choices. "But without the turnips. Many decades ago in prison, I promised myself I'd never eat a turnip again, and I never have. Not even once. Except once by accident. I thought it was a prune."

"Very good, sir."

"But it wasn't. It was a turnip. Hey, also bring me a shrimp cocktail and some more rolls, please. Belov is cleaning us out."

"Of course."

Belov produced a bottle of bourbon from a bucket where it had been sitting in ice. "To a job done," he said as he poured me a glass. "Whether we can be calling it well done or not well done is of no importance. It is a job done."

"I can get behind that."

"I have a concern I am wanting to ask you about." Belov toasted. "The girl, Grace Redfield – she is Lonagan's companion."

"She is."

"Then she most certainly knew about . . ."

"About the late-night cannibalistic romps," I said, helping him out.

"She almost certainly knew. Ms. Bok questioned her this morning for an hour. She claims she had no idea. He would not seem himself, as she put it, and he would stay out for an hour at a time, but she claims she had no idea. I believe she is lying."

My soup came. It was delicious. Something about soup can lift your soul. Even the smallest bowl can give you hope. The rolls came. "Pass the rolls," I told Belov. "And yes, she's lying. She might not have known what was going on, but she knew something was going on. When Lonagan would come back to the cabin, he'd be covered in blood. I questioned her in her cabin two days ago, and I asked to use their bathroom. She wouldn't let me. I think it was covered in blood. She knew."

"You understand, this case is to be turned over to the Russian maritime police. I am considering whether or not to involve Ms. Redfield in their investigation. If her name is put forward as a possible accomplice, she will be taken into custody, possibly for a long time."

"Normally I'm not in favor of incarceration," I said. "And in this case, I'm definitely not in favor. Look Belov, this was a strange thing. Nobody could have seen it coming. What would you do if you came home one day and found your lady friend, Sarah Ivanova, munching on a femur. Would you call the police?"

He seemed to think about it for a moment. "I would not. I would have great concerns about Sarah Ivanova's health and sanity. But no. If I called the police, she would be jailed, and I would be a sad lonely man. No, in all likelihood, I would take the femur from her and suggest energetic lovemaking."

"That's my thinking. So what say we give Grace a pass here? Her chances of taking up with another arctic cannibal are slim. She has learned a valuable lesson."

Belov nodded. "Unfortunately, we have another lesson to be learned, a lesson about the value of powerful relatives."

I turned to see Georgie Orbelani walking toward us, so I kicked out a chair for him. "Sit," I told him. "I'll buy you a drink. Hey, you're a bartender. Let me ask you something, do you know how to mix a Corpse Reviver?"

"Never heard of it," he said as he took his seat.

"It's nice; Brandy and Crème de Menthe, but I take it a step further. Add equal parts root beer and regular beer at the same time, also a hint of cardamom, because I had this bottle of cardamom on the spice rack and I never used it for anything, so I thought I'd give it a try. Then, I like to use a chilled forty-ounce tumbler. The result is very refreshing; I call it Henry's Special Corpse Reviver. You could garnish it with a thing of celery, but I almost never have celery lying around."

"Fascinating. Is there something you wanted to say to me, old man, before the police take you in?"

I finished my soup, taking my time. Belov looked uncomfortable. "There is something I wanted to say," I told him, "but my salad is here, and it looks wonderful, so I'm having a hard time concentrating."

"Make it quick. I've already spent enough time with you."

I took one bite. Now, I'm not a salad man, and though I've never admitted it to myself, I'm not a warm beet man either. But something about this salad worked. "I'll make it quick, Georgie," I said. "We'll be in port shortly, and when we get there, I'm going to have you arrested for the murders of Rose DeSilva and Captain Boris Tolstoy."

Belov growled but Georgie only chuckled. "You actually are as senile as you look," he said. "Lonagan killed them. He ate them. Do you not remember that part?"

I took another bite. "He ate them yes. But you killed them. You saw Lonagan late one night, just some drunk passenger loitering around, maybe. But he was there the night you killed Rose, wasn't he? You didn't see him at first but he was there in the darkness, all crazy, all out of his mind in some drug-induced state, but he was there. Once you killed Rose, he was really there. Maybe he smelled the blood. I don't know how it works, but he came right toward you. You're an edged-weapon sort of man, Georgie. So you probably had a mind to kill him too. Until you saw what he was after."

"You have an imagination," he said.

"What is this?" Belov demanded. "Our investigation is being concluded. This is over."

"Not over," I told him. Then I turned back to Georgie. "It must have been a surprise. But like I said, you're a smart man. You were quick to see the value of this flesh-eating turn of events. So you started watching Lonagan, getting a sense of how he moved, what his triggers were. After that, it was simple. Get the captain to meet you in the Beluga Bar, stab him, and then wait for Lonagan to go to work. Same for Sasha, only I got in your way. You threw a vase at me, which is mean. I'm an old man. But I'm pretty sure I shot you. Want to lift up your shirt for me?"

"Doubt that."

"I could make it happen."

He turned to Belov. "Doubt that too."

Belov lowered his eyes.

"Doesn't matter," I told him. "Rose had to die, didn't she? She disrespected you, threw you aside like last night's warm beet salad. But anyone who touched her also had to die. You know what, in some twisted way, I think you loved her."

He chuckled angrily.

I had to press him. "Well, if it wasn't love, then you were obsessed with her, but she didn't give a rat's ass about you. You wanted to have a life with her, but she wouldn't have settled down with you if you were the last man on the ship."

"You don't know what you're talking about."

"You had a nice run, and now it's time you went back to the pokey. Life in prison for you; I hate to tell you, Georgie, but that second marriage isn't going to work out."

He glared at me. "You've got nothing."

"Watch your temper," I told him. "You still have a few hours of freedom left. If I was you, I wouldn't waste them. Now get the hell out of my sight. I'm trying to eat my lunch."

"You've got nothing," he repeated, but it didn't exactly roll off his tongue. He left.

"What is this?" Belov was fuming. "This is not as we agreed. We agreed you would be apologizing. You say now that he is the killer. Do you believe this?"

"I do." I would like to have discussed the issue further, but just then our entrees arrived. Medallions of venison with sausage dumplings never looked so wonderful.

CHAPTER THIRTY-TWO
DAY 4- AT SEA - 3:00PM

"It looks kind of like Philadelphia," I told the waiter, "only it's smaller and not too similar. Hey, do you have any nuts?"

I was sitting out by the pool drinking a White Russian because it made sense, up here in the arctic end of Russia. I was exhausted. I was just nodding off but I popped awake when something passed between my face and the arctic sun. I opened my eyes and gazed upon a heavenly body.

"You look like an angel," I told Maud Munvez, "and quite possibly the sexiest angel I have ever seen."

She was wearing her one piece, getting ready for her afternoon laps. "Can I sit with you a moment?"

"I would be heartbroken if you didn't."

She leaned forward and I had one of those moments that men sometimes have, one of those moments in which time slows nearly to a stop while your thoughts race, close to the speed of sound. I thought about how this could go if I played my cards right. I could woo. I always could woo. It's a skill I have. It's not because I'm especially good-looking, which I am, or especially fit, which I am, or especially debonair, which I am. No, it's just attitude and confidence. I have those by the bucketful. I can woo. And I saw me wooing Maud Munvez. I watched the hands of my life's clock spin in fast-forward. I saw Maud and me laughing together over cocktails. Later at dinner I'd throw a few hints out there about the future. They'd be just off-the-cuff references, mind you, but they'd hit home. "I'll be heading down toward Biloxi for the winter," I could say. "I know a wonderful seafood place in Panama City that I think you might like."

That's the kind of thing I'm talking about.

The hands of the clock spun and spun and I saw me and Maud Munvez back at Rolling Pines. Maybe we would spend part of the year there, and part down in Florida, who knew? The important thing was that we would be a couple. We would have our lives intertwined. We would love each other, nurture each other, and love each other again every afternoon.

"Are you going to say something?" she said.

"What, now?"

"You have been staring at me with your mouth open. For a minute I thought you had a stroke."

"No, no. No, I was just thinking."

"About me?" she asked coyly.

"Oh, yes. Maud, I won't lie. I have half a mind to smuggle you back to my condo and have my way with you for the foreseeable future. To be honest, I take a little something for the blood pressure, and tonight, I think I'm going to need two of them."

She blushed. "You're quite the smooth talker."

"You're a beautiful woman. You make me feel young. I swear, looking into your eyes right now, I feel like I'm seventy-five."

"Stop." She looked down. "If you were seventy-five, I wouldn't be interested."

"Say again."

"I don't know. I've always loved older men."

How about that! "Maud, you just made my day. Hey, how about you let me buy you dinner tonight, in Russia? We'll have some drinks, eat like tsars, then we'll see what the evening brings. Maybe we'll go clubbing."

She smiled. "That's the best invitation I've had this

entire cruise."

"Then I'll ply you with liquor and have my way with you."

"That's very forward."

"What, now? Did I say that part? I thought I was just thinking that."

"No, you said it."

"Oh well, the cat is out of the bag."

"I love it when men talk about cats."

"Do you?" That was one hell of a transition, but a man must go where a man must go. "I can talk about cats all day, Maud. I'm a huge cat fan. In fact . . ." I got out my wallet. I had my *Cat Fancy* ID in my hand when Murray Abramowitz showed up.

"How is my girl?" he said, kissing Maud on the lips. "Afternoon, Henry."

Maud looked uncomfortable.

"She asked me to move in with her," he told me triumphantly.

Maud shrugged meekly.

"And I'm going to take the young lady up on her offer, I decided."

"It's not like we were finalizing anything," Maud interrupted. "We were hashing out some ideas. And there's also the issue of the cats, remember?"

"I remember," Murray said, "and you know what? I think I can live with the cats. I can pretend they're rodents or something. But the point is, I'll live with them because Maud, you're worth it."

She gave me a pleading look.

I stared at the card in my hand, a card with my picture, naming me the editor in chief of *Cat Fancy* magazine. That card was an ace. All I had to do was throw it down on the table and I'd walk away with the entire pot. And that's where my metaphor broke down, because Maud wasn't a pot. I slipped the card back into my wallet. "He's right," I said. "You are worth it. I think you guys are going to be great."

Irina Bok came trotting toward me. I could tell something was wrong. "I need you now," she said.

"I have to go."

I followed Irina, running, to Brice Laird's cabin.

"He is alive but he is failing fast," she told me. "There was a 'Do Not Disturb' sign hanging on the door, but the housekeeper went in anyway because we were docking shortly."

The door was partly open. A security guy opened it for Irina and I followed. Inside was a disaster; blood everywhere. The doctor was there. He had an IV going and was administering fluids.

Brice looked ashen. His eyes were open but vacant. His sheets were soaked in blood. He looked at me and managed half a smile.

"Single stab wound to the abdomen," the doctor said. "If we had gotten here in time, maybe . . ."

"Who did this?"

Brice lost consciousness.

"Give him something," I shouted.

"Working on it." The doctor had the housekeeper applying pressure to the wound but she looked like she was going to pass out.

"Let me do that." I took her place as the doctor hooked up another bag of saline.

"Is he going to die?" Irina asked.

"I think so, yes," the doctor said. "Normally a single stab wound to the abdomen is survivable, but this went all the way through."

"I need to talk to him," I said. "Can you wake him up?"

"Are you serious?"

My hand was soaked with blood by that point so I

grabbed a clean towel and pressed it to hold down the bleeding. Brice's eyes shot open as I did so.

"You're going to be OK, Brice," I told him. "You're too mean to die."

He grinned. He started to say something but his voice was just a whisper. "Happy now, Henry?" he finally managed.

"No." I shook my head.

"You used me as bait."

"Did Georgie do this?"

Brice smiled. "You still can't do your job without me," he whispered. "I won't tell you."

"Oh, come on. Let me get him for you. You don't deserve this. I can make him pay."

"I don't care anymore, Henry. Don't you see? I don't care."

I stared at him. "You're dying, Brice. You know that, don't you?"

He grinned. "It was bound to happen sooner or later, though I had been hoping it would be later."

"Nothing you want to get off your chest?" I asked. "Something you want to tell me maybe? Don't you want to meet your maker with a clear conscience?"

He chuckled and he winced from the pain. "I don't believe in anything more than you believe in, Henry, so don't waste your time."

"You killed Halene, didn't you? Just tell me that. Just admit you pushed her over the railing."

He said nothing for what seemed like a long time. "There is one thing I'd like you to know, Henry, but you'll need to come closer. It's hard now for me to talk."

Irina Bok took my place compressing the wound, and I moved closer, moved my face an inch from Brice's. And he whispered what he had to say: "Henry, what did the man say to his portly wife when hiking in bear country?"

I pulled away. "Are you serious? You want to tell a

joke?"

He seemed to lose consciousness again but a moment later his eyes half opened. He wigged a finger summoning me near. I moved close and looked into his eyes as he spoke.

"He said, 'all I need is you.'"

I shook my head. "You're a sick old fuck," I whispered back but I don't know if he heard me.

Irina Bok chased me out into the hall. "This is Georgie, isn't it? He did this."

"Yeah."

"I'm going to have him brought in," she said.

"Don't bother," I told her. "I got this."

CHAPTER THIRTY-THREE
DAY 4- IN PORT AT PETROPAVLOVSK - 5:00PM

Georgie actually planned it pretty well, I realized, as I headed for my cabin. We were sailing into the harbor. The pilot and the authorities were already on board clearing the ship's paperwork. Docking and disembarkation would commence in about an hour.

That 'Do Not Disturb' sign was clever. It might have bought Georgie all the time he needed to get off the ship, if the cabin stewardess hadn't ignored it.

But she did ignore it. And Georgie was still on board. The problem with murderers is that deep down, they're just normal, work-a-day insane people. And insane people lack the mental stability of the sane, the kind of even keel that cuts through need and want and all manner of crazy.

Here's what I mean – we were in Russia – how hard would it be for him to just shimmy down some rope and vanish into the tundra or whatever it was they had up here in the ass end of Russia? That's what any sane person would do. And that's why I knew Georgie was still on board. And I knew exactly where I could find him.

It was dark when I opened the door to my cabin. I noticed the window curtains were drawn, which they should not have been. And I knew why. The bed had been made, my socks lined up nicely on the chair. I locked the door behind me and stood by the minibar.

"I haven't got all day," I called out. "I'm a old man, Georgie, and I'm going to need to use the bathroom soon. If you stink it up, I'll be very upset."

He stepped into the room. "You knew I was coming for you?"

I yawned. I was still tired. "I did. So let me tell you how this is going to work."

"No, let me tell you how this is going to work." He moved slowly, evenly. "First, you're going to take your gun out and toss it on the bed."

"Why would I do that?"

"Because if you don't, I'll gut you." He pulled a mean-looking knife from his belt. It was curved and gigantic. It looked like something a headhunter might keep around for religious holidays or three-day weekends.

"OK, that's persuasive." I took out my gun and lobbed it onto the bed. "Let me ask you something. Did you love her, or was it something else?"

"Something else." He moved toward me. "I can't explain it exactly. She was unlike anyone I had ever met. So alive."

"Well sure, before you killed her."

"You wouldn't understand. Being with her, I didn't care about anything else. I didn't care what we did, I just wanted to be near her. I didn't care if we had sex or ate peanuts curled up in a deck chair. I just wanted to be next to her."

"And then she got tired of you."

He shut his eyes. "I think so, yes. I didn't know why. I still don't know why."

"Maybe she saw something in you that she didn't like."

He looked up at me. "Like what? We never fought, we never even argued. What would she not like? There was nothing."

"Nothing? We all have our faults. Take me for example. I'm easy going. I like the good life; fine wine, food in abundance, naked girls. But I'm also a little fat. I've got no problem with sitting in front of the TV for nine hours at a shot as long as there's something good on. I can't stand housework. I'm slovenly, and every once in a blue moon, I might drink to excess."

"Yeah, you're a piece of work."

"And you, Georgie, you have your faults too. For starters, you're a murderous piece of dogshit. You think maybe Rose saw that when she looked into your eyes? I did." I opened the minibar. "Can I get you a beverage?"

"Looking for this?"

"One sec." I reached around for my backup pistol, the one I keep in the minibar, but it wasn't there. I was pretty sure I kept it in the minibar. I wondered if I had moved it.

"Looking for this?"

"What, now?" I looked up and saw Georgie holding my backup pistol. Nuts.

"You think you're pretty smart, don't you?"

I nodded. "I do, though I'll be honest with you, this isn't going the way I had hoped."

"Payback," he said. "I'm all about payback." He pulled open his shirt to reveal a giant purple bruise right above his hipbone. "You shot me, remember? I keep my wallet in my front jacket pocket." He pulled it out to show me where my bullet had lodged.

"That's a fat wallet," I told him. "You carry too much stuff around. So work me through this; Rose was dating the captain but stepping out with you. Then she got tired of you and went back to the captain."

He nodded. "I couldn't let that go. I couldn't stand her being with someone else. You don't know what it's like to want someone so much that you're . . ."

"But she ended it, right? I mean, she dumped the captain as carelessly as she dumped you."

"Yes."

"She didn't love him. So what did you have against

him? He was probably going through the same thing you were, except without the homicidal rage. Why did he have to die?"

"I just couldn't let it go. No way. And then she kissed Sasha on the mouth in front of me. In front of me?" He was trying to keep it together. "In front of me. She kissed him on the mouth and then whispered in his ear, and they left. She even winked at me as she led him away."

"That's cold. That's really cold. Seriously, if a girl did that to me, and I was a merciless shitsack, I think I would have had a hard time with that too. Hey, I've got one last question for you. Why did you go and attack Belov? He didn't sleep with Rose, did he? I can't figure out why you would take a risk like that."

He shook his head. "He was already coming down on me. I think he knew it was me. I saw that I could throw some confusion into the picture. I even had an alibi for when it happened, but you guys never even followed up."

"Yeah, we'll get to it.

"No you won't." He took another step toward me. "I want you to know that I considered just turning away, letting it go, just finding another girl. But in the end, you know what, in the end, I decided to kill her."

I had heard enough of this. "You too, Georgie." I took that little .22 caliber pistol out of my pocket, the one I had taken from Michelle Krilov's bodyguard, and I shot Georgie Orbelani five times. Five times because that was all the bullets the gun had. I didn't know that because it wasn't my gun, but five bullets is what it had. And Georgie definitely wasn't expecting that.

He dropped to the floor and I kicked his gun away, my gun. I kicked that headhunter knife away. Then I sat down on the edge of the bed and I looked him in the eyes. "I want you to know, Georgie," I told him, "I want you to know that I considered bringing you in, arresting you, and turning you over to the authorities."

He coughed up blood.

"But in the end," I said. "In the end, I decided to kill you."

CHAPTER THIRTY-FOUR
DAY 4- IN PORT AT PETROPAVLOVSK - 7:00PM

As the passengers disembarked, I found myself in the Beluga Bar having a Belov with Gimlet, or a Gimlet with Belov, I was too weary to think straight.

"We are several days late arriving," Belov said. "That and paying to fly all the passengers back to Anchorage, refunding all the cruise fares, it will be costing the shipping company a great deal of money."

"It will cost several hundred thousand dollars," I said. "But it had to be done. This particular cruise didn't really work out. Usually cruises are a lot of fun, but this one, this one kind of stank."

"I am agreeing with you," Belov said. "And I am happy to say that I am leaving here tonight."

"So who is going to be captain?"

"Someone is being sent. Not so easy to find a ship's captain at the last minute, I am told. And not so many Russians with cruise ship experience. A British captain is en-route as we speak. His name is Balls."

"Balls."

"Yes, Balls. Weymouth Balls; he has years of experience. I will wish him well, and I also wish never to set foot on the *Nikolai Gorodish* again."

"I'll drink to that," I told him. "Hey who the hell was Nikolai Gorodish anyway? Who was the ship named after?"

He shook his head. "I have no idea."

"Is that right? Hey, do you know any good restaurants here in Russia? I want to meet girls."

Belov frowned.

Irina Bok took a seat next to me. "Nikolai Gorodish was the Soviet Union's foremost expert on arctic whales," she said. "In the summer of 1948, at the height of the Cold War, he was harpooned on an ice floe in the Bering Sea by Japanese whalers. They claimed it was an accident."

"Hell of a way to go," I said.

"Yes. Gorodish is considered a martyr by Soviet environmentalists."

"A harpoon, you say. Did it go through him?"

"Yes." She turned to Belov. "You will be pleased to know that the authorities intend to interview Grace Redmond about Oscar Lonagan's state of mind, but they have also validated her exit visa, so she is still scheduled to leave tomorrow on the flight to Anchorage, along with Mr. Unger and the shaman, neither of whom have any identification papers."

"So what is the problem?"

She flagged down a hostess and asked for a diet soda. "Colonel Peszhenko of the maritime police is in charge of the inquiry. He is just now on the bridge reviewing our documents. He will send for each of you when he is ready, but so far he has three concerns. The first, why is James Ember still in custody?"

I frowned. "Never heard of him."

"He is the chef," she said forcefully. "Chef Ember. You met with him repeatedly."

"Yes, yes. It's coming back to me."

"Did we not let him out?" Belov asked. "I am thinking that we released him from the brig many days ago."

Irina shook her head. "No, he is still there."

I took another drink. "I think we forgot about him."

"Yes," Belov agreed.

"And the second thing," Irina said, "is the issue of the gun you used to kill Georgie."

"What of it?"

"Where did you get it?"

I frowned. "Why is that important?"

"It's important because it is not on the manifest. You didn't list it when you came on board, and we have no record of it. Also, the ammunition is illegal in Russia, and in the United States, I might add."

"Illegal," I repeated.

"The bullets are hollow points but there's a sulphur core. They burn after penetration, providing maximum stopping power from a very small gun. Where did you get the gun?"

I didn't really want to say. "Just something I had around."

"No," she said. "Try again. I understand that you two are leaving the ship, but I have to work here, and I cannot have this issue still unresolved."

"Well I don't want to say," I told her.

"Say something."

"OK. I took it off Georgie."

"Really?" She squinted.

"We tussled, Georgie and I. I hit him, he hit me. We rolled and we rocked. In the end, I was the stronger man. Powerful, I work out with kettle balls and sometimes a jump rope."

"So it was Georgie's gun. That is what you are telling me."

"That's right."

She shook her head. "Fine. And the third issue . . ."

"Let me guess, they're balking at paying Unger for that whale."

She grinned. "In fact, the claim appears to be valid. Mr. Unger has already given them the routing numbers to his bank in Dutch Harbor."

"Good for him," I said.

"No, the third issue concerns Brice Laird." She turned to face me. "Apparently he has no medical insurance other than Medicare, and that does not cover a medevac from Russia to LA."

"Medevac?" I chuckled. "What the hell do you need a medevac for. Shove the body in a carton and mail it. Hey, he was a movie actor, so you could probably send him media rate." I laughed for about six minutes.

"I do not think that is going to work," Irina said finally.

"Ah, hell. I don't even think he has any family. Just dump him over the side."

"He is still alive."

"What, now?"

"Yes, they moved him by ambulance to the hospital and they have him stabilized, but as I said, he has no insurance, and because we brought him here, we have to pay for his medevac."

Belov groaned.

"He's still alive?" I couldn't believe what I was hearing.

"He lost a fair amount of blood. Apparently both his large intestine and small intestine were punctured, and one kidney was nicked, but he will likely survive."

"Well I'll be goddamned. Of all the people out there who had to not die today, I can't figure out why he had to be one of them."

"He is strong," Irina noted. "He has a few years left in him."

"This reminds me of a story," I told her. Belov leaned in.

"So there was this old man, the richest man in the city, and he was miserly. He had three daughters, and those three daughters loved him, but their husbands did not. All the husbands could see was the money."

"They were hoping the old man would die," Belov chimed in.

"Exactly. So one day when the daughters and their husbands came to visit, the old man pretended he was dead, and they cried and cried. The husbands were so happy that they drank and drank, and soon they were fast asleep. But what they didn't know is that the daughters had a secret. They were each in love with the boy who took care of the old man's elephants."

Belov frowned. "Why would the old man have elephants? Was he a zookeeper?"

"What? No, he just had them."

"This is a story from America?" Belov frowned. "I have visited one time. I visited Chicago and Baltimore. I saw no men who keep elephants."

"Some do in Baltimore," I told him. "So anyway, once the husbands had passed out, the boy who took care of the elephants came into the room and began to console the daughters. And they needed consoling, I can tell you that much."

Irina had closed her eyes. "Are you making this up?"

"No. So anyway, it turned out, of course, that the old man wasn't dead, and he had the husbands all arrested or killed, I can't remember, and years later, when he finally did die, he left all his money to the elephant boy, who lived happily ever after comforting the three daughters."

"And this really happened in America?" Belov looked doubtful.

"I don't remember where it happened, but it was a nice show. I saw it on Spicy Bombay. I remember it because I watched it twice."

Epilogue
Rolling Pines Community for Active Seniors

I flew out of Russia the following morning with the rest of the passengers. Our flight was delayed so that Brice Laird's medevac plane could get out. Brice was facing some down time, but he was going to make it. I didn't know how I felt about that. I hoped I'd seen the last of him.

I made it back to Rolling Pines the following morning. I was beat. I mixed myself a tot, and played my records. I called Bernice Babbich from around the corner to see if she wanted to have dinner with me at the Italian place, and she did. I was looking forward to it, but that wasn't until 4:30. I had the whole day ahead of me, so I turned on the TV. I spent a few hours watching Spicy Bombay because they always have something special on. Then I turned to the news.

I had this idea that I was going to see something about a whale that was towing some length of harpoon cable across the arctic. I never did, of course, but I also never did stop thinking about Daddy Unger's bowhead whale. I hoped he was still swimming or diving or doing whatever whales do for fun.

But I did see some news of interest on the BBC site. British naturalist Oscar Lonagan was reported to have suffered a nervous breakdown, resulting from an extended period of isolation while doing research on arctic flora. "We're taking him home for some well-deserved R&R," reported his wife, a patrician-looking English woman. "He has been alone for too long."

Later, I was playing around on the internet and out of curiosity, I looked up Nikolai Gorodish. Turns out that harpoon didn't kill him. Turns out he lives over in Jersey, so I got his number and gave him a call. We made plans to meet up at the Olive Garden in Perth Amboy to talk about the Aleutian Islands.

Then I read an article from the Anchorage Daily News website. Thus far no leads had been found as to the curious case of Drs. Martin Donaldson and Peter McDade of Brooklyn, New York. The two dentists had been found dead in their remote campsite on Nunivak, possibly resulting from a murder/suicide pact. Anybody who had any information was encouraged to contact the Alaska State Trooper hotline.

That same website also had a story about the end of the Pribilof Sago bloom. They interviewed one of the local shamans who said that the summer of the rabbit was almost over.

So we had another seventy years until the next bloom, if history is any guide. I thought about this as I prepared a cheese plate. That meant that we had about seventy years before the next windigo came along. I hoped he wouldn't think about taking a cruise. Because if he does, I'm going to come for him.

If you enjoyed reading **Aleutian Grave**, be sure to check out the other Henry Grave novels. Available at www.amazon.com; or order from a bookstore near you!

The Glencannon Press
ISBN: 978-1889901497

When retired FBI profiler Robert Samson is murdered onboard the cruise liner Contessa Voyager, Henry Grave is sent to investigate. Samson was giving a series of lectures on cold case crimes he felt he could crack. But he got cracked first. Henry has just five days before Voyager reaches Miami. There, the FBI will question the passengers, but the case will have grown cold and the killer will walk free unless Henry can find him first. With the help of a television actress, a cosmonaut, and a Venezuelan general fighting extradition, Henry draws on skills honed in a Nazi prison camp to track down a couple of passengers who might have their own reasons for taking this particular cruise, reasons unrelated to the sumptuous meals, delightful shipboard activities, and exciting ports of call.

BookYear Mysteries
ISBN: 978-0983135401

Mediterranean Grave explores crime on the high seas, and establishes a valiant and original protagonist. Henry Grave is an investigator for the Association of Cruising Vessel Operators. A World War II P.O.W., Henry is as cunning as he is charming, and at 84 years of age, he fits right in with his fellow passengers. The cruising yacht Vesper is anchored off the Greek island of Thera, in the caldera of an ancient volcano when Henry comes aboard. An Egyptian federal agent was onboard to guard a valuable Minoan cup, but the agent was murdered and the cup, stolen. With the help of a Nicaraguan soap opera star, a New Age spiritualist, and a blind pickpocket, Henry draws on skills honed in a Nazi prison camp to track down a killer who might have his own reasons for taking this particular cruise, reasons unrelated to the sumptuous meals, delightful shipboard activities, and exciting ports of call.

12 million people take a cruise each year.
Most have fun.
Some die.
Henry Grave investigates.

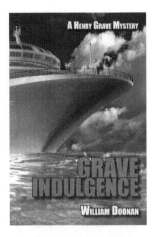

BookYear Mysteries
ISBN: 978-0983135418

At 1200 feet long, the cruise ship Indulgence is the largest in
the world. Accommodating 5400 passengersand 2100 crew
members, she is nearly as populous as the Pacific island na-
tion of Nauru. At 226,000 tons, she weighs as much as four
and a half Titanics. Indulgence is anchored off Helsinki, Finland, preparing to take on passengers for her inaugural voyage when Henry comes aboard. Indulgence is one day old, and
nobody has yet been murdered on board. The same could not
be said about day two. With the help of an Arabian prince,
a voodoo priest, and a displaced band of hunter gatherers,
Henry draws on skills honed in a Nazi prison camp to track
down a killer who might have his own reasons for taking this
particular cruise, reasons unrelated to the sumptuous meals,
delightful shipboard activities, and exciting ports of call.

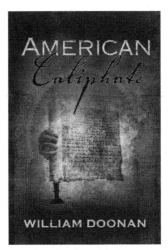

Oak Tree Press

ISBN: 978-1610090438

Archaeologists Jila Wells and Ben Juarez are not thrilled at the prospect of returning to Peru; the ambush that nearly cost Jila her still haunts her. But the ruined pyramids at Santiago de Paz hide an important document that would shock the Islamic world. Professor Sandy Beckham is assembling a distinguished team to dig quickly through the pyramid complex, following clues found in a diary written five centuries ago.

In the diary are details of an illegal expedition to Spanish Peru. Convinced that Spain was forever lost to Islam, Diego Ibanez intended to bring the word of Allah to the pagan Americans. Landing on Peru's north coast, he learned that the fires of the Inquisition burned even hotter there than they did in Spain.

As the archaeologists brace for the ravaging storms of El Niño, Jila and Ben hurry to complete their excavations. But they're not the only ones interested in this project. Should the document be discovered, a challenge could be made to the throne of Saudi Arabia. And the House of Saud has no interest in sharing power with an American caliphate that might now awaken from a five hundred year slumber.

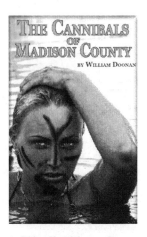

THE CANNIBALS
OF
MADISON COUNTY
BY WILLIAM DOONAN

A Kindle Short Story
ASIN: B00I2WJXGA

Jess remembered stepping out of the wreckage. Parts of the
airplane still burned. Judging by the vegetation, she suspected they were deep in the Amazon.

"Can you help?" someone shouted. Jess found him. It was
Billman from the home office. "Are you a doctor?" he asked.

"No, I'm Jess. We met in Rio. I'm a corporate headhunter."

"That's too bad," he said, and he died.

She searched around but found no other survivors. She
wrapped herself in a blanket and got afraid.

The Jipitos came in the night. Jess woke to find them standing over her, thirty of them. They were naked and carried long
spears.

Jess stood up. She should have been scared but she wasn't.
The Jipitos grinned, revealing rows of sharpened teeth. Jess
grinned back, already becoming something new. She would
spend the next four years learning just how satisfying head-
hunting could be.

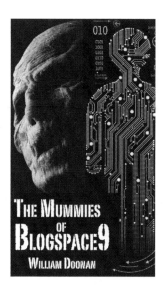

BookYear Mysteries
ISBN: 978-1494778071

"None of us knew what was at stake. And that's the thing about archaeology - you never know what you'll find when you start digging into an ancient pyramid. Maybe some burials, but surely not a five hundred year-old secret worth killing for.

Had I known at the onset that seven weeks later most of my friends would be dead, I would have left Peru in a heartbeat. But of course I didn't know that.

I didn't know that a demonically-possessed Spanish Grand Inquisitor would haunt us, or that a pair of undead conquistadors would help us find the secret to putting down mummies.

And surely, I wouldn't have just sat around had I known that something was watching from inside that pyramid, some malevolent force that could animate the dead.

But it's all true, as you'll come to realize. My name is Leon Samples. I am twenty-eight years old and I am damned."

ABOUT THE AUTHOR

William Doonan is a professor of anthropology in Sacramento, California, where he lives with his wife Carmen, and his sons Will and Huey. To contact William, or to learn more about Henry Grave mysteries and other novels, please visit www.williamdoonan. com.

Made in the USA
San Bernardino, CA
18 May 2020